To Claim My Own

JOY CLEVELAND

ELECTIO PUBLISHING
first century principles.
a twenty-first century approach.

MW01254857

To Call My Own
By Joy Cleveland

Copyright 2019 by Joy Cleveland
Cover Design by eLectio Publishing

ISBN-13: 978-1-63213-702-9
Published by eLectio Publishing, LLC
Little Elm, Texas
http://www.eLectioPublishing.com

Printed in the United States of America

5 4 3 2 1 eLP 24 23 22 21 20 19

The eLectio Publishing editing team is comprised of: Christine LePorte, Lori Draft, Sheldon James, Court Dudek, and Jim Eccles.

Publisher's Note

For the One who calls me His own

ACKNOWLEDGMENTS

Everyone's story has a beginning, and mine began with Eugene and Ellamae Elder, my parents, who taught me early on how much God loves me. I will always be grateful for their love and "due diligence" in my life. I would not be the person I am today without them. Thank you, Mother-Dear and Daddy!

Some people are blessed with "oak trees"; I am blessed with a "stone mountain"—my stalwart husband Mark, who has put up with me for thirty-four years. Thank you, dear, for always being there, for your expertise, and for giving me a computer. Now, look where we are.☺

I not only received a five-star husband when I said, "I do," I received five-star in-laws, William and Laverne Cleveland. They have always loved me as a daughter even though I still can't make decent biscuits. Grandpa Cleveland is now partying with Jesus. We continue to miss him, and we continue to treasure our spunky grandma.

When I signed up for my "Mom Job," I had no idea I would fall hopelessly in love with my four "little Darlins" who are now quite big: Laura Beth, Ben, Katie, and Ellen. Not only did they bring noise and happy chaos into my life (and tons of laundry), they later brought home my wonderful "in-love" kiddos: Chantal, Zach, and Tim, and then, the "cherries on top," my precious granddaughters, Adeline and Ada Grace. May noise and happy chaos live long in my home! Thank you, kiddos, for giving me "kid lessons," for your ideas, for helping me proofread, and Ellen for the title and help with particulars. I'm still hopelessly in love with you all.

Some writers carry a fear of "exposing themselves." Who am I to think I can write a (gulp) *novel*? I eventually "confessed" to Diana, Pam, and Nancy, and what wonderful cheerleaders and encouragers they are. Thank you, girls!

Instruction and inspiration came from three of my teachers: Sharon Steffan, Jacqueline Greb, and Ann V. Miller. These ladies stoked the writing flame that grew into a fire. A heartfelt thanks goes to them.

Every now and then, something strange and crazy happens: we get a "yes." My "yes" came from eLectio Publishing. I will always be grateful to these kind folks for this strange and crazy opportunity, and a special thanks goes to Christopher for his patience with this old lady.

And for those who are reading this, I want to thank *you*. I know your time and resources are valuable, and I would not wish to waste either of them. My prayer is that this story will somehow bless you, and if you happen to be in a dark place, that it will give you Light.

PROLOGUE

May 7, 2002

AN EERIE, FINGERLIKE MIST rose from the lake, luring Karis to the water's edge. She stepped off the trail, shivering in the chill, arms bare. The shoreline was deserted except for a furry creature ambling along the rocks, caught in the shadows of clouds shifting in the morning sky. Below, tiny waves lapped by her tennis shoes, echoing off the stone bluffs that enclosed the inlet.

Why had she come? To forget? To remember? She glanced at her watch and felt the sadness seep in.

Out of habit, she rolled up her jeans and removed her shoes, wincing at the pinpricks of the coarse sand along the bank. She forced each foot into the murky water, ignoring the cold and the sharpness of the pebbles. A merciful numbness crept through her toes and up her legs. As she took another step, her foot grazed an object that floated to the surface. A mass of gray and brown, stiff, yet soft. Karis choked back a sob. Its eyes were open.

"I wouldn't go out too far unless you're a good swimmer. There's a blind drop-off," a voice called from behind.

But she already knew that.

A fisherman appeared in the haze. An older man, he carried a tackle box and fly-fishing pole. He seemed harmless enough, but she looked toward the trail anyway.

He must have sensed her discomfort. He backed away, tripping on an exposed tree root. And then he was gone.

The moment passed, but the emptiness lingered.

Against the marble sky, a red-tailed hawk suddenly screeched. Karis fought for breath, willing her heart to still. She looked down again. The dead bird was gone. In its place, a single mottled feather bobbed on the water. She picked it up and tucked it in her pocket, not really knowing why.

If only the pain would go away . . .

CHAPTER ONE

Eight years later
Harbor, Missouri

"WHAT ABOUT THE BACK ROADS?" The elderly woman looked up, a spark in her opaque blue eyes. Under the fluorescent light of the exam room, she seemed especially thin and frail, her face wizened, but hopeful.

"You don't give up easily, do you, Evelyn?" Karis steadied her stroke patient as the woman struggled into her cardigan. "But no driving includes the back roads."

"You sure know how to ruin a girl's day."

"I want you safe." Karis guided the woman's weakened left hand into the arm of the sweater. "Besides, your daughter would never forgive me if I let you hot rod around Harbor."

"I suppose Gertie can pick me up for my meetings, but she's such a slowpoke." The widow opened the shopping bag hanging from her walker and removed a foil-covered plate. "I made orange rolls. I want you to have some. No hurry with the dish."

Karis smiled and took the proffered gift. "Evelyn, you are going to make me fat."

"That's the point, honey." The woman looked over her glasses.

"Let's see you again in two weeks. And thank you so much for the rolls." Karis held the door of the exam room and watched the woman totter down the hallway toward the checkout desk. In her Hawaiian shirt, capris, and white tennis shoes, she looked so much like Nana. The memory caught Karis off guard. She swallowed the sudden lump in her throat.

A splash of late afternoon sun illuminated the stack of charts on the counter. Karis eased onto a stool, relieved to be off her feet if only for a few minutes. Without a local doctor for over two years, patients had stormed the community clinic as soon as her name went on the sign out front. Budget cuts had delayed the transition to electronic health records. Never-ending paperwork had followed. Two months after opening, Karis had barely unpacked and knew she needed more sensible shoes. Fresh paint on the clinic walls wouldn't hurt either. Beige had never seemed so uninspiring.

A sudden burst of laughter erupted from the second exam room. Her nurse stepped out five minutes later. "There's an add-on, Dr. Henry. An itchy rash, and man, oh man, he's—"

"That's all I need, Lauren. Thank you." She plucked the chart from the young woman's hand and whisked open the door to the exam room. "Hello, I'm Dr . . ."

Her throat constricted as his gaze swept over, lingering on her unbuttoned lab coat. The windowless room seemed to grow smaller and unbearably warm. For a split second, she grappled for an excuse, any excuse to back away, but Lauren moved in behind and took up her post.

Karis forced herself to step to the counter, to open his chart, to act normal. As she fumbled for a pen, the chart slipped from her hands. Lauren bent over to help retrieve the errant papers, but her pen rolled across the floor. She froze as he picked it up and held it out, a cordial smile forming below the dark eyes.

She grabbed the pen, wishing her hand wasn't shaking, and then studied his chart. "You have a rash, Mr. Montes? Where is it located?"

He didn't answer, but took his sweet time pulling off the navy polo. Above the dimpled chin, his mouth pulled sideways. Lauren was practically bug-eyed.

He would have made an excellent cadaver.

Karis swallowed and stepped closer, trying to ignore the faint scent of his cologne. Musk. Still musk. She blinked away the suffocating memory. Tiny red papules peppered the muscular chest. Most likely an allergic reaction. She backed away, breathing again, shielding herself with his chart. "Have you eaten any new foods or tried any new products recently?" She named the usual culprits.

He seemed preoccupied.

"I asked you a question."

That slow, easy smile again. "Yes." His voice sent shockwaves down her spine.

"Yes, what?"

"Yes, I've eaten something new recently."

"What is so amusing, Mr. Montes?"

He straightened, effecting a serious expression. "I beg your pardon. Crayfish."

She noted his answer, but still couldn't shake the feeling that he was laughing at her. "Have you noticed a similar reaction with other shellfish? Or more serious symptoms like swelling? Trouble breathing? Crustaceans are a common allergen."

No answer. She glanced up. Now something akin to a George Clooney smirk. She started scribbling in his chart. "I suspect you have a mild case of urticaria or hives which is probably caused by a food allergy. Avoid shellfish in the future. The hives will probably disappear in time. In the meantime, you can use an over-the-counter antihistamine to control the itching." She slapped the chart shut and prepared to leave the room. "Have a nice life."

"Aren't you forgetting something?"

She spun around. "I never forget anything."

"I requested a complete skin exam. You know, just to be safe." He pointed to the chart. "I never forget anything either, *Dr.* Henry."

She removed an exam gown and then shut the drawer. It clanged loudly. He was doing this on purpose. "Take everything off but your undergarments, *Mr.* Montes."

Out in the hall, Lauren's face was one big question mark, which Karis refused to answer. She'd be rid of the man as soon as possible and forget the day ever happened.

When she stepped back in, he sat with the gown gaping open in front.

"It's supposed to open in the back."

As he stood and pulled the gown off, she caught sight of the fitted, black boxers that left little to the imagination. She felt her cheeks burn. Lauren pretended to wipe imaginary spots off the stainless steel sink with a paper towel, but kept glancing sideways.

He seemed to enjoy the awkwardness. He donned the garment again. "Better?"

"Face the wall."

When he turned around, she saw the ponytail. A leather band secured the unruly black hair. Always one for attention, he'd apparently tired of the textured, curly crop he'd been so meticulous about. She pushed the mass to one side. His upper back was well-toned—no surprise there—and heavily freckled, further evidence of sun exposure aboard what? A new yacht?

And then there was the tattoo, emblazoned across his right shoulder. No doubt he wanted some kind of reaction.

He had two moles on his upper left extremity. She pointed them out for Lauren to document the size and appearance and then pulled the gown back into place. "Show me your hands."

Besides heavily calloused palms, his right thumb was bruised and swollen.

"You should wear gloves when you lift weights." An obsessive bodybuilder, he'd paid his personal trainer a fortune.

"I didn't get these lifting."

She continued the exam. It wasn't her business how he hurt his hands.

On his left posterior thigh, she found the one thing she hated to see on any patient—even him. The nevus was textbook—asymmetric, black, suspicious. "How long has this been here?" She pulled out a hand mirror and showed him the reflection.

"No idea."

"Lauren—"

"Got it." Her nurse produced a 6mm punch kit and 4-0 nylon sutures from the upper storage cabinet and then drew up anesthetic in a syringe.

A swift knock. Belinda, her receptionist, poked her head in the door and spoke to Lauren, who nodded and waltzed out. Karis swallowed, backing away, hating that she felt intimidated. "That spot needs a biopsy."

He crossed his arms and leaned against the exam table, looking down at her. His head was mere inches from the swiveling arm of the overhead light. "You really get into this whole doctor thing, don't you?"

She felt blood rush to her face as she held out a consent form and pen. "This gives me permission to perform the biopsy."

He signed the paperwork with a deft hand. "Anything else . . . you might want?"

She lowered her voice. "Why did you come here?"

"I had a rash."

"You know what I mean."

"Karis . . ." For a brief moment, the smirk melted way.

"Lie down on your right side. This will sting." She sterilized the site, uncapped the syringe, and jabbed the needle into his quad. He held his breath, but didn't move. Positioning the biopsy instrument, she punched out a cylindrical piece of tissue and dropped it in a small bottle of formalin.

"The results will be back next week."

"And then what?" He casually looked over his shoulder as if he were lying on the beach.

She secured the sutures. "I may need to take a wider margin. Unfortunately."

"And why is that?"

"Because this could be melanoma."

"More slicing and dicing. I bet you can't wait."

Karis pressed the foot pedal of the waste can and threw away her gloves. "This is not a joking matter. Melanoma is cancer that can metastasize. People die from it every day."

He sat up and placed a hand over his chest. "Duly noted. And what if the results aren't so . . . catastrophic?"

"In two weeks, the sutures come out, you go on your merry way, and if you ever need a doctor again, find one closer to home."

He shortened the distance between them. "I'm looking at her."

She flinched at the warmth in his voice. "Do me a favor and buy some sunscreen."

Just when she'd finally put life back together, Clay Montes had to show up.

CHAPTER TWO

WHY HAD HE COME TO HARBOR, of all places? The small town was hardly the mecca of tourism. Had he run out of vacation options?

Karis could barely concentrate on the drive home. Her mind kept replaying that toxic moment when she opened the door, his dark eyes boring into her. She ran a red light and quickly checked her rearview mirror, expecting to see flashing lights but relieved when none appeared.

Buddy danced at her feet when she opened the front door of her house on Waverly Drive. A bit rundown, the small 1940s white cottage seemed to be hiding among giant maple trees and the other more elaborate houses in the older neighborhood. But it had felt like home the minute she walked in. The next day, she'd found Buddy on a morning jog.

Dropping her brief case and purse, she scooped up the black cocker spaniel and held him close while he licked her chin.

"I missed you, sweet boy."

He barked, wiggled down, and ran for the back door of the kitchen. After doing his business by the apple tree, she fed him on the patio. He inhaled his food as usual. As a rescue dog, he was the epitome of gratitude, her supreme confidante, and loyal to a fault.

Her phone buzzed. A text from Eden. En route to summer school, she would arrive within the hour. No time to check email. But then again, the possibilities terrified her. She changed out of her suit and ran down the basement steps to put a load of towels in the dryer. She was just draining the pasta when she heard a car. She turned off the stovetop and looked out the dining room window. Eden was parking the old white Bonneville. A sudden pang. A lifetime ago, she had played Chinese stoplight in that car, cruised Blake's Lotaburger in that car. She should have known they'd give the car to Eden.

Karis shook the memory away and slipped on her flats. Eden had the radio cranked up and the backseat crammed with boxes, her pillow pet perched on top.

"What have you done to your hair, you crazy girl?" Karis walked around the car and pulled her sister out, gathering her in a warm embrace. She smelled like French fries.

"I had Tiffany do it this morning on my way out of town." Eden touched the top of her head. "It's kind of smurfish." As she talked, she pulled out a ponytail holder, held it in her teeth, and wove her long blonde hair into a single braid, offset by the blue lock. "Hey, I saw the lake. It's gorgeous. We should rent a boat and go fishing."

"What about the historic homes tour? I thought you wanted to—"

"Karis, chill. It's the weekend. We don't have to plan every second, okay? Could you get my bag and that cactus?" Eden slung her backpack over her shoulder and tucked a tie-dyed pillow under her arm. "Wait 'til you see what's in back." She popped the trunk.

"You're nuts." Karis shook her head at the dismantled futon.

Her sister was all smiles. "I've got a bigger room this summer."

"Eden, I don't have a bed for the guest room yet. It's been so busy—"

"Stop worrying, Karis. I can sleep on the couch." Eden looked down the tree-lined street. "What is this, the land that time forgot? But your house has, um, what do they call it? 'Potential?'"

"I'd say 'good bones.'"

"And it's cozy, kind of like a shoebox."

"It's affordable." Karis lugged the suitcase up the front steps, following Eden who had already tossed her sandals by the front window and her backpack on the forest green sofa.

Eden stood there, gaping at the wallpaper. "Holy cow, I feel like Gulliver. These flowers are ginormous, but the stone on the fireplace is nice, and this is pretty cool." She pressed her foot by a heater vent several times, eliciting a cow-like moan from the hardwood floor.

"I hope to strip the . . ."

But Eden had moved into the tiny dining area, and then the even tinier kitchen. Karis followed her.

"What's with the bird feathers?" Eden stroked her cheek with the blue jay's feather. Eight others, of varying types and colors, lined the windowsill above the sink.

Karis pretended not to hear the question. Her sister had such a short attention span anyway. In the next breath, the feather returned to its place, and Eden began rummaging through the honey oak cabinets. Buddy barked at the back door. Karis set down the cactus and let him in. He ran to Eden.

"Hey Bud, want to go to college with your auntie?" She knelt to scratch Buddy's ears.

Karis shut the cabinet doors. "Eden, do you want to see the upstairs or eat first?"

"You have to ask?" Her sister had flopped on her back to let Buddy lick her face.

Fifteen minutes later, with the citronella candle burning, they watched the lightening bugs swell in the waning light. The evening air was muggy and warm. Buddy camped out under the patio table, positioning himself between their feet. Her sister had eaten three servings of pasta, two slices of focaccia bread, not one taste of the crockpot chicken con broccoli, no fruit salad, and now wanted more cherry cola. Karis refilled her glass, reluctantly. "Women cannot live on carbs alone, Eden."

"You sound just like Mom."

Karis set down the two-liter bottle. "How is she?"

"The same. Sad. Still wanting you to call."

"The office keeps me pretty busy."

"Oh, that's original."

Karis pushed back her chair and snatched Eden's plate. "Do you want any ice cream?"

"Hey, I'm sorry. I just wish—"

"Don't hold your breath, Eden."

*****

Just before midnight, Karis closed her laptop. She'd hit another brick wall. Removing the velvet jeweler's box from its hiding place, she held it close as a tear slid over her cheek. Was it any use?

*****

"Taste this." Eden shoved the cup in Karis' face. "I got two extra shots."

The lake area was unusually crowded due to Harbor Lights, the town's annual festival, which boasted carnival rides, food vendors, and a vintage arts and crafts fair. Her sister had almost knocked over an elderly couple when she saw the coffee shop along the boardwalk. Karis took a sip and handed it back. "I don't understand how you can drink that sludge."

Eden surveyed the dock. "They're kind of low on boats."

"If we'd gotten here at eight like I suggested, instead of ten—"

"Oh stop, you didn't want to fish anyway." Eden slurped her latte. "We could go bowling. It's probably not busy."

"I already bought the bait, Eden. And fixed the poles."

"Okay, okay. Sorry." Her sister tossed her mane back. "There's a guy over there checking us out."

When had her sister become so boy crazy?

Karis left the small cooler with Eden, but didn't trust her with the poles. "I'll be right back. Stay out of trouble."

The boat rental office doubled as a tiny convenience store and smelled oddly of bacon. Two waist-high shelves showcased a variety of gas station food while the glass-fronted refrigerator bulged with soda and beer. A lanky college student leaned over the front counter, fiddling with his phone. He didn't look up when Karis inquired about rentals. Nope, no fishing boats, only one-man kayaks, but she could come back in three hours. Right. Three hours to follow Eden all over Missouri. She'd rather clean out her gutters.

The screen door squeaked open behind her and then slammed shut. Fully expecting a new demand from her sister, she spun around. "Eden, I . . ."

She swallowed, her pulse quickening. Business casual had morphed into a black Nike T-shirt and jean shorts. Clay pulled off his sunglasses. It felt like "that summer" all over again. She was working at the marina when he walked through the door.

He gave her a once over, his eyes finally returning to her face. "My boat's outside."

She straightened. "No, thank you."

He glanced at the poles. "I'm about to go out. I can take—"

"I said, 'No. Thank you.'"

"Karis, look, I'm—"

Her sister burst in. "Well?"

Karis stormed past her. "We're fishing on the shore. In the shade. Don't argue with me."

She didn't stop until she'd marched past the beach area and located a secluded inlet under a grove of pine trees, a good mile from the dock. Eden had griped the entire time while Karis refused to speak. They were both drenched with sweat.

"Hey, why are we stopping, Karis? Let's hike around the other half of the lake. It's only like, a thousand degrees out here."

Karis tried to give her a water bottle. "Your face is red."

"Imagine that."

"In case you hadn't noticed, the lake is a sea of humanity." Karis opened the Styrofoam container and pulled out a night crawler. "I assume you want me to bait your hook."

Eden crossed her arms. "Who was that guy back there?"

"Nobody."

Eden toed a rock in a semi-circle. "So you're not going to tell me about Tarzan?"

"Don't call him that."

"What should I call him?"

"Here's your pole."

Her sister tossed it aside with great ceremony and picked her way over the sandstone ridges to the water.

Karis felt anger squeeze her chest even as the chasm between them widened. "What are you doing, Eden?"

But it was her mother's voice she heard in her head. *What are you doing, Karis?* Fifteen years old, she'd walked out, slamming the door.

Eden turned around and kicked off her flip-flops, looking more like the defiant six-year-old Karis had babysat years ago than a senior in college. "I'm going to join the sea of humanity. They're way better company than you are." She split the water with a perfect dive.

*****

No fish, not even one bite, but at least Eden had stopped giving her dirty looks. Karis packed up after two hours and took Eden home to shower, cool off, and return to the harbor. Her sister now wanted to "do the festival" not take "some boring tour for old people." She proceeded to bounce around the grounds like a pinball, finally landing in the food court at dinnertime.

The north lot was a mish-mash of sizzling grills and multicolored tents under which everything from burgers to gyros to walking tacos tempted the noisy crowd. The heavy smell of fried foods filled the amusement park air.

In the adjacent park, a monstrous white canopy provided cover for the makeshift dining area where rows of picnic tables obliterated the grass. A live band played swing tunes in the nearby gazebo while the town's Young-at-Heart Club danced. For some reason, the older couples all wore Hawaiian shirts. Karis looked for Evelyn, but didn't see her. The couples' prancing brought a smile and an ache. Just like Nana had been with Papa.

Eden wanted a Pizstick, a spiral of garlic bread wound on a stick with pepperoni and cheese. Lauren's family, the Romanis, had invented the bestseller, and with the heavy crowds, Lauren was helping out at their booth. Karis waved at her from the back of the line, but when Sabina, Lauren's mother, spotted her and Eden, she grabbed Karis' arm and propelled them to the front. Two plates containing Pizsticks were doled out with accompanying Italian sodas. Sabina waved off her money and kept telling her to *buon appetito*, "enjoy your meal."

Karis wasn't surprised when Eden bypassed several empty tables for the one with the highest testosterone level. A group of twenty-something guys were ripping apart turkey legs in true Viking style. Karis frowned at the beer bottles and situated herself across from Eden.

Within seconds, her sister had acquainted herself with Cooper, a blonde Adonis who claimed to be a physics student at Mizzou. Eden, the great "math-hater," suddenly couldn't hear enough of Bernoulli's Principle, the graduate student's research project, supposedly. Watching the two, Karis felt like an old schoolmarm and wondered what Mom would think of Eden's flirting. Karis slid off a section of the warm bread, trying to appreciate the garlic and buttery taste, but expecting trouble at any second.

It came soon enough. Eden stood and announced that she "needed" chocolate. Cooper offered to accompany her on her quest. Karis palmed her a five-dollar bill and gave her a warning look, which she seemed to ignore. If she wasn't back in five minutes . . .

A warm body slid in to her right.

Musk.

The bread turned to paste in her mouth. She scooted to the left as much as possible, suddenly angry with Eden for creating yet another awkward moment.

Clay set two plates on the table, one holding a large T-bone steak, the other two ears of corn. He glanced her way, a smooth expression on his rugged face. "Catch anything this afternoon?"

Maybe if she ignored him . . .

He opened his water bottle and motioned toward Eden, who clung to Cooper's arm as they ambled toward a frozen custard stand. "You two could be twins."

His arm bumped hers as he sliced into the steak. She jerked it away. He speared a bite. "And you look comfortable. Not that you don't look nice in—"

"I presume you're not having any trouble with your stitches."

The fork halfway to his mouth, he looked amused. "Would you like to check? Here?"

"You are impossible."

He chewed quietly. "That guy with your sister, where'd she meet him?"

"I'm sorry, how is this *your* business?"

Clay took a swig of his water bottle. "He's trouble."

"So says the pot."

"Karis, if you would just listen."

Eden chose that moment to plop into the opposite seat, a devilish grin on her face. Cooper nudged in next to her like a lost puppy. She savored a bite of chocolate custard that had been buried under cookie crumbles, and then looked at Clay with bright, bunny eyes. "You're the guy from the dock. I'm Eden. This is Coop."

Coop? Karis felt like yanking Eden's ponytail. The girl had apparently lost all sense.

Clay put out his hand. "Clay. Nice to meet you." But his smile didn't quite reach his eyes. He only nodded toward her sister's diversion.

Eden's slender fingers, sparkling with iridescent blue nail polish, traveled to Cooper's overly large bicep. "So, Karis, since you don't want to stay for the sky lanterns, Coop can drive me home. He's got a Harley."

"Eden, I—"

"Actually, Eden, you can join Karis and me. We're taking my boat out. The view's much better on the water, I hear." Clay didn't blink.

The two men eyed each other. Karis bristled at the flagrant lie, but Eden seized the opportunity as a robin would a worm from the road. "Oh, I don't want to intrude. I'll just stay with Coop."

Like Karis would let that happen. She sent a pointed look her sister's way and then confronted Cooper's intense, green eyes. "Actually, Eden is leaving now." And then to Clay. "And so am I. Why don't you and Coop take your boat out? Maybe compare notes?"

Clay leaned in, his voice low. "I was just trying to help."

Eden's face was stonelike. She glared at Karis and then flashed her cell phone to Cooper, no doubt passing on her number. Hopefully, she wouldn't throw a fit or say something inappropriate.

"Eden, let's go." Karis gathered her plate.

*****

Eden stared straight ahead all the way home and stormed into the house before Karis could even put the car in park. Buddy wrestled with the drapes at the window. As Karis opened the front door to let him out, the floor above creaked. What was Eden doing in her bedroom? She went up the stairs to see her sister, rifling through her top dresser drawer.

"What are you doing?"

"Getting my running shorts—the ones you *borrowed* last year."

"Shut that drawer. I'll get them."

Eden picked up the black velvet box. "Hey, what's in here?"

In two quick steps, Karis grabbed the box from her hand. "That's private." She tucked the box away, slammed the top drawer, and opened up the bottom one, removing a pair of black shorts. She thrust them at Eden, who plucked them from her hand, spun around, and headed down the stairs. Within minutes, Karis heard the front door open and slam. Buddy started barking. She rushed downstairs to see Eden, lugging her suitcase and backpack across the yard. Her heart sank.

She ran outside. "Eden, it's late."

Her sister unlocked the car without looking up. "I don't care. I'm leaving, Karis."

"Look, I'm sorry. I didn't mean to be so—"

"I hardly know you anymore. Where did you put my big sister, the one who loved just being alive?"

"Eden, we all have to grow up sometime."

"Why? So I can be like you? No thanks." She threw her luggage in the back, slammed the door, and slid in behind the steering wheel.

"Are you coming back after summer school?" Karis hugged herself.

"I don't think so." Her sister snapped her seatbelt and shook her long hair out.

"What about the B&B?"

Eden started the car. "What about it?"

"Am I still invited?"

"Of course, you're invited, but you should know that Mom's coming."

"How is that possible?"

Eden applied lip balm. "Dad's dropping her off."

"I'll have to check my schedule."

"Get happy, Karis. You're no fun anymore." She started to close the driver's door, but then stopped. "I almost forgot. Mom found this." Eden handed her a sealed envelope and drove off, squealing the tires as she turned the corner.

Karis glanced at the envelope illuminated by the streetlight, her stomach turning sour. She hardly felt the mosquitoes ravaging her ankles.

CHAPTER THREE

"YOU GONNA SIT THERE in that air-conditioned truck all day or give us some help?" Lou tapped on the window.

Clay put away his cell phone and slid out. "Sorry, Lou. What's the verdict?"

"Termites. Foundation's rotted. It's all got to come down."

Clay swigged his water. "Guess your fears came true. Did you reclaim much?"

"The trailer's full. We pulled up the floors in the bedrooms. Lots of nice hickory and the kitchen cabinets were solid, but that's about it."

"What about the container?"

Lou hooked his thumb toward the rear of the lot. "Out back in the alley. The city wouldn't allow it on the street, but Jake called ten minutes ago. He's coming with the truck."

Clay surveyed the dilapidated house. According to the city inspector's report, it had suffered years of neglect, wind and hail damage, and most recently, a meth dealer. Plywood covered every window. A large portion of the roof had caved in by the chimney. The yellow paint was long gone, and inside, they'd found a virtual petting zoo of mice, rats, and squirrels. "What a waste."

"I know, but we're getting this party started. We can't save 'em all." Lou lifted his Cardinal's cap and wiped sweat from his brow. "Besides, it's hotter than an habanero out here. There's Jake."

A red truck with *Sanctuary Homes* written on the side pulled into view. Lou gave a thumbs-up to Frank, who attached earplugs, cranked up the excavator, and attacked the front porch.

The crew was down to the basement remnants by three o'clock, when Lou called it quits. Clay was more than happy to sit by his truck with a two-liter jug of ice water. He'd never worked as hard in his life as he did with these guys. His shirt was soaked through. The June sun and humidity had been merciless.

Lou sidled up to him, swigging his own water. At sixty-five, the older man wasn't heavily built, but could still outwork guys half his age. He limped slightly from a Vietnam War injury. Taking off his cap, he wiped down his baldhead. "You've been awfully quiet this afternoon."

Clay finished off his water. "I saw that lady doctor last Friday."

Lou eased his frame against the truck. "How'd it go?"

"I went in with a rash and came out with skin cancer. Didn't see that coming. She's going to carve on me again this Thursday. I may have to take a couple of days off."

"I expect me and the boys can manage without you."

"But it's not just that." Clay straightened. "Maybe you could pray I'd keep my mouth shut."

Lou raised an eyebrow. "Now, we're talking miracles."

Clay laughed and felt the tension in his neck ease.

Lou nudged a rock with his boot. "Any idea how you got skin cancer?"

"Bad luck, I guess."

"No such thing."

"Well, as you would say, maybe God's got something up His sleeve."

Lou smiled. "There may be hope for you yet, Montes."

*****

Of course it was melanoma. Karis tucked the pathology report back in Clay's file. He'd been scheduled for Thursday's last excision slot, and she'd been dreading his appointment all day long. She filled her mug with the grainy dregs of the coffee pot and listened to the footsteps outside her office.

"Right this way, Mr. Montes."

Did he realize what he was doing to her?

Her courage faltered. She took a deep breath and told herself he was just another excision. But the past continued to torture—his designer clothes, the Italian leather shoes with names she'd never heard of and couldn't pronounce, the cars, an endless supply of credit cards. Standing next to him, she'd felt shabby in her college T-shirt and cut-off shorts. It shouldn't matter what he thought of her. She was a professional now with a wall full of black framed diplomas and certificates. But she had still put on her nicest outfit as if she had something to prove.

Clay seemed engrossed with the floor tiles, but came to attention when she entered the exam room. He'd had enough good sense to wear loose athletic shorts, which negated the need for any awkward undressing. She assumed her medical persona. It had saved her before.

"I presume Lauren has already informed you of the procedure. It's very similar to last week. I'll take another half-centimeter margin since the pathology report showed melanoma in situ, or non-invasive, which is good, but—"

"You need to check the lymph nodes in my groin first. Lauren explained that too."

"It's standard protocol. Don't make this harder than it already is." She could see the amusement in his eyes, but at least he had the decency to look away, a ghost of a smile pulling his mouth sideways.

She palpated the area quickly, her pulse hammering in her ear. Normal. She stepped back, again relieved, but just being near him . . . she had to get out. Outlining the excision site with a blue marker, she quickly applied Betadine. "Lauren will get you numbed up now."

She waited outside the door, pretending to check a file. Several waves of laughter rippled the air. Irritated, she stepped out of earshot of the exam room.

The door soon opened. Lauren meandered out, her cheeks flushed, a wide smile on her face. Karis handed her the pink message note that Belinda had left by the microscope. "The diabetes patient from yesterday morning is on line two. Take the call. I can manage by myself." The last thing she needed was her nurse ogling the patient instead of doing her job.

The young woman picked up the phone when Karis gave her a pointed glance.

When she entered, Clay looked her way, his features pensive, and then he watched her like Dr. Anderson had. The neurotic physician had scrutinized her every move during the two-month surgery rotation, taking pleasure in doling out criticism in front of the other residents. She had picked herself up every time. She would do it now. After re-prepping the site with more Betadine, she put on a mask and snapped on sterile gloves to organize the instruments and tray. The drape came next. As she tried to steady her shaking hand and breathe normally, Clay repositioned himself to view the procedure. A trickle of sweat slid down her back. "Most people don't like the sight of their own blood."

"I'm not most people."

How well she knew that. She brought the blade to his thigh. "You'll have a scar. There's no way around it."

"Seems fair. I gave you one, you give me one."

"I'm not doing this on purpose." Her first stroke was shaky and uneven. She staunched the blood with gauze, wishing she could wipe the moisture from her neck.

"But it is one of the perks of the job. You can always get back at anyone who hurts you."

"I don't need your commentary."

The second stroke was deeper, properly angled to complete the ellipse. Using forceps, she lifted the tissue and cut away the underlying remnants. After dropping the specimen into the formalin bottle, she sutured the site, noticing for the first time his bare left hand.

"There is no wife, in case you're wondering."

Karis swallowed, trying to keep her voice even. "I guess she got the kids then."

"No kids."

She dropped the forceps and needle driver, her hands still shaking. They clanged against the metal tray. Gathering ointment, gauze, and tape, she made quick work of the dressing.

He stood up. "Any plans this weekend?"

Her mind lurched back to "that summer" again. He'd asked the same question. She had just stocked the bathhouse. He'd been standing there, waiting for her, the sun yawning over the pine tree ridge behind him.

She pulled her lab coat around her. "You can quit the act."

He was suddenly serious, his brown eyes capturing hers. "It's not an act."

"No? Now that you've got a tattoo, you're what? A changed man? Like I would believe that."

"What's happened to you, Karis?"

"I learned my lesson the hard way. You always want something, don't you?"

"You're right." He stepped closer. "I just haven't figured out how to get it."

"I should have known."

Clay's face registered frustration. He hissed under his breath. "I don't want to sleep with you, okay?"

Lauren poked her head in. "I can finish up, Dr. Henry."

Karis gave her a brief nod and left the room, inflamed. Clay Montes never stopped until he got what he wanted. How well she knew that.

*****

It was a lie. Of course he wanted her. Any red-blooded American man would take one look at Karis Henry and want her. Clay tried to strangle his thoughts. She had been beautiful at twenty, but she was stunning now, a woman with all the right curves in all the right places. Even with the loose-fitting blouse, he could tell she had— Clay gunned the engine of his truck and tore down the highway, trying to put as many miles as he could between himself and Harbor, Missouri.

God help him. He was such an idiot.

The fancy doctor talk and icy exterior must be a cover-up. It was those amazing, blue eyes that gave Karis away, offset by smooth, flawless skin and exquisite cheekbones. He couldn't stop looking. But why had she hacked off her hair?

He felt a fresh loathing for himself. Instead of conducting himself as he'd intended when he walked into her office, he'd lost his cool. Just like the old Clay. He knew he should control himself, but every time he saw her or smelled her, he wanted her, and all of his noble, holy thoughts turned to ash.

He drove to St. Louis, not really knowing why. By sunset, after circling the city on the I-270 loop, he drove back to his camper. He was a fool. The first thing he saw when he flipped on the light was the open book on the dinette table. At first, he'd thought the gift from his father a complete waste of time—as if knowing anything about his ancestors would somehow impact his life. *The Spanish Conquistadores: Men Who Lived by the Sword.*

But the more he read, the more the truth set in. He was just like them. He'd spent his entire life in conquest, claiming and taking what wasn't his. Life had become a game. But a waterlogged Mercedes had changed all that. The police had found the CEO's body still buckled in his seat belt when they pulled the car from Lake Michigan. As the last person seen with the man, they'd hauled Clay down to the station for questioning. Released hours later, he'd drowned himself in booze. The death was ruled a suicide, but Clay knew the man's blood was on his hands. He'd pushed too hard and played too dirty. Even now, he could still see the man's widow and three kids. God have mercy on his soul.

The next day he had wandered around downtown Chicago for hours, realizing how empty his life had become. A street preacher found him at dusk, staring down a flock of seagulls on the Navy pier. The man gave him a bottle of water and a Hostess Twinkie, mumbling something about "living water" and "the bread of life." Clay told him where to go, but that seemed to ignite the man's passion. He grasped Clay's collar and begged him to listen. The Innocent died for the guilty. There was forgiveness. There was release. In the Blood. Repent. Confess. Clay tried to block out the sound, but the words took on a life of their own and seared his mind even as he stumbled back to his condo and long into the night, when sleep proved impossible. Someone was stalking him, breathing down his neck, permeating his room. Finally, in desperation, he surrendered to the Innocent One, this Jesus.

Two years later, he was still trying to conquer his old nature, still trying to make up for his past, and still trying to get Karis out of his head. It wasn't happening. He'd started searching for her, but with no luck. As a last resort, he hired a private investigator, his old buddy. The man was thorough, if not a bit reckless, but the whole thing felt wrong. It was the old way of doing things—data collection, surveillance, invasion of privacy, and knowing Grayson, probably illegal. But he couldn't stop.

Karis popped up in Harbor with all her medical credentials, just an hour from the St. Louis office. It had been easy to point the *Sanctuary Homes* Board in the direction of the town. Rural areas were crying out for help, and Harbor was no exception. Clay had assumed everything would just fall into place. But she was so different from the lake girl he'd dreamed about for the last decade—so hard, so sharp.

He tried concentrating on the July budget, but by midnight, after hours of looking at the same columns, he shut his computer. What was the point?

CHAPTER FOUR

THE ENVELOPE STILL SAT ON the mantle, where she put it after her sister left. Every time she looked at it, she felt ill. She recognized Aunt Ernie's scrawl on the outside. Did the woman even now want to torment her? Those months still haunted, the nightmares swooping in at unexpected times. Karis had tried to leave, but there was no place to go. Penniless and devastated, she held on to a small thread of hope, but soon realized the depth of the lies. *Suffering was God's will*, her aunt had spouted. And freedom only brought emptiness, the cruelest punishment of all.

One lonely year after another passed. She had buried herself in medical school and residency. Exhaustion kept the demons away. It was survival.

*****

After sleeping poorly, Karis dressed and came into the office early, hoping to find an escape from the neurotic thoughts of Clay. Had two weeks really passed since his last appointment? When she saw his name in the nine o'clock time slot, dread pooled and the memory continued to taunt.

Clayton Emmanuel Montes. Cloistered at the private college, she hadn't known men like him existed. The summer she met him she had been a camp counselor at Camp Jubilee at Somerset Lake. One Saturday, after the kids had packed up and left the camp, Mr. Allison had let the staff go waterskiing. Clay had been standing on the deck of his expensive lakefront home on Timber Trace Ridge. When he waved at her, she lost her grip on the rope and tumbled backward. The next thing she knew, he was by her side, completely soaked, helping her back in the boat.

The next day, Clay showed up at the marina and asked about docking fees. With his dark hair, bronze tan, and imposing presence, he was the twitter of all the female staffers, and Karis couldn't help noticing too. She had never met anyone like him—funny, handsome, charming . . . dangerous. He came every weekend and always seemed to find reasons to bump into her, whether she was cleaning cabins or stocking the bathhouse or mowing the lawns. Every time he saw her, he would ask her out, but she always refused. Why would someone like him be interested in someone like her?

After the Fourth of July, she had gone for an early morning swim in a secluded cove and encountered Clay out rowing. She'd tried to duck away and pretend she didn't see him, but he quickly pulled alongside in his canoe. She could hardly keep her eyes from wandering over his bare chest. He invited her to join him, and she hadn't refused. They spent the morning together on the water. She'd been shy, but the more he teased, the more she let her guard down.

He was originally from Springfield, an only child. He'd graduated from Southern California Institute with a degree in architecture and finished an MBA at Northwestern University two years later. He would start a new job with a Chicago firm in September. Karis hadn't needed to ask about his financial status. From the three boats he owned to the Corvette in his driveway to the extravagant vacation home, she knew he was loaded.

After their early morning encounter, he'd suggested lunch at the marina, and then dinner in Branson the next week, and finally two weeks later, dessert at his home. Her first kiss happened on his back deck. His lips were warm and gentle. He had wanted more, but she insisted they stay outdoors. He'd been the perfect gentleman and honored her wishes.

But on a sultry evening in mid-August, everything changed. He invited her to dinner, swearing that her life wouldn't be complete unless she tasted his specialty, grilled New York strip. That night, his eyes seemed to smolder. By the water's edge, they ate and laughed, and Clay suggested a swim. She hadn't brought her suit, but he smiled, handed her a wrapped box from Lord and Taylor, and told her he'd meet her at the dock. She went inside to change, not knowing what to expect. She pulled back the delicate tissue paper to find a black bikini. Every coherent voice inside her head told her to march outside, give the box back, and head to her cabin.

But she didn't.

"Dr. Henry?"

Karis shook her head, coming to awareness. Lauren was giving her a funny look.

"Did you hear me? Two patients are waiting."

Karis donned her white coat and followed Lauren into the first room. Thankfully, Clay was not in it. She checked the middle-aged woman, noting the labored breathing and recent fever. She ordered a chest x-ray and blood work and gave directions to the hospital in nearby Landover. After the patient left, she checked Clay's chart. Just his name set her stomach roiling.

He sat on the exam table, staring at his hands. He looked up when she walked in. "I'm sorry about the last time. I didn't mean to—"

"It doesn't matter."

"Of course it matters."

"Let's just get this over with." She washed her hands at the sink. "The final path report was fine." Lauren entered with a suture removal kit and then left to draw up vaccines for a pediatric patient.

"The scar won't be bad. It should fade in the next year."

He nodded, keeping his gaze on the wall. She snipped off the knots and pulled out the loose strings with forceps. Next came the dressing. "That's it."

Clay stood, his eyes holding an emotion she couldn't decipher. Something about the way he was so quiet was unnerving. She almost preferred his belligerence. She checked the note in his chart. "You need a follow-up exam in three months. It doesn't have to be with me. I can forward your records."

"Is that what you want? To get rid of me?"

An awkward moment passed. He continued to stare. She swallowed and looked up, her voice weak, but determined. "You are the biggest mistake of my life."

There, she'd finally said it to his face after thinking it a thousand times. But why was she shaking?

A muscle twitched in his jaw. He pinned her with a dark gaze. "I'll see you in three months, if not before."

She backed up. "What is that supposed to mean?"

He moved closer. "It means I'll do whatever I have to do, Karis."

He stared at her a moment longer and then left the room. The chart blurred before her eyes as she felt herself caught in an undertow with nothing to hold onto.

Hours later at home, she sat on her bed with a sense of doom, Aunt Ernie's cursed envelope in hand. She couldn't open it, much less bring herself to read the contents. It was all coming back. The woman's weathered face rose in her imagination. How could anyone be so cruel and unfeeling and call themselves a Christian? She went downstairs and flipped on the stove burner. Hadn't she dealt with enough to last a lifetime? She set the envelope on fire, watching the paper blacken and curl.

*****

You are the biggest mistake of my life.

Her words continued to torture with every nail he hit, with every board he cut, their weight pressing harder and harder into his thoughts. He became more determined, almost obsessed.

He had to fix this.

On Tuesday evening, the sink in his trailer backed up. Clay filled a basin with water at the bathhouse and was headed back to his campsite when the red Camaro caught his eye. His pulse quickened. The private investigator held a cigarette out the window, its smoke curling in the late afternoon air. The short man was always trying to kick the habit. Apparently, he still hadn't. He got out, looked around, and smirked. "What's with the Grizzly Adams gig?"

Clay straightened. "Lots of fresh air. Clears the mind."

Grayson looked at the basin. "And no modern plumbing? I would have thought that—"

"Why are you here?"

"You know me, can't leave a stone unturned."

"I thought we were finished." He'd paid an exorbitant fee for the man's "services."

"You always like things so cut and dried, Montes, but the world isn't like that. I found a pretty tasty tidbit on your lady doctor. Couldn't pass it up. For another five hundred . . ."

The man was a leech. "No thanks."

Grayson pulled on the cigarette and exhaled. "Turns out she has a little secret. But then again, don't we all? Who could forget Key West?"

Clay set down the basin. "Just stop right there."

"But man, it was fun. You were such a—"

"Dead and buried, Grayson." Clay swung open the door to the trailer and reached inside for the stack of dirty pots. Maybe the leech would take the hint.

"May 7, 2001 mean anything to you?"

"I told you, I'm not interested."

"Oh, I'm pretty sure you'll want to know this." Grayson threw the cigarette butt down and crushed it with his shoe.

All the blood sucking was starting to get on his nerves. Clay slammed the door and took the pots to the picnic table. "Alright, what?"

Grayson lit another cigarette and followed him, kicking a rock into the fire pit. "It's her kid's birthday."

A red-winged blackbird burst out from a nearby thicket, sending a jolt down Clay's spine. He whirled around and stared at the man, his mind racing backward, reliving, rehashing. It was simple addition, and she had been a . . . *Oh, dear God.* What had he done? "Are you telling me—"

"Hey, with five hundred on the line, would I make this stuff up?" Grayson checked his cell phone. "Which is what you now owe me, Papa Bear."

The old, dark passion stirred.

Grayson took another puff. "So . . . I'm guessing she kept you in the dark."

"There's the road, Grayson."

The man exhaled. "Or maybe some other guy got in the oven."

"Keep talking like that, and I'll bust your face."

"Whoa, Montes, chill." Grayson held up both palms. "This kind of thing happens all the time. You need a drink, man."

"You have no idea what I need."

Grayson produced a manila file from his car. "It's all in here with some pretty impressive photos, I might add. You've got yourself a real live mermaid. And for the record, she is smoking hot. I wouldn't mind taking her for a—"

Clay's fist caught him in the jaw and sent him sprawling. The cigarette fell by the road and smoldered. Wide-eyed and disoriented, the man shook his head and slowly came to his knees. Blood trickled from his left nostril. He wiped it away and stood shakily. "Defending a lady's honor. That's a new one."

"Just get in your car."

"Five hundred tomorrow, Clay, or I press charges. Understand?" Grayson took out his keys. "Man, whatever happened to the old you?"

Dead and buried. And now desperate.

*****

Over the next two weeks, he'd left a dozen messages, but Karis hadn't returned his calls. Maybe that Belinda person never gave them to her. The woman seemed preoccupied every time he called and then annoyed. But more than likely, the messages were crumpled or ripped to shreds in a trash can somewhere. He punched in the office number again and then ended the call abruptly. He got in his truck. If she wouldn't talk with him on the phone, she'd talk with him in person. It was time for some answers. He headed downtown with the AC on high.

He tapped the steering wheel as he drove down Main Street. Years ago, he would have thumbed his nose at Harbor. The dated storefronts, some begging for new paint and others for an owner, were glued to each other like in a thousand other backwater towns. Lampposts peered out between trees, uprooting the sidewalks. On the corner of Third Street, an antique store struggled to survive across from Ed's Diner and the Bullfrog Bar, which sat next to an insurance office. The locals still referred to the ratty garage at the end of town as "the filling station." Revitalization efforts were ongoing, and Nelda's, the ladies' boutique, looked promising. Ditto for the record shop, of all things.

But Feather Lake was the town's redemption—miles of shoreline, coves, and picturesque bluffs, and wildlife of every sort. Lou was downright giddy when his fishing boots touched the water. He could practically smell out the fish. But few boats plied the choppy waters on this stormy afternoon. Rain was coming soon.

Clay parked on a side street where he could see the rear exit and parking lot of the medical clinic. Apparently, the boxy brick building, with a 1960 cornerstone, had been a post office in its previous life. A twenty-foot flagpole hugged the southwest corner, and he'd noticed a couple of old-timey mail slots in the waiting room. The back alley was a virtual dump.

The file folder taunted him from the passenger seat. That she loved the lake was no surprise. The pictures told the full story—Karis walking along a path, swimming at sunset, wading at the beach, sitting lakeside on a bench. She was always alone, always somber, but where was . . . The need to know plagued him. *Oh God, help me.* He put away the pictures and covered the file with his jacket.

When five o'clock came, the back door opened. He recognized the nurse and the Belinda person. As they both drove off in their cars, Clay studied the 2002 Mitsubishi Spyder convertible left behind. Karis had always seemed like the eco-friendly Prius or even the sedate Buick type. Maybe there was another side to her.

Another hour passed. Streetlights flickered on. Clay left his truck as darkness settled. Leaning against one of the ancient oaks, he faced the rear of the building. He didn't want to come out of nowhere and scare her to death. The back door opened at six-thirty.

Karis came to an abrupt stop when she saw him, seemingly shocked and then animated with anger. Well, he was upset too. He walked to her car and tried to remain calm. "Just curious why you can't return my calls?"

She took out her keys, but he stepped in front of the Spyder. Her eyes sparked. "This feels like stalking."

"We need to talk."

"You have a lot of nerve showing up like this."

"What other option did I have?"

"I don't take personal calls at my office." She tried to step around him.

"Karis, look." He took a deep breath. "I know about the—"

A motorcycle raced by, the revved up engine splitting the night air.

"Baby." It came out too loud.

She flinched and then backed away, eyes wide.

"Why didn't you—" Clay stepped closer.

Her lower lip quivered.

"I wish you would have told me."

Her voice shot out as her eyes ignited. "Told you? You were engaged to be married."

"Still, I could have—"

"What? Thrown money at me? Like you fix all your problems? How dare you show up now with all these questions." She removed her phone. "I'm calling the police."

He stepped aside. "Karis, believe me when I say how sorry—"

"Save it." She struggled to unlock her car. As she slid in, he grabbed the door before she could shut it.

"Where is he now?" The question came out of nowhere.

The fire left her face. He moved his hand just before she slammed the door.

CHAPTER FIVE

ON THE FRIDAY AFTER THE Fourth of July weekend, an evening thunderstorm hit, leaving Clay's campsite a virtual war zone— branches down, upended camping chairs, his cooler halfway to the bathhouse, and the trailer canopy ripped beyond repair. But he didn't really care. He stretched and took off jogging. He had to clear his mind.

He'd always enjoyed confrontation, the adrenaline high of the fight, besting his opponent at every turn. And he always won and always managed to throw the last punch. But now . . . He had called Grayson and apologized for his surly behavior. The man had laughed and said something about Clay auditioning for *Survivor*. But he still felt ashamed and out of control.

He set a punishing speed as the incline of the road increased, winding around the bluff and then down by the lake. A few boats trolled in the dampness of the early morning, but the woods were still.

At mile five, heavily winded, he slowed his pace. A truck pulled up beside him.

"I thought we were fishing this morning?" Lou called to him from the open window.

Clay gasped for breath, running alongside. "Lou, sorry. Totally forgot."

"No problem. Just help me eat these." Lou held up two boxes of Zippy Donuts.

"Looks like you bought 'em out."

"You know I can't resist maple long johns." Lou sipped from his travel mug. "Their coffee's pretty good too. You want a ride?"

"No. Almost done."

"Don't kill yourself."

Clay saluted as Lou drove off. When he arrived at his trailer, Lou tended a morning fire in the pit area for "ambience." He threw another log on the flames and then sat in a camping chair with his feet propped up on a large stone, the donut boxes stacked on his lap.

"How'd you manage a fire?" Clay stretched his quads.

Lou surveyed the donuts. "Found some dry wood under your trailer. Found your gas tank too. Sometimes, all it takes is a little encouragement."

"Good thing it's so damp out here. The ranger might question your tactics."

Clay went inside and grabbed a water bottle from the fridge. Lou tossed him a box as he sat down by the fire. He debated between an apple fritter and a cruller. "Guess we're not worrying about our cholesterol today." Lou's doctor had recently chewed him out.

"Don't ruin the moment, Clay." Lou crammed half a donut in his mouth and groaned in delight.

"How'd your RV hold up?"

"Better than your canopy." Lou chewed and slurped his coffee. "But my side view mirror is busted. I'm going to St. Louis this morning. You need anything?"

"We're not shingling?" Work would be a welcome diversion. The apple fritter melted in his mouth. Must be half grease.

"Not with more rain on the way. Besides, the guys need a break. So do you. How's the cut?"

Clay moved his bandaged finger. "Not bad." For one second, he'd lost his focus with the jigsaw, but he refused to go to the clinic. What would he have told her? *I'm an idiot because of you.* He had let Lou doctor him with the steri-strips instead. He guzzled his water bottle and then crushed it, the plastic crackling in his hand.

"So, what's eating you?" Lou was on his third long john.

"Come again?"

"Your finger. You almost cut it off this week. That's not you."

Clay studied the laces of his running shoes. Lou was like a giant oak tree, unmovable, unshakable, a tower of strength and strong character—the very opposite of himself. "It's not pretty."

"Pretty is overrated. I much prefer honest."

A few cobbled clouds shifted as the sun's rays skimmed the steeples of the pine trees, warming the air. Clay breathed in the scent of the woods, mingled with the smoke of the fire. He couldn't deny how much he enjoyed outdoor living, a far cry from his earlier penthouse life. He'd sown more than a few wild oats back then. At times, he owned the entire countryside. A V of geese honked by. Clay watched them until they disappeared behind the bluff. "You ever do something you regret?"

Lou looked off in the distance. "What a dumb question."

Clay sighed. "You know why I wanted the Harbor project?"

"Something tells me that lady doctor has something to do with it."

"How'd you guess?" He chucked a piece of bark in the fire.

Lou sipped his coffee. "Well, you—"

"I got her pregnant ten years ago." Clay forked fingers through his hair. "I just found out last week."

To his credit, Lou didn't flinch. "And now you're wondering . . ."

"What am I supposed to do with that information?"

"What you should always do. Get down on those ugly knees and pray."

"And then what? Do nothing? This whole 'wait on the Lord' thing drives me crazy."

Clay jumped up and started dragging a large branch to the fire pit. He'd get out the chainsaw later. Lou watched him with a look of concern. "Would ya stop before you hurt yourself?"

"I have to do something, Lou."

"Then maybe shut your craw and listen to some reason."

Hours later, Clay had a good-sized woodpile and a million Bible verses to look up, but he still felt like a caged animal.

*****

It had been a long week of sleepless nights—the nightmares, the nausea, the hopelessness. Karis felt wired by Friday's end. She'd hardly eaten lately. She downed her fourth cup of coffee and ducked into the exam room.

The mother of four rubbed her extended stomach. "I just know it's a girl. I can feel it, but Dr. Henry, I can't have this baby 'til after July thirtieth."

Karis moved the Doppler monitor over the woman's abdomen, finding the heartbeat. "Why is that, Lourdes?"

"Because that's when we move into our new house on Dewberry Court." The woman clasped her hands as she lay there, smiling at the speckled ceiling tiles. "I can't believe it. Two bathrooms! Two! An answer to prayer, that Mr. Montes. "

Karis' hand jerked. "I'm not sure I follow you."

The woman went on to chatter about these nice men from St. Louis who were building houses. The family had been cramped in a small apartment for over two years. Lourdes' new home was on the southern fringes of town close to the county line. A bunch of old houses had been torn down to make way for the new development.

Karis pulled on gloves and checked for dilation and effacement. "You're at two centimeters and starting to efface. The heartbeat is still good and strong, and baby is in the right position. I'm not sure you'll make it to your move-in date."

"Oh dear, I must pray harder."

Karis remained silent and helped the woman up to a sitting position. "You are a natural at this, Lourdes. I'm sure whatever happens, things will work out. Try not to overdo, okay? It's fine to let Julio help with the housework."

"Like I would let that man touch my vacuum!"

"I'll see you next week."

Karis returned to her office and shut the door, pressing fingers to her forehead. How could it be Clay? And yet . . . is that why he was in Harbor—on some do-good mission to ease his guilty conscience? She dumped her lunch in the trash and reached for her ibuprofen.

*****

Saturday morning was rainy. What better day to strip the gaudy living room wallpaper? Karis started peeling the loosened edges by the front window while Buddy chewed the remnants that fell. She finally secured his leash to a staircase post to keep him from gagging, but his whining grated on her nerves.

Clay knew. She'd always wondered what would have happened if he knew. Would things have been any different? The thought offered no comfort.

By noon, her fingers ached, and only half the front wall was finished. What had possessed her to start such a task? She poured coffee and sat down at the kitchen table. Buddy folded himself at her feet and started snoring. The rain had stopped, but clouds remained, casting the house in a quasi-darkness that matched her spirit.

How had he found out, and what did he want from her now?

She opened her laptop and typed in *Sanctuary Homes*. A website popped up, detailing housing projects for low-income families, the disabled, and seniors. He was involved with a nonprofit? The very thought was ludicrous. It was probably a front for organized crime or some investment scam. Karis shut her laptop and went in search of a box cutter. For some reason, slashing the wall felt very good, almost cathartic.

Two hours later, she still felt restless, hounded by thoughts that threatened her sanity. She opened the fridge and stared at the empty shelves. She needed food. Maybe she would take the southern route to the county market. She got in the car and drove, knowing she really wasn't going to the store. The sign for *Sanctuary Homes* soon appeared. A new concrete road snaked through a handful of houses that stood in varying stages of completion. Most of the lots were barren and riddled with stakes. A lone black truck sat in the drive of a white ranch-style home with blue shutters. Karis checked the address and parked just short of the drive, noting the Missouri license plate of the truck. She frowned at the letters: SAMSON.

At that moment, she heard the crunch of gravel and glanced sideways to see Clay, heading toward the truck with two wooden doors balanced on his right shoulder. When he saw her, he froze.

She could hardly control the words that spewed out of her mouth. "Don't you think 'Samson' is a little presumptuous?"

He set the doors in the bed of the truck without answering and then removed his work gloves. He seemed totally at ease in ragged jeans and a red T-shirt. It was unnerving.

"My father's name is Samuel. I'm his son. Sam's son. That's not presumption. It's just fact."

"You know what I mean."

Clay leaned an elbow on the back of the truck. "Do I? Are we talking Bible now? I thought that was off limits with you."

"Why did I ever come here?" She threw up her hands and stalked to the driver's door of her car.

He followed her. "Why did you come?"

She backed against the door. "To see for myself. If what I heard was true." She could smell his sweat. He was much too close. She swallowed.

"Any other reason?" His gaze was suffocating.

She pointed at the house. "Why this?"

"Just keeping a promise."

"What happened to your big plans? You were going to crush corporate America."

His face softened. "I've tried to tell you."

"Oh, of course. You're a new creature now with a tattoo to prove it—all cleaned up and born again. Hallelujah!"

She wished for the old Clay, the one who could turn cold and selfish, the one who used people. She would know how to handle that man, but not this.

He answered quietly. "Yes, to all of that."

"Well, good for you." She fumbled for her keys, shocked when she felt his finger under her chin, willing her to look up. Powerless, she fought back tears as he raised her face. She would never survive this. She would never survive him. His calloused thumb brushed her lips, causing a shudder. She hated the quiver in her voice. "Stop. Please."

He didn't listen.

She felt her knees weaken as he searched her face, leaning closer, his voice tight. "You're right. Samson was a powerful man, and he made a big mistake, many mistakes. But in the end, he got something right. I'm just trying to get it right, Karis."

He opened the car door for her. After she slid in, he shut it just like a . . . she couldn't say it, couldn't think it.

*****

She wiped away the moisture on her face as she drove home, the skin burning where his thumb had grazed. He would ruin her again. She could see it in his eyes. The intensity. The hunger. And part of her desperately wanted it, wanted him. She slammed on the brake at a four-way stop. What was she thinking? What had possessed her to seek him out? He would always win. He was born to win. And he would crush her heart like he did before.

A car honked from behind. She gassed the accelerator, causing the car to lurch forward.

And yet . . . he had held back. Could he really be telling the truth? Was he really different? Or was it all a put-on? He was a consummate liar.

Without warning, she saw her younger self, wracked with guilt, standing on the porch of his lakefront home the night after she'd done the unthinkable. When she rang the doorbell, a beautiful woman wearing a strapless yellow shift had answered. Everything about the woman was exotic—her long black hair, her violet eyes, her smooth olive skin.

Karis had mumbled something incoherent when she noticed the large diamond on the woman's left hand. The woman gave her a funny look.

"Who is it, babe?" Clay pulled the door back, shock evident for a split second and then a quick recovery. "Oh hi, Karis. Everything okay at the marina?"

She stood there bewildered, the ugly truth slowly coiling around her heart. Somehow, she breathed. Somehow, she spoke in a normal voice. "There's a bad storm tonight. Mr. Allison wanted everyone to know."

The woman wrapped her arms around Clay's waist and kissed his neck, her voice sharp and possessive. "We have a phone."

"Thanks for the heads up." Clay gave her an easy smile and closed the door.

But that wasn't all he gave her. Three weeks later, she'd snuck into the dorm bathroom after midnight, fearful someone might see. Shutting herself in a stall, she removed the test with shaking hands. She knew it would be positive. She was always regular. Within weeks, her world fell to pieces. All because of one night with him.

The liar.

*****

Her lips were soft and moist. How easily he could have let his fingers slide into her hair and take her in his arms and drown himself in . . . *Oh dear God, what was he doing?* He shouldn't have touched her, but he couldn't help himself. And yet, she had let him. Could that mean— He shook his head.

You are the biggest mistake of my life.

How could he ever fix that?

She had bewitched him that summer and left him yearning for something he couldn't even define, something outside himself. He pursued her relentlessly, and then slowly, like a rare bloom, she opened up about her faith, her love of God, and her dream of helping others, making the world a better place. She wanted a family, five kids. Secretly, he found her amusing and naive, her aspirations laughable. But he'd played along so he could get exactly what he wanted. And he had. And now this.

God have mercy.

CHAPTER SIX

DELICATE WILLOWS CANOPIED the winding road up to The Wisteria House B&B, their leafy limbs shimmering in the rays of the July afternoon. Karis slowed and admired the beauty of the place. How she wanted to enjoy the weekend. She'd made a mess of things with Eden two months ago. They'd hardly talked in the ensuing weeks. Of course Eden had twelve credit hours, a part time job at the library, and tutored her roommate Ashley, but still . . . Maybe the weekend would be a chance for reconciliation, but with Mom coming, Karis hardly knew what to expect.

She removed her small suitcase and Eden's cactus from the back seat and picked her way along the cobblestones leading through the well-tended grounds to the front porch. Impressive from a distance, the stately Victorian was breathtaking up close. Boasting a turret and numerous chimneys and peaks, the three stories of the "Grand Dame" were pale blue with white gingerbread trim. The inviting wraparound porch and gazebo practically begged for company. Perhaps she could try out the porch swing tomorrow before anyone awakened. Just as she reached the top step, Eden flew out the front door, breathless.

"What do you think of the house?"

"It's exquisite."

"Don't look so serious, Karis. We're going to have a good time."

"Can I have a hug?"

"If you put down that cactus and promise to laugh at least once this weekend."

Karis set the pot on the porch and then slid her arms around her baby sister, squeezing tightly. "I promise. It's so good to see you."

Eden grabbed her elbow and started dragging her through the front door, the cactus forgotten. "Wait until you see the inside."

Karis scooped up the prickly plant just before a pleasant middle-aged woman wearing a black and white polka-dot apron met them in the spacious foyer. "You must be Karis. I'm Deanna, Ashley's mom."

Eden took the cactus back as Karis shook the woman's hand. "Such a lovely home. Thank you for having us."

"It's the least we could do after all Eden has done for Ashley. Her dyslexia has really been a challenge."

Eden piped in. "But she's doing great. On track for graduation."

"I look forward to meeting her."

"Which should be any minute now. I sent her to the store for pancetta." Deanna glanced at the grandfather clock by the formal dining archway. "I hope you'll excuse me. We're totally full this weekend and I still have some prep work. I gave Eden the keys to your room. Do make yourself at home."

As Deanna returned to the rear of the house, Karis followed Eden up the staircase. She stopped on the second floor by *The Bluebird Suite*. The room featured intricate mahogany pieces and a massive bed with a tulle canopy. An overhead chandelier cast soft diamonds of light on the pale blue comforter and matching floor-to-ceiling drapes. Karis had never seen such a beautiful bedroom.

"You and Mom are in here."

Karis' chest tightened. "Where are you staying?"

"With Ashley in the 'Nanny Attic.' Put your stuff down. I want to show you something."

Eden was off again. Karis followed her to a small door at the end of the hallway that opened to a narrow, carpeted stairwell. At the top, a cozy room housed two twin beds, tucked on either side of a gabled window that overlooked the back garden. On the other side of the room, squeezed between a plain wooden door and the room's sloped ceiling, was a tiny bathroom, all in white, with a claw-foot tub and pedestal sink.

Eden stood expectantly in front of the wooden door. "Just wait 'til you see what's behind this. You'll freak out."

"Bats?"

"See, Karis, you can be funny." Eden smiled and then made a grand gesture as she opened the door. "No, the secret library. In the turret."

Karis stepped over the threshold in awe. Two crimson wingbacks sat by a single window with an oval table in between. Inches away, an elaborate mahogany staircase spiraled downward with custom bookshelves lining the circular walls. Every shelf was stuffed to capacity.

Eden pointed below. "The door at the bottom opens to a passageway that ends in the pantry of the kitchen. The story goes that in 1846, the lady of the house wanted to read at night without disturbing her husband, so this turret was added. But in reality, the guy didn't want the servants to see him sneaking around the kitchen at all hours of the night. Rumor has it he weighed four hundred pounds. Ashley and her brother used to throw sticky balls into a trashcan at the bottom."

A car drove up outside. Eden rushed to the window. "Mom's here. We can go down the turret stairs. It's faster."

Karis froze. Her sister was halfway down the steps. "I'll stay here, Eden."

Eden stopped and looked up. "Karis, they just drove three hours. You can at least stick your head out the door and say hi."

"I need to call the hospital."

Eden scowled. "You just don't want to see him, do you?"

Karis swallowed. "You don't understand."

"Of course, I don't understand. No one tells me anything. Go ahead. Keep your grudge. Ruin the family. See if I care."

As the sound of her footsteps fell away, Karis felt the guilt resurface like a creature from the deep. She had only spoken to her mother sporadically through the years. And what would she say now? Anytime she opened her mouth, they wound up arguing. This whole trip was probably doomed.

Standing back from the window, she watched her mother embrace Eden while her father opened the trunk and removed her mother's old brown suitcase. He looked leaner with more gray, but still appeared strong and imposing. In the next moment, he hugged Eden warmly. Daddy's baby girl. Her father cast a glance toward the house. Was he looking for her? Cursing her? The pain sat heavy. He pecked Mom's cheek. Karis turned away, not wanting to see anymore. A moment later, she heard the sound of wheels on gravel. She blew her nose and called the hospital, hoping for a reason to leave. If only Lourdes would go into labor.

For dinner, Eden had made reservations at a bistro not far from the B&B. Ashley would be helping her parents, so it would be the three of them. Karis mentally squirmed, fearful of where the conversation might lead. She went down to the suite and glanced in the mirror of the chifforobe just as she heard Eden on the steps.

"Mom, they don't want us to pay. Ashley's mother made that clear."

"Honey, I don't feel right taking up a room when this is their livelihood."

"Then crochet an afghan for their parlor or something."

"Oh, Eden." Her mother sounded slightly winded.

Karis turned around as they entered the room. Her mother paused, hesitant.

"Hi, Mom."

In the next moment, Lorna Henry had her arms around Karis, whispering, "Oh, how I've missed you."

"Me too, Mom." Something ached inside.

Her mother cupped her face with warm, soft hands. "I'm so glad you came, but you look tired. Are things still hectic?"

Eden interrupted. "Can we talk about this at the restaurant? I'm famished, and we're supposed to be there in fifteen minutes."

Lorna smiled. "Some things never change."

Eden insisted on driving the Bonneville and zipped along curvy back roads until Mom asked her to slow down. Karis noticed she clutched the armrest. From the backseat, she studied her mother's dark bun, threaded now with a few silver strands. Did she ever want to cut it? Did Dad ever let her pick out her own clothes? She'd been wearing that same floral skirt since 1998.

When they arrived at the quaint eatery, they were ushered to a small table by a corner window. Black and white checkered napkins held silverware in pockets over a crisp, white tablecloth. A cluster of tea lights flickered beside a vase holding three red roses. Piano music played softly in the background. The waiter began filling their water glasses.

Eden fiddled with the salt and pepper shakers, smiling up at the twenty-something man. "I hear you make your bread in-house. Can we get some soon . . . Stone?" Eden glanced at his nametag.

The waiter gave Eden an appreciative look. "Absolutely. I'll be right back."

Sitting next to Eden, her mother put on reading glasses and studied the menu. "They have some nice pasta, a little pricey, but lots of options, Eden."

"I'm having spaghetti."

Karis smiled inwardly. Eden's choice was untainted by any vegetables. "What about you, Mom?"

"You know me. I can't pass up a good salad."

"Where do you think he got the name Stone?" Eden started folding her straw wrapper.

"Maybe a movie from the eighties." Her mother took a sip of water.

Eden straightened. "Here he comes again. With bread."

Stone sat the bread near Eden. She smiled at him and flounced over her menu, ordering extra Parmigiano cheese with her spaghetti.

Just as Stone finished taking their order, Eden requested more butter. She pulled her bread apart. "You know, Karis, he kind of reminds me of your friend. Not as tall and no ponytail, but definitely dark and handsome."

Mom looked at her, eyebrows raised. "You've got a friend?"

Karis suddenly thought of *Katie Kiss 'n' Giggles*, Eden's favorite doll growing up. Karis had often hidden the double-A batteries to silence the doll. How she wished she could do that with Eden. "No, I do not."

"That's not how it looked at the festival that day." Eden gave her a meaningful glance, which her mother pretended not to notice.

Mom straightened her napkin. "So, Eden, how's your term paper coming?'

"Fine. Only three more novels to read, and then I can finish my analysis. I'm so glad I didn't live back then."

With her double major in psychology and women's studies, Eden had finagled a term paper that explored Jane Austen's personality. What she would do with her major once she graduated was anyone's guess. Karis kept suggesting Human Resources. Eden thrived on social media.

The butternut squash soup was delicious, but Karis struggled to eat. Her mom seemed to be picking at her salad too.

Her mother speared a tomato. "Have you thought about Thanksgiving, Karis?"

It was four months away, but Mom kept bringing it up. Karis swallowed and set her spoon down. "I'm working the day after, so I won't be able to come. And you know the other reason."

"Karis, your father has—"

"Let's talk about something else, Mom."

Her mother remained quiet for the rest of the meal and let Eden babble on about the theater department's upcoming performance of *The Sound of Music.* Eden planned on auditioning.

When they arrived back at the B&B, the front porch glowed with twinkle lights. Ashley was waiting on the steps. Within seconds, Eden had introduced everyone, and then pulled Ashley to the car. The two headed off to meet up with friends at a local coffee shop for some live music.

Her mother shook her head as they drove off with the radio blaring. "Where does she get all that energy? Just watching her makes me tired."

"It'll catch up with her someday. Thanks for supper, Mom."

"Thank your father."

Karis remained silent.

Her mother glanced at the sunset. Strands of peach and lavender clouds striped the horizon. "This is strange, isn't it? Being here."

"How is it that Dad let you come?"

"I think it was Aunt Ernie's doing. She talked to him before she . . . I'm sorry you didn't come to the funeral."

"He didn't want me there."

"Karis, he . . . What did Aunt Ernie's letter say?"

"I don't know. I didn't read it."

"Oh, Karis." A look of disappointment shadowed her mother's face. "Nana thought Aunt Ernie confessed in that letter. What she did with . . . him. She had a friend in some adoption agency."

Karis suddenly felt faint, unable to breathe. "Why didn't you tell me?"

"Why didn't you just read it?"

"I don't know. I thought . . ."

"She's the only one who knew, Karis, and now she's . . ." Her mom sighed and brushed Karis' bangs to one side. "Sweetheart, look what this is doing to you. Can't you let it go?"

Karis turned away. It would be dark soon. Already, a few stars twinkled. "How am I supposed to do that?"

"You know how. I taught you how." Her mother sighed. "Why can't you meet your father halfway?"

A whisper came out. "It still hurts. I still hurt."

Her mother pulled her into a hug. "Oh, honey."

"I don't have any hope left, Mom." A silent tear made its way down her cheek.

*****

Karis had dreamed of him — the smoothness of his cheek, his tiny fingers, his hair as soft as butterfly wings, his little pug nose. He smelled soapy and fresh. She took him outside, wrapped in a towel so they could soak up the morning warmth together, but she didn't see the animal. In the next moment, she was running through woods, clutching him to her breast, heart beating like mad, and the animal was gaining, gaining . . .

Hands squeezed her shoulders. She opened her eyes to see her mother hovering and worried. "What's wrong, honey?"

She shook away the darkness and came to full consciousness. "Just a bad dream. That's all." But she felt spooked. There had never been an animal before. "What time is it?"

"Just after seven. I tossed and turned all night. I was thinking about having some coffee in the sunroom and then crocheting." Mom was already dressed.

"Let me put on some clothes." She sensed that her mother wanted company, but the coffee would also do her pounding head some good. "I guess we won't see Eden until noon."

"Not unless she smells bacon. I think she came in after midnight."

They found an elegant silver service in the dining room with coffee and hot water for tea. Deanna had also set out some pastries for the early risers on the buffet. A full breakfast would follow at nine. Mom added cream and sugar to her cup and then opened one of the French doors to the sunroom. White wicker furniture graced the small space while the lavender floral cushions lent a cottage air. Karis eased onto the loveseat beside her mother, cradling her cup.

"Deanna tells me they roast their own coffee beans." Her mother took a tentative sip. "What do you think?"

Karis blew on the dark brew and then brought it to her lips, sipping. "Outstanding."

Her mother smiled. "I never thought you'd be a coffee drinker. Sometimes I find it hard to believe that my children are all adults."

Karis noticed the yellow yarn in her mother's basket. "So, what are you making now?"

Her mother exhaled slowly. "A baby afghan. I don't suppose Micah told you yet."

"Micah doesn't talk to me, Mom."

"Well, they just found out. Clara is still in the first trimester."

"When's the baby due?"

"March." Her mother's eyes held an apology.

"That's wonderful." Her tongue felt like soggy toast. Her younger brother was going to be a father. A legitimate father.

"I'm sorry, honey."

"What are you sorry about? You're getting a grandchild."

"I will always be sad—"

"Please don't, Mom."

Her mother blew her nose. Karis looked out the window at the shifting clouds. Was a storm coming? A wind stirred the willows and swayed the geranium pots hanging along the porch. Eden's plans to visit the craft fair today might get blown away. Not that Karis really wanted to go.

Her mother swirled her cup and cleared her throat. "So, about this 'friend' that you don't have. Is there something I need to know?"

What would Mom think if she knew Clay was lurking around Harbor? That he was actually the . . . She had never dated before Clay and she had never dated anyone since that summer. How could she? He'd left her broken in a million pieces. "No, Mom, there is nothing you need to know."

"How long will you stay at the clinic?"

"At least a year. I signed a contract, which will take care of twenty-five percent of my loans. Then I can renegotiate for another year.

"And after that?"

"I don't know. Africa? South America?"

"Running won't solve anything, Karis." Her mom crocheted with renewed vigor, the hook pulling and bobbing. "I would like to see you settled. Happy."

Her phone went off. Lourdes was in labor. At least someone would be happy.

*****

Lourdes had barely made it to the hospital in time. While the nurse tried a third time to start an IV, the veteran mother burst out, "I need to push!"

Karis motioned the nurse away. "Forget the IV." Grasping the writhing woman's knees, she spoke firmly. "Not yet, Lourdes."

The baby's head was crowning. Lourdes moaned and grabbed Julio's arm as his eyes darted back and forth from the mirror to his wife's drenched face.

"Help her sit up." Karis maintained a calm tone, even though her heart was racing.

Two nurses scrambled. The next contraction took hold.

"Now, Lourdes!"

Her face a contortion of red pain, the woman strained against the stirrups. Her husband stroked her arm, his brow furrowed. "Mi querida. Lo siento, lo siento."

"That's it, Lourdes. Baby's head is out. Now, wait for the next contraction." Karis cupped the infant's head.

Seconds later, Lourdes threw off Julio's arm, and with a long, guttural groan, pushed the baby into Karis' waiting hands. Karis began suctioning. The baby responded with a lusty cry.

Beautiful, perfect, and strong.

"Congratulations, Lourdes. You have a daughter." Karis lifted her up. "A daughter with a great set of lungs."

Lourdes held out her arms. A nurse slipped a wrap around the neonate and set her on the mother's chest. Julio beamed. While the new parents cooed over the tiny baby, Karis finished up with the umbilical cord and placenta and then slipped out, leaving instructions with the nurses. She felt a little frenzied and weak. The B&B was over an hour from the hospital, and she had raced to get there in time, frustrated when the officer pulled her over. When she had showed him her badge, he'd grudgingly let her go without a citation. But now, it was all catching up with her. She headed toward the cafeteria. After two cups of coffee and a piece of toast, she checked on Lourdes with plans to return in the evening.

*****

As the water pounded her back, Karis found herself crying. Hot, salty tears. Every delivery stirred the memories, but Lourdes' little Isabella was so like . . . Karis grabbed the handle of the shower door for support. There had been no epidural, no pudendal block, nothing to ease her pain. Labor had been long and hard. Aunt Ernie finally dumped her at the indigent hospital. *If you can make a baby, you can check yourself in.* It was after midnight, and she would only get one night. They gave her an enema and sent her to the bathroom. All patients got enemas, the nurse said. Hospital policy. Scared and shaking, she'd sat alone, afraid the baby would come out in the toilet.

"If you'd stop writhing and focus, things would go faster." The doctor's gravelly voice had been terse. The hours ticked by as she moaned, twisting through the pain. Finally, at 6:47 a.m., she grabbed the bed's railing, and with a final, fiery contraction, strained and pushed the baby out.

"A healthy baby boy."

He'd wailed in the cold delivery room, and Karis shivered, spent and exhausted, but felt for the first time that she had done something right. The nurse worked quickly, and when she placed the baby on her chest, all the sadness and heartache fell away.

Beautiful, perfect, and strong. She vowed to keep him. No matter what.

Ten fingers, ten toes, big-little feet, feather-soft black hair, brown-gray eyes that melted her insides—his cry brought tears to her eyes. He was hungry. She put him to her breast, but the nurse swooped in and stole him away.

They let her stay the remainder of the day in the maternity wing. Her roommate had just given birth a few hours before. Three bouquets sat on Tamara's side of the room. The young husband gushed over his wife, stroking her cheek, holding her hand. They kept the dividing curtain closed and talked in hushed whispers. Later, the nurse brought a squalling infant for Tamara and a pill for Karis to dry up her milk. Aunt Ernie's doing? She flushed it down the toilet and kept asking for her son. They finally brought him, and she held him close, memorizing every inch of his tiny body. Somehow, she would make things work.

But two days later, her arms were empty, her breasts full, and her heart shattered.

"He's going to a good Christian family, Karis. Something *you* can never give him." Aunt Ernie's words had cut her in two.

"But—"

"Be happy you're not on the street."

Karis scrubbed herself, willing the water to wash away the pain. She thought of the charred ashes from Aunt Ernie's letter and felt sick. Had the woman actually admitted what she'd done with her baby? Drying off, she dressed and opened the top drawer of her dresser, feeling for the little jeweler's box, needing to hold it. She'd stolen Aunt Ernie's scissors the day after her son's birth while the woman was out feeding her goats. Sick and feverish the next day, Karis had slipped in and out of a heavy sleep. When she finally came to consciousness, she could hear Aunt Ernie singing and playing "Wonderful Grace of Jesus" on the piano. But there wasn't any. Not for her anyway. She reached for the warm bundle at her side, her hands grasping cold, crumpled sheets. Panicking, she stumbled out to the living room. Aunt Ernie had glanced up and belted out the last line of the chorus, a triumphant expression across her face.

The velvet box. Nine feathers to mark his birthdays. A pittance. Lifting the lid, she touched the lock of silky black hair. Where was her little boy now?

*****

Karis could hear the voices echoing down the hall, all in rapid-fire Spanish. Laughter erupted, then a baby's cry, then a shushing, and then more Spanish. Lourdes had a large family. Karis stopped by the nurses' station and checked her patient's electronic record. It was always a relief to find mother and child doing well. She stepped toward the noisy room but stopped when she heard Clay's low voice, fluent in his father's native tongue. What was he doing here? She listened for a few moments, unable to discern his words, her heart pounding. Each time she saw him, she felt more exposed, like he was ripping off clothes from her soul. She backed away and headed for the elevator. The physician's lounge would be deserted this time of night. She'd check on Lourdes later after the family reunion was over. She punched the *down* button several times, debating whether to take the stairs. As she glanced back, Clay came out of Lourdes' room. They both stared at each other a moment, and then she quickly opened the stairwell door and fled.

An hour later, she stood beside Lourdes' bed, admiring the flowers and balloons and stuffed animals that crowded the window seat. Lourdes held the sleeping Isabella while Julio hovered nearby, totally enraptured. He hadn't left her side all day. Lourdes had told her.

Oh, to be loved like that.

Karis felt the ache growing. She ducked out of the room, blinking away tears and longing for things she would never have.

CHAPTER SEVEN

IT WAS ANOTHER LONELY SATURDAY. Karis rarely slept well anymore. She looked at the clock—4:34 a.m. The dream lingered—the hazy blue sky, the smell of pine, Somerset Lake, her brother Micah playing by the shore, Eden napping on a blanket near Mom while she and Dad fished. They had caught bluegill and walleye and cutthroat trout. She had reeled in an eighteen-inch largemouth bass. Dad had beamed and got out his camera. He was so proud of her.

She stared at the ceiling, listening to the hum of the clock radio, an idea forming even as she argued with herself. The living room was still a disaster. The wallpaper had claw marks and gouges where she'd stripped off sections and damaged the dry wall. She should tackle it again, but what did it really matter? No one saw it. Buddy remained asleep as she tiptoed out. At Wal-Mart, the cashier, a curly-headed teen, looked at her curiously as she pulled out her credit card. He scanned the granola bars and the carton of night crawlers.

"Make sure the lid on that thing is tight. One time, those little boogers got out in my mom's fridge. She nearly killed me."

The image of a slimy worm shimmying across her Greek yogurt made Karis feel nauseous. She scribbled her signature, grabbed the bag, and left.

Back home, she packed up the fishing supplies and put Buddy on his leash for the two-mile walk. The sun was just hitting the treetops when she arrived at Feather Lake, but the August heat already felt like a thick, damp blanket.

She breathed in the moisture, appreciating the stillness. The lake was her sanctuary. She had spent hours hiking the trails, swimming and when time allowed, fishing. She was hoping to buy a kayak soon. She followed the sign to the visitor's center. Buddy strained at the leash as they descended the wooded hill and veered to the right, nearly choking himself when he spotted a squirrel. Acorns and pine needles peppered the trail. A few birds called. She tied Buddy around a young maple and went in to find a trail map, hoping to explore a new area along the northern bluffs.

When she came out, her heart nearly stopped. Buddy was nowhere in sight. The leash hung from the tree trunk, its metal clasp snapped. She looked in all directions and fought the sick feeling in her stomach. Ditching her fishing gear, she retraced her steps to the place where he had first barked at the squirrel.

She called his name, weaving between trees and undergrowth until she arrived at the water's edge, but still no little black dog. She tried to quell the panic. He'd always come when she called.

She headed west, calling and hoping and trying not to imagine home without her shaggy companion. She would find him. She had to. Thirty minutes later, she scrambled up the rocky trail to Boone's bluff for a better vantage point. As she neared the top, a familiar rabid barking sliced the air. She prayed he hadn't found a coyote or a raccoon. She ran toward the commotion. With heart pounding, she ducked through the woods and burst into a clearing.

Clay.

Hands on hips, he towered over her dog, a perturbed look on his unshaven face. His eyes swerved to hers, clearly surprised. Buddy's teeth were bared, a bad sign. She ran for him, catching him by the collar, and yanked him toward her, relief and frustration rushing in. Kneeling down, she scooped him up and clamped his jowls shut. "You naughty boy." She ventured a look at Clay. "I'm sorry."

"No harm done."

An awkward moment passed. She noted the orderly trailer and campsite, the other trailers down the gravel lane, the bathhouse in the distance. He was *camping*? "How long have you been here?"

"Since June, about the time I came to your office." He bent over a cooler and removed two water bottles, thrusting one her way. "Here."

Karis suddenly realized how bad she must look. With little sleep, no makeup, and a frenzied jaunt through the woods, she could only imagine. She took the bottle. When their fingers brushed slightly, she jerked her hand back. "Thanks for the water."

She turned to go, but something stopped her. Clay didn't move, nor did he smile. His eyes seemed to fill with regret, and the misery she saw there mirrored her own. She glanced away. "I shouldn't be here with you."

A slight breeze rustled the nearby oaks.

"What will it take, Karis? What can I do to make you believe I'm not who I was?"

It was on the tip of her tongue.

He blew out his breath. "Forgive me. Please."

Karis backed away, needing more air, the familiar pain squeezing her chest. Was he insane? She'd lost everything because of him. "Forgive you?"

"I will always be sorry."

She hugged Buddy tighter. He yipped. "You have no idea—"

"It's the reason I came here."

"And you think a one-line apology will just erase it all?" Her voice shot up an octave as her mind stripped him back to his cocky, younger self. Anger ignited. "Was I some kind of diversion? A game to play while you're fiancée was, what, unavailable?"

His jaw tightened.

"How could you do that to me?"

He tried to take her hand.

"Don't touch me!"

He raised his palms and backed off, his face pained. "I'm sorry."

It didn't matter. "Forgiveness is the last thing I'll ever give you."

CHAPTER EIGHT

KARIS STARED AT THE BEIGE brick building. The two-hour drive to Althorpe in pouring rain had done little to calm the storm raging inside. She had sworn never to set foot on the grounds of this place, never to lay eyes again on the person within. But she was desperate now, desperate and obsessed. She had to know for her own sanity.

Oak Ridge Nursing Facility—rising three stories at the foot of a wooded hill— stood like a fortress. If not for the pear trees lining the front sidewalk and the yellow daylilies in full bloom, the facility could have passed for a prison.

A woman in scrubs sat behind the reception counter, a pair of reading glasses perched on her frosted hair. Without looking up, she typed at a computer. "May I help you?"

"Ernestine Henry, please."

"Sign the Visitor's List." The woman pushed a clipboard across the counter but continued to peck at the keys. "She's in 16C. Someone will have to let you in."

An ancient, red-faced man ambled up to the counter and removed a cookie from the pocket of his denim bib overalls. He held it in fingers twisted with arthritis and then pinned Karis with rheumy eyes. "Lookie what I found in my slipper. You think them elves done it?"

The receptionist glanced over. "Harvey, where is your walker?"

The man broke the cookie all over the counter and then mashed the pieces with both thumbs. "Now we got ourselves some magic dust." He glanced up at Karis. "You want some?"

"Oh, Harvey." The woman sighed as she watched him swirl fingers through the crumbs. She picked up the phone. "Hey Susan, can you come and get your boyfriend?"

Harvey began licking his fingers. "Tastes like oats."

Karis handed the clipboard back to the receptionist. "You her daughter? Granddaughter?"

Karis shifted uncomfortably. "Niece."

"You can wait over there while I call C floor."

Karis murmured her thanks and crossed to the beige couch that faced a large picture window. Mauve pillows matched the patterned wallpaper, and white Priscilla drapes muted the afternoon light. For a moment, it felt like being back in Nana's living room. What would Nana think of her coming here?

"Ma'am?"

Karis turned. A nursing assistant stood by the arched entrance to the floor's central hallway.

"You here for Ernie?"

Karis nodded and stood.

"Right this way."

The woman keyed an elevator, holding the door open when it arrived, and then pushed the third floor button. "She just had her nails done—one hand's plum, the other scarlet red—but she don't let anyone touch her toes. She's kinda fidgety today."

The elevator dinged. The woman used a different key to open the door. "Here we are. Just take a left and follow the hallway 'round to Room 16. If you pass the showers, you've gone too far.

"Thanks."

"Oh, and when you're finished, tell Billie at the desk. She'll let you out."

Karis started down the hallway, trying to ignore the foul odor and moans coming from behind the closed doors. Overhead, fluorescent lights cast the walls in a chalky hue, giving a haunted house feel. As she turned a corner, a woman dressed in dark pants and a baggy sweatshirt crawled along the wall, her silver hair a chaotic mass. When she saw Karis, she scurried away like a rodent in the attic.

Karis paused outside Room 16, her heart beating wildly. She had last seen her aunt on May 10, 2001 when the woman had dropped her off at the bus stop with a one-way ticket to Mandalay. When the old Buick had disappeared, Karis stepped to the ticket counter to trade in the ticket. There was no way she was going home.

After she rapped on the door and waited, she slowly turned the handle and peered in, shocked by the emaciated form in the center of the room. Dressed in a blue nightgown, the woman looked dead, as if she was lying in state, except that her lips were moving. The gray hair that had always been neat and tidy in a bun was now white, cropped, and boy-like.

As Karis inched closer, the woman's shriveled face came into view. "Aunt Ernie?"

Her aunt's head jerked suddenly. She looked toward Karis with cataract-coated eyes, a guttural sound coming from the back of her throat.

"It's Karis."

Her left eye rolled back just as she grabbed Karis' wrist, her chilled fingers a claw. "Sing!"

Terrified, Karis tried to pull away, but the woman was still strong. She swallowed the fear. "What would you like?"

"Sing!"

The hymn came easily, and the melody seemed to awaken the woman's memory. She sang each verse perfectly, just as she had years ago when she pounded the piano and demanded that Karis harmonize with her sultry alto voice. It had been a ritual after supper. It had been torture.

As the song continued, her aunt's fingers loosened, and Karis backed away out of reach. The woman still scared her to death. With the final amen, her eyes closed. Karis took a deep breath.

"Aunt Ernie, what did you do with him? The baby."

Her lips moved again. Karis fought the rising frustration. The stroke had ravaged her body, and the dementia her mind. Was there any hope at all? Mom had said she had lucid moments. Maybe there was a chance.

"The baby, Aunt Ernie. Where is my baby?" She felt like shaking the woman.

Her aunt's eyes popped open and shifted right, then left, and finally settled on Karis. A single word came out.

Horrified, Karis felt the floor reeling. She stumbled out the door, rushing into the hall bathroom just before she vomited.

CHAPTER NINE

CLAY TAPPED THE REMINDER postcard against his knee. With the Internet exploding and the rage over cell phones, mail was kind of old school, but he still liked it. It fit Karis' personality, although he was pretty sure she hadn't put the stamp on it herself. He let his eyes wander over her diplomas. Medical Doctor, The University of Missouri School of Medicine. Resident, Washington University. Board Certification in Family Medicine. Licensure in Missouri. By all accounts, the woman was at the top of her game.

Another twangy country song played over the waiting room speakers. Clay felt like pulling the thing out of the wall. Who picked the music anyway?

It had been three months since Karis had cut on him, and three weeks since he'd felt the sting of her parting words by his trailer. Behind the swinging door, she was probably cursing him for not going to another doctor for his follow-up exam. That would have made her happy, but he wasn't ready to give up yet.

"Mr. Montes."

Clay followed Lauren to the first exam room. He found it interesting that her hair matched her purple scrubs. She had him sit on the table and answer a few questions while she fluttered her long black lashes at him. Clay kept his answers simple and unengaging.

The young nurse had probably been in diapers when he got his driver's license.

After she stepped out, Clay surveyed the room. It was orderly and clean and smelled of a familiar germicidal agent. But overhead, an annoying sound clanged from the room's central duct. It was probably closed, given the room's subtropical temperature. Clay stepped up on the table. After wrestling the jammed vent open, a burst of cool air flowed out and the noise stopped.

"What are you doing?" Her voice was ice.

Caught in what was not his finest moment, he stepped down and tucked in his shirt as Karis shut the door.

"Your vent was closed."

He tried not to stare, but she seemed off-balance and pale. The white coat practically swallowed her. She kept her face hidden. Something was wrong. She wiped her nose with a tissue. Clay assumed a neutral stance, fearful she might misinterpret any concern as patronizing.

She opened his chart. "Please just put on a gown and don't give me any trouble."

Good thing he wasn't evaluating her bedside manner. "Are they still in here?" He pointed to the exam table.

She wouldn't look at him but nodded and left the room. He pulled open a drawer, pulled off his outer garments, and donned a gown.

She returned with Lauren, who seemed to read her mind, first scribbling in his chart, and then flipping through a file for updated literature on melanoma. When Karis finished the exam, she sent

Lauren to the next patient and left the room while he dressed, returning after a few minutes.

She focused on his chart. "I didn't see anything suspicious."

"That's good, right?"

"You should be checked again in three to six months."

"Should I—"

"Not with me." She swayed and grabbed the doorframe for support.

Clay came to his feet. "Are you okay?"

The question seemed to undo her. She backed against the wall looking like a trapped animal, swiping at her eyes. He felt so helpless, standing there in a gown no less, doing nothing. Clearly, she needed help. He took a step toward her. Her head snapped up, eyes red-rimmed. "Promise me this is the last time."

The overhead fluorescent light flickered and buzzed. They stood there, staring at each other, a blade ripping his insides as he took in her tortured expression.

"I can't."

Her face fell before she slammed the door.

*****

She rushed to her office and shut herself in, slumping over the desk, hands to her face. How could she keep this up? She'd come here to start over, to keep the pain at bay, and to find relief from the past, but instead, the demons had followed.

A knock on the door. "Dr. Henry?"

Karis blew her nose and cleared her throat. "Yes, Lauren. Come in."

"Mr. Montes asked me to give you this." She put a folded piece of paper on Karis' desk. "He's gone, by the way."

Karis nodded. "Have a good evening."

As she heard Lauren leave, she stared at his scrawl. The worst demon of all. She ripped the note to shreds.

*****

Clay looked at his lifeless phone for the tenth time, hoping her number would light up the screen.

Lou gave him a sour look. "Put that thing away and enjoy the moment, Clay."

Right. Ninety degrees and one hundred percent humidity. Lou was nuts. Clay slid the phone into his pocket and massaged his neck. His other hand was going numb, holding Lou's infernal Big Bass fishing rod. "Whose idea was this anyway?"

"Be a man, Clay." Lou tightened his line.

It would probably start raining any minute. They'd been in Lou's trolling boat since daybreak. His legs kept cramping.

Clay shifted his weight and stared at the water, looking for any sign of activity. "I've got some Spam in my trailer." Lou loved Spam for reasons beyond normal comprehension.

"Oh, ye of little faith." Lou steadied his pole. "But if we can't sweet talk these babies, we'll thaw some liver. I need to use it up. We can fry up some onions too. Open a can of peas."

Over his lifeless body. "I'm still thinking Spam for lunch."

Off to the right, a sudden movement caught Clay's eye. A doe picked her way through the trees. Two others followed with wary, halting steps, stirring the wet leaves along the bank. Clay remained still, but motioned to Lou with his eyes. The older man looked over, smiled, and was about to reposition when his pole lurched forward. Lou lurched with it. The deer bounded away.

"Got something!" Lou started reeling, his eyes bright with excitement. "It's ornery. Maybe a big ole catfish!"

Clay watched Lou wrestle with his line, the bobber keeping beat with the serpentine movement. Ten yards out, the line snapped suddenly, and Lou let out a wail. "Oh, I could taste it!"

"If I buy us some burgers, can we call it a day?"

Lou started reeling in the torn line. "When am I gonna make a fisherman out of you, Clay?"

"When I'm not sopping wet."

"Next comes ice fishing, you know."

Clay's head jerked around. He should probably tell Lou the conclusion he'd come to during the night. Thoughts of Karis had haunted him—the way she had looked at him, the despair on her face. He hadn't slept one second. Maybe it was time to admit defeat and give her what she wanted. "About that. I'm heading back to St. Louis next month. Thought I'd start working on plans for the spring. We're looking at the Ashland area."

"But we're not finished here. We've got four more houses."

"You've got a full crew, Lou. You don't need me."

Lou set his pole down and turned, his face shadowed under the floppy fishing hat. "So you're quitting?"

The comment prickled. "Of course not. I just thought I'd get a head start on—"

"Stop!" Lou waved his hand back and forth as if to shut him up. "May I remind you that this whole project was your idea? What happened?"

"What do you mean?"

"You know what I mean. What happened with her, because that's what this is really all about."

"She refused my request."

Lou gave him a pointed look. "And now, just like that, you're walking away from everything?"

A surge of anger cut through Clay's chest. "Hey, I have bent over backward. I live in a trailer. I—"

"You know, you should listen to yourself sometime. You talk about *you* quite a bit. Well, maybe this isn't about *you*, Clay. Maybe there's a bigger picture here."

"What do you want me to do?" He was ready to hurl the fishing pole to kingdom come.

Lou's spine seemed to stiffen. "Figure it out. Did you come here for forgiveness or did you come here for something else?"

"I don't know anymore."

"Oh, I think you do. You just haven't said it out loud yet."

"She wants me gone."

"What does God want?"

"No clue."

"Well, ask Him. If you wanna keep your life, you gotta give it away."

"I thought I was doing that."

"You are such a wuss." Lou picked up his pole.

Clay's line jerked suddenly to one side. "I've got something."

Lou sprang up, dropped his rig, and started coaching Clay. When a fifteen-inch trout surfaced, the man almost capsized the boat.

Lou pulled out the hook, a lopsided grin on his face. "Time to get down to business." He slapped Clay on the back, their earlier conversation apparently forgotten in the joy of the moment.

"Oh, great."

Hours later, after Lou had stuffed him with two bass, three crappy, and a "big ole catfish," Clay sat by a campfire, his friend's words replaying themselves. He stared at Grayson's picture of Karis wading in the lake, holding her shoes, hair shimmering in the sunlight. She was beyond beautiful, but the sparkle was gone. Had his selfish act caused this? Was there more he should do for her? And what did it really mean to give your life away? He stared at the four words Grayson had scrawled on the bottom of the last page of his report, and that's when the idea hit him. It was crazy and scary, but maybe it was the answer.

He looked up at the cloudless night sky. "Lord, I'm a regular screw-up, and if this isn't Your will, shut me down." Orion was just visible. The hunter. Maybe it was a sign.

*****

The woman behind the desk kept giving Clay funny looks. Did she not like his choice of reading material or was it the plaid shirt? He adjusted his weight in the flimsy waiting room chair. The next time she glanced his way, he gave her a big smile and then flipped to another page of the *Better Homes and Gardens* magazine. The bacon-wrapped steak looked good.

The small waiting area was old and outdated with faux wood paneling and a brown speckled floor tile, no doubt "hip" in the seventies. A window offered the only natural light, plus a dismal view of the parking lot. A nice bamboo shade would help that. Clay refilled his cup again, while peering at the messy bulletin board behind the water cooler. Pictures, flyers, announcements, and government notices—Clay read a few and felt like he'd been punched in the stomach. The whole place gave off a depressing vibe. He'd been waiting over an hour for Ms. Leila Stipes, a social worker with the agency. He'd probably have a full beard by the time—

"Mr. Montes," a small woman called out. Her short, graying hair just touched the collar of her blue blazer. "Right this way, but watch your head. I do apologize for the wait."

Clay ducked under the doorframe and matched the woman's clipped pace to an office down the hall. As he sat across from her, he couldn't help but appreciate the meticulous desk. Not one speck of dust. Hopefully, he would get somewhere this time.

She tented her hands. "So, Mr. Montes, you're interested in adopting?"

He shifted uncomfortably on the hard wooden chair. No one had asked *that* question before. "Uh no, I'm just trying to find somebody. A boy."

The woman blinked twice behind her oval-shaped glasses. "Why?"

Clay swallowed. "Because . . . I recently found out that I . . . am possibly his father."

"Possibly?" Ms. Stipes watched him, probably waiting for him to squirm.

"Actually, I know I'm his father." The memory of that night with Karis returned. The taking. Her shame. His indifference. He suddenly felt like a kid in the principal's office. He'd been there enough times, but this was different—he was turning himself in, admitting guilt. He cleared his throat.

Ms. Stipes folded her hands neatly on the desk in front of her. "You still haven't answered my question. Why do you want to find him? Are you just curious or concerned or—"

"Of course, I'm concerned about him." The words slipped out too sharply.

"We have rules, Mr. Montes, to protect children and the families that adopt them."

Of course, the *rules*. "Are you saying no?"

"I just want to be very clear."

"Look, I swear I'm not trying to break any rules or mess up anyone's life or safety or well-being or whatever else you're trying to protect, so let's just cut to the chase. He was adopted in St. Louis, and I've been to three agencies already. He was born on May 7, 2001 and his mother's name is Karis Henry."

"You do realize that once an adoption occurs, the records are normally sealed.

"Yes, Ms. Stipes."

"So I can't make you any promises."

"I get that, Ms. Stipes." Did these people think he was stupid?

The woman removed a sheaf of papers. "Here are some online resources you might find helpful and some general information."

He already had a file full, but he politely accepted them.

Ms. Stipes clicked a pen and pulled out a yellow legal pad. "Chances are, though, if we find him, there is very little I can share with you. Keep that in mind."

"I take it you don't believe in happy endings."

"This isn't Disney World, Mr. Montes."

CHAPTER TEN

KARIS HELD THE REFRIGERATOR door open and shivered. She'd turned up the heat in the house but still felt cold. Her neck hurt, her throat hurt, her whole body hurt, and she felt like she was in a fog. Belinda had come to work with a cold on Monday and sneezed on everything. Lauren had urged the receptionist to go home, but as a single mom, money was tight. Karis shut the door and opened a cabinet, removing a can of soup. While it warmed in the microwave, she sipped a diet soda, hoping it would calm her stomach.

The phone rang. Someday she would get caller ID when she wasn't watching every dime, but until that day . . . She picked up to answer.

"Honey, what's wrong? You sound sick." Her mother had laser hearing.

"I've probably got a virus, Mom. That's all.

Her mother suggested all the home remedies.

"Mom, I'm a doctor."

"But you're still my little girl." A few seconds of silence. "I was hoping you would reconsider Thanksgiving." Karis could hear the determination in her voice. It was hard to keep saying no.

"I have thirty patients to see on Black Friday, and it's a six-hour round-trip drive to Mandalay. Even if I drove down on Thursday, I'd only have a few hours before I'd have to drive back. "

"Your father really wants you to come home, Karis."

"I went to Althorpe."

"Oh, Karis, I told you I'd go with you."

"She's pretty bad off."

"Did she even know who you were?"

"Probably. In a strange way."

Karis could feel tears threatening. She wiped her nose on a tissue.

"Did she say anything?"

She still couldn't bring herself to talk about it. "Not really."

"I'm so sorry, honey. Please come home."

She must be feverish. "I'll think about it."

She dropped the phone and stumbled for the couch, feeling dizzy. As she slipped into a troubled sleep, Clay's face rose before her. He came toward her, hand extended, and reached into her chest, pulling out her heart. As he grabbed it—pulsing, bloody, and black—she cried out, *How can I still be alive?* He backed away then, holding a little child's hand.

She came awake instantly. The room was black, the couch cushion soaked through—from sweat? Tears? She didn't know which. A profound sense of emptiness hovered. She stared at the ceiling. "Why won't You help me?"

Eden jogged toward her in the parking lot. Karis locked the car door and zipped up her jacket, turning as her sister almost knocked her over with a hug. "You came!"

"I told you I would."

A sudden wind lifted Eden's hair and sent it flying in all directions. She caught it in one hand and held it to the side. Cheeks red, she waved to a group of girls across the quadrangle. Students filled the leaf-covered lawns and sidewalks that crisscrossed the center of campus.

Eden tugged on her arm. "I have to be at the theater in thirty minutes for makeup, but I want you to see my room."

They wound their way to the red-bricked dorms on the south side of Kingston College. Carver hall, the smallest and newest, housed senior women on three floors. Eden took the stairs to the third floor and proudly opened her door with a "ta-da."

Karis had to smile. Eden loved origami. Paper cranes hung from the ceiling, the curtain rod, and the doorframe and were tied to strands of Japanese lanterns that circled the walls. Even the futon was adorned beneath her messy lofted bed.

"Don't light any matches."

"Is that all you can say?"

"It's beautiful, Eden."

"Ashley started knitting. Look what she made." Eden picked up a navy sweater with gold trim from her roommate's bed. A mountain of throw pillows suffocated the turquoise comforter. "She's going to make caps for hospital preemies next."

Karis wanted to ask about her studies but held her tongue. "That's very nice."

Her sister checked her phone. "Do you want something to eat? There's marshmallow pies by the fridge."

"No thanks, I'm not hungry."

"I've got to go." Eden ran a brush through her hair and then handed her an envelope. "Here's your ticket. I'm so excited!"

Karis watched her waltz out the door, singing "Climb Every Mountain." She was a perfect *Maria.* Oh, to be young and carefree.

Outside Eden's window, "The General" still obscured Brookings Hall. Karis had studied under the giant oak many afternoons, a soda tucked between her legs. She had loved this college, loved to hear Old Gray chime on the hour, and loved the smell of the roses in the prayer garden. Now, it seemed like another life.

A door down the hall slammed suddenly. Giggling erupted. Karis locked Eden's door and took the long way to avoid Brookings. Her old dorm would just bring back the memories.

The theater doors had just opened when she arrived. Finding her seat in the lower balcony, she admired the new acoustic ceiling and the plush red velvet drapes that matched the red theater seats. A paisley patterned, jewel-toned carpet graced the aisles leading up to the stage. Random instruments warmed up from the orchestra pit. Karis closed her eyes, looking forward to the escape. *The Sound of Music* was her favorite.

Someone slid into the seat next to her and squeezed her elbow. She glanced sideways, surprised. "Mom?" And behind her, Dad.

Karis felt the air spark with tension. Mom hadn't said a word over the phone. And Eden hadn't told her either. In fact, Eden had lied. Her father held up one hand to wave. She looked away, feeling trapped. Her mother tried to make small talk until the production began. Karis answered in a controlled voice, but ignored her father. He occupied himself with the program.

A lump formed in her throat. He looked hurt.

Mercifully, the orchestra began playing. Eden was spectacular, the other cast members outstanding. With the final curtain, Karis said a quick goodbye to her mother and stood, trying to maneuver her way through the throng as quickly as possible. As she neared the stairwell, she felt a hand on her arm.

"Karis."

She wouldn't face him.

"Can we talk?"

Blinding tears stung. She jerked her arm away. It was too late for that.

CHAPTER ELEVEN

"WHAT DO YOU MEAN 'what are my intentions?' I've already told you. I just want to find him."

Clay was in her cavernous office again, the sun angling through the blinds and creating slits on the speckled carpet.

"Mr. Montes, there is no need to speak in that tone." Leila Stipes laced her fingers together and glared back at him. The woman sat like a judge behind her desk, a giraffe mug within reach. It seemed odd.

Clay shifted in the chair. "I don't understand. You just told me your agency handled the adoption."

"Yes, we did, but—"

"But what?"

"Things don't always turn out as planned, Mr. Montes." She straightened the already neat stack of Post-It notes that sat by a burnt orange ceramic pencil holder.

"Okay, so what didn't turn out?"

"Certain . . . details."

Clay felt like throwing something. The pencil holder would shatter nicely against the wall. "So why did you call me here?"

"Mr. Montes, have you ever babysat?"

"Excuse me?"

"Have you ever been around children?"

What was this? A day care job interview? "Not much."

"Do you have any experience whatsoever with children?"

"Your point, Ms. Stipes?"

She sat back in her chair. "I don't feel comfortable giving you any more information."

Clay struggled to control himself. "Because I haven't done any babysitting?"

"It's easy to become a father." She gave him a pointed glance. "As you probably know. But it's hard to actually be one. You don't seem to care about children. I find that disturbing."

Did the woman ever blink? Clay bit back a retort. The silence in the room was palpable as their eyes locked. But a small voice niggled. Wasn't she right? He looked down at his balled fists. Hadn't Lou tried to tell him that he was a self-absorbed jerk? *If you wanna find your life, you gotta give it away.* He'd waltzed in here thinking he'd locate a child, give Karis an update, make her happy and then what? Waltz out with forgiveness and a hot date? Leila Stipes would throw him out if he admitted that. And she should.

How could he have been so unfeeling? So like his old self? He was looking for a child that he was responsible for. His child. *Lord, forgive me.* Chastised, he stood and stretched his hand across her desk. If nothing else, he would end this well. "I'm sorry for my rudeness. I know I have a lot to learn. Thanks for your time."

He turned to leave, but she wouldn't let go. For a tiny woman, she had a firm grip. That stare again. "Mr. Montes, do you know anything about soccer?"

Here we go again with the psychoanalysis. He sighed. "A little."

She finally released his hand but continued to stare at him with narrow green eyes. "Have you ever coached soccer?"

"Ms. Stipes, why don't you just spit it out?"

She stood there with her eyebrows pinched together as if weighing her next options. "Mr. Montes, I live in a world where I constantly have to judge character. I don't quite have you figured out, but I've got a proposition for you."

Now what?

"If you help coach a soccer team after a comprehensive screening, I'll reconsider your request."

Clay eyed her. "You can't be serious."

She gathered herself up and squared her shoulders. "Humility goes a long way with me, Mr. Montes." A pull of her mouth sideways softened her face. "Besides, my sister could really use a man."

Oh, great.

*****

"I do appreciate your coming." The short, sturdy woman in the straw hat smiled up at him. Except for the green eyes and height, she looked nothing like her sister Leila. In the next instant, she laid a hand on his arm and squeezed. "But I don't need your assistance. I've been doing this for years. Why don't you go have a hot dog?" Another big smile.

Nothing like a rebuff from Mrs. Santa Claus. She turned away and whistled for her team, the Fighting Bulldogs, to change drills. Her "team" was little more than a ragamuffin ensemble of boys, all differing in size and ethnicity. Clay bit back the choice words he had for the sixty-something woman. If she only knew how much trouble he'd gone to—the eight-page application from her sister, the character references, the interviews, the drug test, the background check, the hour drive this morning to fight for a parking space with a woman in a teal minivan. She'd honked when he attempted to swerve in and kept honking when he hadn't backed up fast enough. Heads swiveled to watch. He hated being part of a "scene." A quarter mile away, he finally located a spot to park. People were everywhere, walking and running haphazardly. A child carrying a camping chair had whacked his leg. And then, fifteen bucks to be admitted to an event he was supposed to help with. So no, he did not want a hot dog.

"Mrs. Kandar, your sister—"

"Moira will do just fine."

He cleared his throat. "Moira, your sister—"

"Meddles." Another smile, this one pasty. "You know, this really isn't a good time, Cliff. The game is about to start."

"It's Clay, and—"

"Hassan, tie your shoe!" the woman called to a small boy with olive skin and black hair. He glanced toward Moira and then dropped to the grass, securing his cleat. Behind him, a tall, stocky redhead booted the ball and hit a Latino boy in the stomach. The boy's face registered pain and then rage. He charged the redhead, tackled him, and started hammering his torso with punches. The other boys were quick to encircle the fight to enjoy the show.

Moira took off, half hobbling, half running, clutching her hat. What would she do? Blow kisses? By the time she reached the brawl, the redhead had flipped the Latino boy to the ground and had him pinned, his knees pressing into the boy's shoulders. Moira tried to pull him off, but he pushed her away with such force that she fell backward.

Sure the woman didn't need help. Clay sprinted into the fray. He grabbed the redhead around the waist, hauled him up, and locked his arms behind him while the other boy yelled obscenities but didn't advance. Thankfully, no one was bleeding. Moira stood slowly and limped toward the two. "Tad, Lucas, next time I will definitely sing."

What in the world did that mean?

She caught her breath. "And because of your little stunt, you two will sit out the first fifteen minutes of the game."

Clay would have suggested laps, suspension, or even jail time for the miniature thugs.

The redhead groaned. The other boy spat out another obscenity and kicked at the ground by Moira's feet. "Darlin', that just cost you another five minutes."

Darlin'? Really?

"Now everyone go get a drink before the game starts." She smiled through clenched teeth. She must be in pain.

As the boys ran toward a yellow five-gallon cooler, she dusted off her hands, but grimaced when she put weight on her left foot and struggled to walk.

"Here." Clay offered his arm. "You might need to have that ankle looked at."

"I'm fine." But she seemed relieved when he escorted her to the bench and helped her sit.

He crossed his arms. "I know you don't need my help, but—"

"I need nachos."

"Excuse me"

"Please get me nachos. Here's a five."

Had he heard right? "So that means—"

"That I'm hungry, Cliff, Clay, whatever your name is."

He suppressed a smile, not bothering to correct her or accept the money. The woman was kind of growing on him. "Be right back."

"No jalapenos, please." She fluttered her eyelashes. "What? Don't just stand there. Get going."

"Yes, ma'am."

By the time he handed her the plastic plate, a throng of fans, bearing lawn chairs, had descended upon the two sides of the field, and the bleachers had swelled to capacity. Within minutes, the referee blew the whistle, and the game began. The Fighting Bulldogs struggled to stay in their zones, even though Moira cajoled and pleaded and threw out several "Sweethearts," "Honey-pies," and "Darlins."

By the end of the second half, the Hornets led by five. Lucas had been ejected from the game for unsportsmanlike conduct, another boy had suffered a bloody nose, and Hassan had lost his left cleat, twice. Thankfully, the airborne shoe had not resulted in any casualties. After triple-tying the boy's shoe, Moira sent him back in. The Bulldogs continued to struggle. Clay kept one eye on Lucas and one on the game. With the clock ticking to the last minute, a tall African-American boy recovered the ball, dribbled downfield, and passed to a blond-haired boy who booted it in. The Bulldogs finally scored.

Moira was ecstatic, clapping her hands and waving them over to the sidelines. "I'm so proud of you guys! We didn't win, but that was a great pass, Dante, and a beautiful goal, Seth. And for the most part, you were all good sports. Now, who wants ice cream?"

Eleven hands shot up. She instructed the boys to gather up the balls and meet her at the van if they needed a ride. They scampered off. Clay picked up the water jug and ball bag while Moira chatted with a few parents. If nothing else, he could be her pack mule. Maybe that would appease the unflappable Leila Stipes. Moira finally finished talking and turned around. "You're still here?"

"Where do you want these?"

She studied him a moment. "We've got six more games. I just hope they can win one. It would sure help morale. We're 0 and 3 now." She zipped up her jacket. "Help me to the parking lot, Cliff."

He smiled to himself, noting she hadn't asked. But it was slow going. She was in obvious pain, although she wouldn't admit it. Clay found himself feeling protective of the feisty woman.

He helped her step down from the curb. "If you want my unsolicited opinion, those boys could win the rest of their games, but they need to work as a team. You've got a lot of raw talent and a truckload of energy."

She looked hopeful. "That would mean the world to them."

"If you want, I could try something my football coach did years ago. When's your next practice?"

"Wednesday at four, right here."

"So what all can you tell me about your little cherubs?"

She had big dimples when she smiled, and now she was beaming. "Well, as I'm sure you've noticed, Lucas craves attention, and he'll do anything to get it. Tad, whose nickname is 'Fire-head' for obvious reasons, can be a bully. He and Lucas have a long history of trying to kill each other, but secretly, I think they enjoy their tiffs." She continued to tell him that Gabe, Paul, and Hassan were very compliant and would do whatever they were told. Nicholas and Joaquin were very competitive. Eduardo couldn't stand Josh, so she never played them at the same time. "Dante assisted Seth for the goal. Those two have the best attitude, and you probably saw that Seth is missing his left hand."

"I didn't notice."

Cars were buzzing out of the parking lot. Moira brushed a wayward gray curl aside. "I don't think the boys mind an old woman too much for a coach. At our first practice, I kicked the ball from the goal to the center field line. Of course, I didn't tell them I could hardly move the next day." She took out her keys. "We're going to the ice cream shop on Manchester Road. I'll meet you there."

He decided not to argue. When he arrived, Naomi, a pleasant Chinese woman, greeted him and suggested different flavors. Moira ordered a chocolate peanut butter shake and chatted with Naomi about her collection of orchids lining the windowsill, while the boys scanned the display cases. When they received their cones, Clay helped usher them to empty tables.

A melee soon broke out around the water fountain as Lucas shoved Tad away from the spout.

"Here we go again. I think it's time for a song." Moira hobbled over, planted herself between the boys, and began to sing, prima donna-style at the top of her lungs:

I've got peace like a river,
I've got peace like a river,
I've got peace like a river in my soul.

The two quickly stomped off in different directions.

A devilish grin appeared on Moira's bright red lips. "They can outrun me, they can outshout me, and they can beat me in arm wrestling, but they cannot out-embarrass me." She slurped her shake in victory.

Clay caught a cherry cheesecake drip with his tongue. He'd ordered a double scoop in a waffle cone. He watched Moira chat with each boy. She was a natural with children and obviously loved them. Clay had a feeling the quirky old widow could teach him a thing or two. Maybe that was the plan all along: kid lessons.

*****

Moira had been skeptical of his unorthodox idea but had provided an assortment of objects for the team building activity. When he'd asked her for odds and ends, he had no idea what to expect. But the hula-hoops, swimming noodle, exercise mat, tennis racket, flip-flops, baseball caps, and soccer balls would work perfectly. He'd also bought bags of candy for prizes.

Wednesday was a warm day for the first of October. The boys were in shorts, and Moira hobbled around with a cane in loose-fitting sweatpants. Clay hoped she had seen a doctor, but he would never ask.

As soon as the "minefield" was set up, he explained the rules of the game and then organized pairs with Moira helping to even out the teams. One member of each team coached the other blindfolded member through the minefield. No physical contact was allowed. Each sighted member could only talk. When the pair had successfully navigated the "mines," the roles were reversed. Upon completion, each received a candy bar if they had followed the rules. After all the boys were finished, Clay moved the mines around and changed the pairings. By the hour's end, the boys were full of sugar, but hadn't thrown any punches.

During the last hour, they practiced kicking and passing. Moira had been delighted when he volunteered to run every drill, and the boys had seemed to enjoy running with him down the field. Dante and Seth had almost outrun him.

At six o'clock, Moira blew the whistle and gave them final instructions for Saturday's game. "And don't forget, it's going to be chilly, so wear a long-sleeved shirt under your jersey or bring a jacket. Do you have anything to add, *Cliff*?" Her eyes twinkled.

He gave her a quick smirk. Messing with his name had become their private joke. He faced the group. "Good job out there today, guys. Great teamwork. Remember that on Saturday." Most of the heads nodded. "Alright then, time to practice our chest bumps for the big win on game day."

At his suggestion, the boys were quick to follow his lead. Moira looked concerned and bewildered.

After dismissing the boys to their waiting rides, she turned toward him, hands on hips. "What in the world was all that bumping business about?"

"That's man love language. You wouldn't understand."

Moira rolled her eyes. "Guys are so weird."

*****

Three weeks later, the Bulldogs were 2 and 3, but still tainted with unsportsmanlike conduct during each game. Moira had held out the ultimate carrot—a movie and pizza party if they won a game with no penalties. But it wouldn't be easy. The Panthers were undefeated and highly disciplined.

As the game progressed, though, Moira's bribe seemed to work. The Bulldogs fought long and hard and, to everyone's surprise, controlled their tempers. Tied in the second half with two minutes left on the clock, the bleachers were a writhing mass. Moira kept grabbing Clay's arm and making frantic hand motions, all the while cheering on Gabe and then Nicholas and then Josh. But it was Lucas who somehow miraculously managed to intercept Gabe's pass and score. A frenzy of chest bumping ensued. Clay beamed at Moira. She rolled her eyes and then covered them as the Panthers took possession of the ball.

Seth went toe-to-toe with the other team's star player, #7 Sanchez, but the boy was wearing down. He'd been in both halves. Clay cast a quick glance at the clock as Sanchez found an opening and sent the ball sailing toward the goal. Time slowed. All eyes turned to Joaquin, the goalie. Moira climbed on the bench, grabbing Clay's left shoulder, while yelling in a hoarse voice. Joaquin was small, but quick and wiry. Maybe, just maybe. At the last possible second, the boy threw himself to the right, one hand outstretched, and deflected the ball as the horn blew, signaling the game's end. Clay let out his breath.

The boys went wild and collided with each other, jumping and hollering. Moira almost fell off the bench. Clay caught her just in time. She squealed.

"Good heavens, Cliff, set me down!"

The boys were rushing toward them. Clay knew what was coming when he saw the water jug in Josh and Dante's hands, but did Moira know? He'd causally mentioned the ritual at Wednesday's practice when she was out of earshot.

She screamed when the cold water doused her head. The boys roared with laughter. Clay was quick to take off his jacket and put it around her shoulders. When was the last time he'd had so much fun?

CHAPTER TWELVE

"HONEY, I REALLY WISH you'd call me."

Karis listened again to her mother's message on the landline answering machine. The last thing she wanted was another discussion about the Henry family Thanksgiving.

She set her briefcase on the dining room table, slipped off her shoes, and went upstairs to put on some sweats. Buddy bounded up behind her. The patients had been nonstop, and she was tired.

Just as she moisturized her hands, her cell phone rang. Mom again. She let it go to voicemail. It went off again. There would be no peace until she answered.

"Hi, Mom. I just got in."

"Honey, I've got to start supper soon, but I had to call you. I was cleaning out Aunt Ernie's house and found the most unusual thing––a newspaper clipping from 2001. It was folded up in her old Bible. She wrote your name on the top and starred a couple of the obituaries."

Karis' breath caught. She touched her throat as her heart pounded in her ears. She didn't want to know the sordid details. She wasn't strong enough. She grabbed the sink for support. Mom hadn't put the pieces together.

"I found it rather odd that she would keep something like that. I was going to give it to you at Thanksgiving. Well, anyway, I put it in the mail yesterday. Apparently, there was a couple in a—"

"Mom, I have to go!" Karis punched off the phone and threw it on the bed as if it would burn her fingers.

The mail. She had forgotten.

She walked out to the mailbox and glanced in. There were three envelopes—the electric bill, a credit card solicitation, and one with her mother's neat handwriting, postmarked from Mandalay. With shaking hands, she slid her finger along the top edge.

*****

The storm had come in suddenly Friday afternoon. Karis watched the rain pelt the windows and wondered if the streets would flood again. But the weather hadn't affected the schedule. Patients had streamed in all day.

Finally able to sit in the late afternoon, she poured herself another cup of coffee and shut the door of her office. She removed the obituary page from her purse. She'd read the notice over and over. Anger stirred afresh for the demented woman at Althorpe. Why hadn't she said anything? Was her silence more punishment? God's will?

The agony of not knowing hadn't subsided. If anything, it had grown to invade her dreams and steal her appetite. Her concentration suffered, her sleep suffered, and she could think of nothing else . . . except Clay. She had to get a grip for her patients' sake, but also for her own well-being.

Lauren knocked on the door and peeked her head around. "Hey, do you mind if I bug out early? My mom just called. The restaurant roof is leaking, and Dad is freaking out."

"No, you go ahead. I'll get Belinda to close."

"She's already gone. Sorry, I didn't tell you."

"Don't worry about it. Just go. I can lock up."

"Thanks, Dr. Henry. Hey, be careful by the lake. A car went off this afternoon. I just heard it on the radio."

"You be careful too."

But Karis wasn't thinking about Lauren's comment thirty minutes later as she sped down the country road, her wipers thwacking the windshield. She accelerated as she looked at the Spyder's clock. Most places closed at dusk. When she reached the outskirts of the little town and pulled onto the paved driveway, a man had just shut the iron gates.

She hadn't driven like a crazy woman to be turned away when she was so close. She ran toward the old man, droplets sluicing her face. He regarded her from under his cap. "Sorry, ma'am, I just locked up."

She held out a crumpled twenty-dollar bill. "Just five minutes. I can give you more."

Spiky white hair poked out from his cap like stalactites, crisscrossing his weathered forehead. His glasses were thick, making his hazel eyes enormous. He waved her money away.

"I promise I'll be quick."

A sudden crack of lightning assaulted the darkening sky. Karis jumped and dropped the white lilies. The old man stooped to pick up the pot.

His face softened as he held out the flowers. "Five minutes." Pulling a ring of keys from his tattered overalls, he unlocked the gate. "Stay on the paths."

On another day, she would have admired the order of the place, the well-tended lawn, the engraved stepping stones, and the stalwart trees. Instead, she dashed down the main path to the east garden and finally found them on the last row.

But only two.

Names. Dates. Chunks of gray granite.

Her heels sank into the soggy grass. A quake of thunder blasted. She laid the flowers between their headstones, her throat constricting.

"Where is he?" The words came out strangled.

A punishing deluge answered.

The giant drops whipped her face with no mercy.

CHAPTER THIRTEEN

THE THEATER HAD A CERTAIN zoo-like energy, and while Clay had looked forward to seeing the boys again, he hadn't counted on the buttered popcorn in his lap, the soda on his boots and his head getting bumped from behind no less than six times, but who was counting?

When the matinee ended, Moira directed the noisy gang to the nearby Pizza Shed. With all the junk they'd eaten in the theater, Clay couldn't believe the kids had any appetite left. But Moira ordered five large pizzas, and they soon disappeared. Then the boys were off to the jungle maze, leaving Moira and Clay at the table.

Moira wiped off a side chair and propped up her right foot.

Clay sipped his ice water. "Still bothering you?"

"Every now and then it talks to me and tells me to slow down."

"Maybe you should listen."

She'd finally let a doctor check her ankle. Just a sprain, but she still struggled. She waved him off, shifted in her seat to better view the "monkeys," and then picked up a piece of the giant cookie Clay had surprised the team with. "I did tell you about the Big Brother program, didn't I?"

Several times. "Yes and—"

"Just look how you've impacted those boys in one month's time." She nodded toward the maze. "They like you. They trust you. You show up for them."

"Moira, I—"

"The power of a positive male role model is huge. Can't you see that?"

Not to mention the power of a grand dame. But still, hadn't he fulfilled his end of the bargain with Ms. Stipes? And now her sister was dragging him off like fresh meat in another direction. He watched Lucas try to shimmy up a rope. The boy tried again, failed, and then flung the rope against the adult supervisor who told him to leave the "Gorilla Zone."

Clay sighed. To say no would feel like treason. And then there was Moira across the table with her big, green, twinkling eyes. How could he say no to those? On the other hand, if she only knew his past . . .

He leaned his forearms on the table. "Moira, I'm not exactly positive role model material. You don't know—"

"I know enough, Clay." She covered his hands with hers in a maternal sort of way. "Besides, it's not a life sentence, just a few hours a week."

He paused. She had called him by his real name. First time ever. She must be serious. "I'll think about it."

Moira frowned suddenly at the front picture windows. "Oh, dear."

"What?" Clay swiveled and followed her line of vision. Ominous clouds blackened the sky like Judgment Day. A distant siren blared.

"We must be under a tornado warning. Can you help me get them home?" Worry creased her forehead, a touch of panic in her voice.

Before he could answer, she knocked over a chair as she rushed to the play area, searching for the boys. The next moment she was on her old-timey cell phone, calling parents. Clay picked up the chair and started rounding up jackets the boys had strewn about the tables. After Moira gave him directions, he headed out the door with Tad, Lucas, Seth, and Joaquin.

Before they made it to the truck, the wind whipped up as icy droplets sliced the air. Clay stuck Lucas up front and the others in the back seat of the quad cab. The boy immediately started punching radio buttons and cranked up the volume when he found a rap station.

Clay gripped the steering wheel, knowing the boy was fishing for a reaction, and the bigger the better.

But the reaction came from the backseat. "I hate that song." Tad slapped Lucas' head and pulled his seatbelt from behind. "Turn it off."

"You're choking me!" Lucas flipped the volume even higher and grabbed at the seatbelt.

Clay bit back a sharp retort, any cozy "big brother" thoughts quickly evaporating. He killed the engine.

"Lucas, you want to walk home?"

The boy glanced sideways, a derisive retort on his lips. "No."

"If you don't stop, you will."

Scorn edged his voice. "You can't make me."

"Oh, I can." Clay grasped the boy's shoulder.

He threw off Clay's hand and jerked his head toward Tad. "What about him?"

"You started it. There's the handle."

Droplets drummed the roof of the cab.

"It's pouring rain."

"So?"

Lucas stared at him for several long seconds and then looked bewildered, almost like he'd been struck. Clay didn't budge. The boy finally pushed open the door and slid out. As he was about to shut the door, Clay stopped him. "Hold up, Lucas."

The boy hunched over as the rain pelted his jacket and soaked his face.

"Who burps better, you or Tad?"

"What?" Lucas eyed him as if he'd sprouted antlers.

Tad's head suddenly bobbled in the back seat, and he let out a loud belch. Lucas responded by gulping a large amount of air and eclipsing Tad's contribution. Seth and Joaquin joined in.

Clay nodded. "Hmm. Not bad, guys. Maybe we should have a contest. Think you can keep your hands to yourself, Lucas?"

More derision. "Yeah."

"Alright then. You respect me and my stuff, I'll respect you and your stuff. Get in."

Within minutes, guffaws replaced the earlier tension.

"Almost sounds like a choir in here." Clay smiled to himself. Maybe he didn't know anything about kids, but he would always be the undisputed burping champion of Miss O'Connor's sixth grade class. He let a loud one rip just to impress the boys.

The roads were flooded as he drove to the children's home to drop off Tad and Lucas. The old, five-story brick building was wedged between two businesses in the warehouse district. It had once been an elementary school, Moira had said, but now bars lined the windows. How could a place like this ever seem like home? There was no room to breathe or move. He watched the boys scurry in and felt a tug. If anyone needed a big brother, it was those two.

Joaquin's mom was a single mother who didn't speak English. When he escorted Joaquin across the busy street, Clay spoke a few words in Spanish. She smiled and asked him to wait, returning with a foil-wrapped tamale. Three down, one to go. He told Seth to climb up front and headed toward a southern neighborhood, noting the boy's Green Bay Packers coat.

"So you're a cheesehead."

The boy's face lit up when he referenced the exuberant fans of the popular NFL football team. "Yeah."

"How 'bout the Rams?"

"They're good too."

"You play much football?"

Like a deflating balloon, the boy's face fell. "Nope."

Clay glanced over. He didn't want to make a big deal about Seth's disability. "Why? Because of your hand?"

"Yeah, I guess."

Clay tapped the steering wheel with his thumbs. "Ever thought about kicking? Every team needs a good kicker, and you're an awesome kicker. You know, I played a little football in high school. Maybe we could try you out sometimes."

"I don't have a football."

"Not a problem." Clay pulled into Seth's drive.

"But it's like, almost winter."

"You think that stops the Packers?"

The boy's smile couldn't be any bigger.

"I'll see what I can work out." Clay held up his fist. Seth punched it with his left stub. Another tug on his heart. Swallowing, he watched the boy run in as his mom opened the storm door. Three small children huddled around her legs. The dad was in Afghanistan. Had Moira handpicked these boys on purpose? He wouldn't be surprised. Behind that sweet grandma face was a spine of galvanized steel. He suspected the woman never took no for an answer.

Jesus' words, Lou-style, drifted through his mind again. *If you wanna keep your life, you gotta give it away.*

He put the truck in reverse. "I guess I'm in, Lord."

CHAPTER FOURTEEN

IF HE DIDN'T KNOW BETTER, he could have sworn Ms. Stipes chose to be out of the office every time he called. This week she was in Phoenix at a conference and last week on a court case in Olivette. Could he at least make an appointment? Call her cell phone? No, she was very busy and didn't use a cell phone. She would call him as soon as possible. Right. He put his phone away and pulled into the parking lot of Romani's. Lou was starving for Italian, they were both tired of cooking for themselves, and it was Tuesday's all-you-can-eat pasta buffet. The place was packed.

Lou waved at him from a table in the back, his reading glasses a quarter inch from the end of his nose, a C. S. Lewis book in hand. Clay sat down in the black bistro chair and ordered water when the waitress stopped at the table. She set iced tea by Lou's napkin and two bowls of chicken gnocchi soup at the table's end. Then she invited them to help themselves to the buffet.

"Bless the food, Clay, but make it quick." Lou held his spoon in midair.

Clay heard a loud slurp before he could even say "amen." Lou had been instructed to fast after eight p.m. the night before, in preparation for his blood draw at the lab the next day. Unfortunately, his appointment had been at noon, so the starving foreman had snapped at the entire work crew all morning long.

"Next time you go in for a needle stick, I'm taking the day off." Clay savored a chunky carrot.

"Sorry about that." Lou's soup was half gone. "Say, your tiling job in the shower sure looked good."

"Ned mixed the grout. That makes all the difference."

"Just like frosting. He should have been a pastry chef." Lou pushed back his chair. "The line's not too bad. I'm going in." He snaked toward the buffet through a checkerboard of white and green-topped tables. The buffet had been set up in the middle of the dining area, just off the door to the kitchen.

Clay admired the original brick walls of the refurbished old building. Wide-planked oak floors, large posts, and exposed ductwork in the upper rafters added to the ambience. Three massive wrought-iron chandeliers hung centrally down the length of the dining area. Booths lined the front window. Whoever had done the renovation was a professional. The place was elegant without being overly snobbish.

Clay finished his soup and headed to the buffet. He scooped up a plateful of fettuccine and topped it with Bolognese sauce and a good helping of Parmesan cheese. As he waited for a server to replenish the breadsticks, the front door opened. A burst of cold air snuffed out the candles at several tables as more customers entered. Clay's heart beat faster when he saw Karis with an older man and woman. Her parents? She did resemble the shorter, dark-haired woman. The older man was almost as tall as Clay, but thinner with silver hair. The man helped the older woman with her coat while Karis stood awkwardly, her eyes scanning the dining area. Clay ducked behind the overhead warming light. No sense ruining her evening. She already looked miserable.

A waitress soon escorted the trio to one of the booths by the front window. Clay breathed a sigh of relief and made his way back, undetected. Lou had a napkin tucked in his shirt.

"Hey, you didn't get the shrimp Alfredo. I probably took too much. Here." Lou scooped a sample on a bread plate and slid it toward Clay.

For a moment, Clay contemplated the outcome. Eat shellfish. Get rash. See Karis. Bad idea. Repeated exposure made things worse, and she would think he'd done it on purpose. "Lou, remember the crayfish last summer?"

"How could I forget? Those sweet babies were . . . oh, wait a second. You're allergic." Lou took the plate back and stuffed the shrimp in his mouth. "Sorry."

"Are you around next Saturday by chance?" Clay swirled strands of fettuccine around his fork. "I need a favor."

Lou groaned with delight as he finished off the shrimp. The man's sound effects were downright entertaining. He finally wiped his mouth. "Yep. Shoot."

"So I've been doing this Big Brother thing. Now, Moira thinks the boys need a campout with me this Friday night."

Lou stopped chomping to grin rather obnoxiously. "You?"

"When she found out I live in a trailer, she got this crazy idea, and before I knew it, she was talking about her baked bean recipe."

"So how do I fit in?"

"Fishing on Saturday morning, then maybe hiking. Moira wants a campfire for lunch."

"This Moira sounds a little bossy." Lou snarfed a bread stick and glugged down half of his iced tea. "We'll have to take your boat, Clay. Mine's too small."

"That's what I figured."

Lou stood and peered toward the buffet. "Looks like they just put out some lasagna." The man had a one-track stomach. Several other patrons had the same idea.

Clay had kept an eye on the front booth. Karis sat across from the man and woman. She appeared tense, looking out the window frequently. The woman said something to the man and then spoke to the waitress who stopped by the table with three iced teas and three soup bowls. The man and woman bowed their heads, the man apparently offering a prayer. Karis, frowning, stared at them and twisted the napkin in her lap. She hardly touched the soup.

Lou looked to be in earnest conversation with a guy in a Harley-Davidson cap. Back in his glory days, he had made it to Sturgis every year.

Clay pushed his empty plate to the table's edge. If he hurried, he could probably make it through the line and back before the front booth patrons finished their soup. He moved past Lou and removed a plate. The lasagna was piping hot, the mozzarella cheese slightly browned and bubbling just like Raphaela, his mother's maid, used to make. He shoveled a decent serving on his plate and headed back to his table, but a man in a wheelchair blocked his path. When he turned aside, he came face to face with Karis and the older woman.

Karis jumped, her face paling. "What are you doing here?"

The older woman glanced curiously between him and Karis.

He smiled casually, hoping to defuse the tension. "Dinner with a friend. Nice to see you, Dr. Henry. The Bolognese is excellent, by the way."

He moved on, not wanting to make her more uncomfortable. Lou was still talking. Clay slid into his chair, knowing she had watched where he sat. She didn't look well—hollow cheekbones, darkened circles under her eyes. Had she lost more weight? Her sweater seemed to hang limply on her shoulders.

Lou finally came back with a rather large serving of lasagna. As he motioned to the waitress for more tea, Clay noticed Karis' plate as she skirted tables—it was almost empty. When she returned to her table, the older man made some comment that seemed to cause a few sparks. He soon left for the buffet. Karis slid to the end of the seat, keeping her head down. She swiped at her eyes, just before the older woman sat down and, a few minutes later, the man.

Lou clinked his fork against Clay's glass. "You're staring, Clay. What is it?"

Clay blinked, directing his attention back to Lou. "She's here. The doctor. In that far booth."

Lou twisted in his seat and then back around. "With the couple?"

Clay nodded.

"So . . ."

"I haven't seen her in weeks. She looks . . . unwell."

"Have you found out any more about . . . you know . . ."

"The woman from the agency is still MIA."

Lou looked toward the buffet line again. "You'd think they would have some kind of dessert."

Clay shook his head. "It's a miracle you don't weigh five hundred pounds. There's a big pan of tiramisu by the water pitchers."

"Oh, glory be!" Lou shoved back his chair. "You want some?"

"No, I'm good."

As Lou clamored for the layered dessert, Clay cast a quick glance to the front booth again. Their dinner appeared to be going down the tubes. The older woman picked at her food while the man attempted to engage Karis in conversation. She wouldn't look at him. Clay said a silent prayer, wishing he could do more than just watch from a distance.

"So, getting back to the weekend, you think those boys will get up early to fish?" Lou eased into his chair and sampled his dessert.

"I have no idea."

"What about food? I can get us some donuts on Saturday."

"Moira actually gave me a menu." Clay rattled off as much as he could remember.

Lou snorted. "Kids don't like that stuff."

"Moira has spoken."

"You're a goner. Man, this dessert is to die for. You sure you don't want some?" Lou was off again.

The older woman left the table, disappearing into the ladies' restroom. She returned just as Karis exchanged a few words with the man. His face darkened. Karis stood abruptly and stormed out. Clay's heart lurched. What had he just witnessed?

*****

Her mother wouldn't stop knocking.

Karis finally flung open the front door. Her father sat out in his car with the engine running, the dashboard lights illuminating his somber face. The evening had been a disaster. Why had he pushed?

Mom looked forlorn and tired. "May I come in?"

"What about . . .?" Karis looked toward the car.

"He'll be fine. I won't be long." Her mom sat down on the couch and adjusted her skirt.

Karis hugged herself and stood by the wing back chair.

"Sit down, Karis. Please." Mom took her hand and looked her in the eye. "How long are we going to live in this wasteland?"

Karis snatched her hand back. "You blame me too."

"I don't blame you. I just wish you'd—"

"What? Grovel at his feet? Pretend it didn't happen?" Tears threatened. "I know I was wrong, but haven't I been punished enough?"

Her mother sighed deeply. "And now you mean to punish him."

Buddy whimpered from the back door.

"I can't believe you're defending him." Karis struggled to breathe, her throat aching. "I was so young. How could he have done that?" A choked sob came out.

Mom gripped her shoulders. "I will never condone his behavior, but neither will I condone yours. He was trying to make peace, and you tore into him. Please, Karis, look where this is taking you."

She couldn't stand the disappointment in her mother's eyes. She pulled away. Mom sighed and moved to the door. "So, Thanksgiving?"

Karis wiped her eyes, feeling the weight on her chest press harder. "I can't, Mom."

"Can't or won't?"

CHAPTER FIFTEEN

"LOOKS LIKE A BOMB WENT OFF in here." A jumble of kids, sleeping bags, dirty clothes, and backpacks were strewn about Clay's trailer. "Smells like one too."

"Keep your voice down, Lou." Clay whispered as he eased outside and stepped into the morning chill. None of the miniature bodies moved. He closed the door.

Warmer weather had melted last week's freak snowstorm, but the lake would still be cold.

"You ready? It's past seven. Time's a wastin'." Lou looked a little too chipper in his flannel jacket, three boxes of donuts tucked under one arm.

Clay rubbed a hand across his forehead, trying to ease the pounding. "They didn't go to sleep until two a.m. I felt like duct-taping them to the wall."

"That bad, huh?"

"Let's just say I wasn't exactly having Christian thoughts toward Moira. Hey, didn't I tell you not to bring donuts?"

"That's like telling a cow not to moo."

Clay popped the lid off the nearby cooler and removed a large plastic container. "I have my orders."

"What in the world?" Lou scowled at the contents.

"Whole grain muffins, boiled eggs, fresh cantaloupe." Each muffin was in a red and white, polka-dot paper liner, the eggs and cantaloupe neatly packaged in resealable plastic bags.

Lou picked up a muffin, took one bite, and spit it out. "Good heavens! That tastes like sawdust."

"You should have been here for supper."

Lou opened the top donut box and plucked a maple long john from the lineup. "I'm scared to ask."

"Three-bean chili. And I thought those boys were good at belching."

Lou held the long john out to him. "Here. You need this more than I do."

Clay declined just as a loud bang shook the trailer followed by "Get off me!" In an instant, he'd flung open the door to find Tad standing on top of the converted dinette table bed that Lucas was sleeping on, the upper cabinet open. A metal box stood upended on the floor. Dominoes were everywhere.

"What are you doing?" Clay growled.

"I wanted to play." He'd taught the boys Mexican train last night, but Tad had cheated.

"Get down and pick those up."

Tad stepped on Lucas' leg to hop to the floor. The smaller boy yelled and pushed Tad into the mini-fridge. Fists came out. Clay launched himself between the boys, knowing what was coming. Hauling them up by their sweatshirts, he secured one under each arm football-style, and pushed through the front door to the picnic table, sitting them down on either side. "Lou, give these boys some donuts."

Smiling, Lou ambled over. "Now we're talking." Lining up the boxes, he sat down next to Tad and started pointing. "If you like pure chocolate, I recommend the cake donuts. Otherwise, these jewels are stuffed with raspberry filling. Can't beat that. Personally, I'm a long john man. Say, you fellas drink coffee?"

"Lou, don't you dare!" Clay scowled. Last night, they were rabid squirrels after drinking caffeine-free soda.

He headed back to the trailer. Seth and Joaquin were still asleep. He roused them and grabbed the milk. Both boys soon joined the others. They looked like zombies thirty minutes later, but surely the sugar would kick in soon. After the boys dressed and Tad picked up the dominoes, they took Clay's boat to one of Lou's favorite inlets to try some fishing. Chaos soon erupted. Seth lost his pole and nearly fell overboard, Lucas put worms down Tad's shirt to get back at him for the domino incident, Joaquin kept snooping in the compartments, and and after twenty-three minutes, the boys were bored.

Clay glanced toward Lou, perturbed. He didn't exactly keep toys on his Freedom outboard. "Any ideas?"

The man chuckled as he opened the cooler. "I'd say it's time for a muffin flinging contest."

Following Lou's lead, the boys began hurling "high-fiber balls" at boulders along the shore. Tad had the size advantage, but Lucas tried a javelin maneuver and hit a beached log. When the ammo ran out, Lou magically produced a slingshot from his tackle box and proceeded to show the boys how to launch egg missiles. With the last boiled egg kerplunking near the shore, Lou suggested a spin.

Clay revved up the engine and in seconds, they were speeding around the lake, splicing the water, a sharp wind whipping their faces. The boys roared every time he jerked the boat into a power turn and zigzagged in the resulting wake.

As they neared the northern bluffs, Lou looked over and shouted. "You might want to slow down."

"I'll stay away from the rocks. Don't worry."

Lou glanced back at the boys. "It's not that, it's . . . oh, Lord have mercy!"

"What?"

Just then, Seth, Tad, and Joaquin made a beeline for the front of the boat. Clay shifted to a lower gear and looked behind.

Oh, great. Why did it have to be the raspberry jewels? Lucas was puking on the bench seat.

"Lou, what do I—"

The man waved him off, inching toward the front of the boat, holding his stomach. "Don't look at me. I can't—"

Clay shut off the boat as Lou upchucked over the edge to a fresh chorus of "ewwws" from the three survivors up front. Grabbing a beach towel from the side compartment, Clay doused it with a water bottle. With Lucas hunched over and miserable, Clay had a sudden paternal feeling for the boy. He squeezed out the towel and helped Lucas wipe his face. "How many donuts did you have?"

The boy rubbed his stomach. "Six."

Clay shot Lou a dirty look. "You let him have six?"

"Hey, I told you to slow down."

Lucas hugged his midsection. "I want to go home." At least the boy's clothes were unscathed.

Home? Clay thought back to the old, rundown building in the sketchy neighborhood. How could Lucas consider that home?

"Okay, buddy, Moira's coming soon." Clay guided Lucas to the captain's chair and had him sit while he mopped up the mess with the beach towel. Then he deposited the towel in Lou's fish cooler. Served him right.

Hiking was definitely out. When they arrived back at the campsite, Moira was shaking out a red and white checkered tablecloth that she spread on the table. A vase of fake sunflowers came next. Someone forgot to tell the woman that it wasn't exactly picnic weather. The boys jumped out of the truck and swarmed around her.

A fire was popping in the pit, encircled by his camping chairs that he stored under the trailer. She'd made herself at home, apparently.

Lou eased out of his SUV and sidled up to Clay. "Did she bring ants, too?"

The boys were chattering about the morning. Moira listened attentively, smiling and mussing their hair. If the wasted food bothered her, she didn't show it, but the report from Lucas brought an enormous hug, which he tolerated surprisingly well. Afterward, she passed out juice boxes and string cheese. Lucas got a pack of oyster crackers that she magically pulled out of her purse. The boys started slurping and scrambled for a camping chair so they could sit by a "real live fire."

Moira turned, her eyes twinkling, and patted Clay's arm. "And how is Papa Bear doing?"

"Oh, Papa Bear is just peachy." Clay widened his stance. "Moira, this is Lou Barrows, our foreman on the Harbor project."

Lou stuck out his hand. "Ma'am."

"May I call you Louis? Clay has told me all about you." She was wearing her signature red lipstick again and a Lucille Ball smile. Why did she feel the need to change everyone's name?

"I go by Lou, ma'am."

Clay watched her. *Don't mess with him, Moira, and don't touch him. He doesn't like forward women.*

She stepped into Lou's personal space. Oh, great. The man shifted uncomfortably.

"But is your real name Louis? Louis is a fine name. Think of all the great men with the name Louis. Louis Pasteur, Louis Braille, Louis Renault. You really shouldn't be ashamed—"

"Who says I'm ashamed?" Lou's face reddened.

Moira took his arm. "Would you rather I call you Mr. Barrows? You seem a tad defensive."

"Moira, the natives are getting restless." Clay clapped his hands and rubbed them together. Seth was holding his cheese stick close to a flame, mesmerized as it dripped onto a rock a few inches from Tad's burning juice box. And then there was Lou. Now his neck was red.

"Louis, will you be joining us for lunch?" Moira still clung to his arm, her eyelids fluttering

Was she . . . flirting? No telling what the man's blood pressure was.

"'Fraid not, ma'am."

"Oh, what a shame. Well, do take a brownie. They're sugar-free, gluten-free, *and* fat-free." Oh boy. She squeezed Lou's elbow and removed a brownie from the cooler, placing it on a blue napkin before handing it to him. "I am a certified dietician, after all."

Lou looked traumatized but still managed to mumble a thank you before heading for his SUV with the brownie bunched up in his hand. No doubt it would soon rest peacefully in Feather Lake.

The next hour was a chaotic blur as Moira emptied the cooler of tofu dogs, baked beans, potato salad, pickled beets, and of course, the "healthy" brownies. The boys, however, were more interested in charring the hot dogs than eating them or the "scary vegetables" Moira put on their paper plates. With the last dog sufficiently carbonized, Clay sent the boys inside to pack up their things, while he and Moira cleaned up.

"So, how about a roller-skating party next week?" And in the next breath, "Clay, I'm leaving you and Lou these leftovers. You bachelors need some good food once in a while."

Clay could just imagine Lou's response. "Um, thanks. And yeah, roller-skating would be a blast. Hey, speaking of the boys, I found out Seth really likes football. I was thinking I could help him out. Teach him how to be a kicker."

Moira stopped scraping beets into the trash. "Are we talking about football as in contact sport?"

"That would be correct."

Deep frown lines appeared. "Seth should not play contact sports. I worry about him playing soccer."

"Why? Because he's missing a hand? Kids with disabilities are doing everything these days."

"That's not all he's missing."

"I'm not following."

"He's missing a kidney too, and he also has a ruptured spleen. Think what a blow to his stomach could do."

"Moira, we would just be kicking a football."

"You probably don't like the word no."

Clay crossed his arms. "Seems to me, you let the soccer team get pretty rough sometimes."

Her eyebrows shot upward as she blinked furiously. "Are you . . . *challenging* me?"

"Looks that way."

"Well, consider this." She was fighting for control. "On the one hand, we have football, a sport where the players slam each other to the ground every time the ball is hiked. A sport where the players can hardly move because they're encapsulated in a shell with pads, a helmet, a mouth guard, and God knows what else to keep them from getting hurt, and they still get hurt. On the other hand, we have soccer, a sport with shin guards. None of this slamming, hitting, punching, brutalizing nonsense."

"Moira, I'm sorry, but you're being unreasonable."

Her face went from pink to red. "I am not being unreasonable. I am sensible, realistic, and—"

"Overprotective."

Hands to the hips now. "I do not want Seth hurt, and I do not want *you* filling his mind with impossible expectations."

"Moira, if you could have just seen his face."

She gave him a long, hard look. He glared back. She finally sighed. "*If* the weather's agreeable, and *if* it's okay with Sharon."

"Thanks, Moira."

"And one more thing, if Seth gets hurt for any reason, *you*," she jabbed at his ribs, "are personally responsible."

"Got it."

The boys streamed out of the trailer, backpacks in tow. Moira opened the hatch of the minivan as Clay slid the cooler in, minus the food.

"Boys, tell Mr. Clay thank you."

They responded in unison and then jockeyed for seats. Just before she pulled out, Moira powered down her window. "By the way, Leila said she would call you this week."

Yeah, right. When pigs fly, as Lou would say. In the meantime, a nap sure sounded good.

CHAPTER SIXTEEN

KARIS STOPPED THE CAR in front of the gray house. It looked sad among the barren sweet gum trees and dead grass. Black shutters winged each window, and a wooden planter in front held dormant rosebushes, each stem riddled with thorns and topped with dried, crackly blooms. The carport by the side of house was empty, and behind the chain link fence, a small swing set occupied a corner of the yard. Not the expensive wooden kind, just a standard metal-framed one with a teeter-totter, slide, and two swings.

Brian and Sarah Lawton. This house is where they had lived in 2001.

Karis removed the newspaper from her purse and read their obituaries again for the hundredth time. They were the same age, born in 1962. They both had attended Webster High School and Meramec College. Brian had worked for Boeing in St. Louis as an engineer. He enjoyed gardening, the St. Louis Cardinals, and serving as a deacon at Unity Baptist Church. He loved the Lord.

Karis swallowed and blinked back tears.

Sarah had been a kindergarten teacher, beloved by her class. She was an avid scrapbooker, grew roses, and dreamed of traveling to exotic places. She was the pianist at Unity Baptist Church.

He's going to a good Christian family, Karis. Something you can never give him.

They were preceded in death by both sets of parents and three siblings. Survivors included an infant son, but the newspaper had been cut where his name would have been, seemingly on purpose. A wave of anger crested. Aunt Ernie's cruelty knew no bounds.

Where is he? She wanted to scream at the house. If only it could talk. For a moment, she wondered what would happen if she rang the doorbell, claimed to be a . . . what? The shades were open at the front window. Just one look. That was all she wanted.

No, that wasn't true. She wanted inside. She wanted to know what it had been like for him. Her mind envisioned a bedroom in pale blue, a white crib with little friends nearby—a furry lamb, a plush turtle, maybe some teddy bears. The floor was covered with a soft rug to play on, toys housed in a wooden chest with his name carved on the outside. The closet was filled with tiny little shirts and pants, his dresser holding socks and onesies and jumpers and . . .

What were they like? Brian and Sarah? Did Brian help Sarah care for him? Did Sarah rock him? Did she sing? Did she hold her cheek next to his and breathe in his sweet baby scent? Did her heart ache when he cried?

Karis could feel her throat tightening. She opened her car door, walked to the front porch, and rang the doorbell, her heart racing. Nobody came. She rang it again and then glanced around the quiet cul-de-sac. She tried the door. Locked. She leaned toward the window. Hardwood floors, a tan leather couch, loveseat, a small adjacent dining room, white walls. Innocuous. Deserted.

A gray sedan turned up the lane. She stepped off the porch and quickly walked back to the Spyder. The sedan pulled into the drive of the blue house next door, the older man inside eyeing her. He powered down his window.

"Need some help?"

She shook her head, got in her car, and drove away.

*****

One lone van sat in the parking lot of Unity Baptist Church. The small red brick building was simple and unpretentious and reminded Karis of the church her family had attended when she was a little girl, before Mandalay, before everything changed.

The morning worship at Mandalay had started promptly at eleven o'clock on that Sunday in May 2000. Eden had sat between her and Mom, doodling on the bulletin and then pulling on Karis' bracelet during the sermon. Micah was on the other side of Mom, rubbing one shoe against the other and watching dirt clods fall to the carpeted floor. Mom had given him several warning looks. Karis finally took off her bracelet and let Eden play with it. That day the choir had sang Mom's favorite hymn, "When I Survey the Wondrous Cross." Mom had teared up like always. It was the last time Karis had set foot in church.

The back door opened suddenly. An older woman came out, wheeling a trash receptacle. She headed toward the single-door garage, situated at the rear of the tree-lined property. Slightly stooped, she wore a parka, warm-up pants and neon green tennis shoes. She was humming.

"Excuse me."

The woman stopped. "Not much moving this time of morning. What can I do for ya, hon?" She spoke with a deep southern accent.

Karis swallowed. "Do you attend here?"

She shook her head. "No, I'm just the cleaning lady."

"Do you know how long the pastor has been here?"

"Brother Crandall? Hmm, I would say going on about eight years. He lives right over there." The woman pointed to a white house with green shutters across the street. "That's the parsonage. You could just go and ring the bell."

"Do you know who was pastor before him?"

"Brother Herman Boeker."

"Is he still around?"

"You might say that." The woman pointed to the gated cemetery next door. "Sorry, hon."

Heart sinking, Karis mumbled her thanks and left. Why was she torturing herself?

*****

November had come and gone as the Fighting Bulldogs ended their season 6-3. Meanwhile, Clay arranged to pick up Seth every Sunday for kicking practice. On the first December Sunday, he grabbed a bite to eat after church and then he and Seth drove to the soccer complex. A nearby picnic table served as the goal since all the soccer equipment had been stored for the season. Clay started Seth five yards out from the table and then moved a few yards back once Seth had kicked the football over the top a few times successively. Once he kicked, Seth ran to retrieve the ball over and over. Clay continued to marvel at his enthusiasm and energy. The boy was a natural.

Clay zipped up his jacket as a biting wind tore through the park. "We either need to get some more footballs or find us a gopher."

Seth looked at him puzzled. "Gopher?"

"Someone to *go for* the ball besides you."

"I don't mind."

"Well, you're looking pretty bushed. Why don't we call it a day?"

As they were driving, Seth traced the stitching of the leather seat with the index finger of his right hand and then looked sideways. "Are you an Indian?"

Clay glanced over. He loved the kid's audacity. "No, but I'm half Spanish."

"We just studied Indians at school. You look just like them except they have feathers sticking out of their ponytails."

"Really? Where do you go to school?"

"Dewey."

"Where's that?"

The boy mentioned a neighborhood near Historic Route 66.

"You like school?"

"Not really, but we've got an awesome playground."

"That's looking on the bright side."

As Clay drove up to Seth's house, he noticed a mishmash of bikes and toys peppering the yard of the small brick home.

Seth looked at him expectantly. "Can we do this next week?"

"If it's okay with your mom. Deal?" He held out his hand, palm up.

Seth gave it a resounding slap. "Deal."

The boy climbed out as a petite woman approached Clay's window with a toddler, clutching a stuffed zebra, balanced on one hip. She smiled. "Thanks for all the driving. I think we're almost done with our chicken pox outbreak."

Clay noted a few healing pustules on the little girl's forehead. "I can pick Seth up for the skating party on Saturday, if you'd like."

Seth interrupted excitedly. "Hey Sharon, can I kick again next Sunday?"

She put her arm around him. "If you get your math homework done," she said, then turning to Clay. "And yes, that would be great."

He waved and backed up, almost hitting the mailbox that bore the name Waters, and wondering why Seth called his mother Sharon. These modern women . . .

*****

Moira had invited her church's entire children's department to the two-hour skating party, and the parents had seemed overjoyed to drop them and run. Now if he could just survive until four o'clock.

"I hope you don't mind, Clay. I didn't want any of the kids to feel left out." She hefted a large shopping bag that held small wrapped boxes with polka-dot bows.

Twenty-seven kids. They just kept coming through the door. Next time, he'd get a signed contract that it was *only* a Big Brother affair.

He stood at the counter, hoping against hope they didn't have his size. Nope, they had two pairs. Great. He laced up the skates, thankful Lou was nowhere in sight. Moira had brought a large sheet cake bearing the words *"Happy Birthday Jesus"* in red and green letters. She planned on cutting it midway through the skating.

Clay pushed off with his right foot, his back and neck jerking when he tried to align his left foot and continue in a straight path. Moira stepped to his side. "Have you done this before?"

"Not since the eighties." Both his arms flew out in a flapping motion as he tried to balance and move toward the rink.

"Just do what the kids do. You'll be fine." She gave him a little push.

Off he went, hurtling toward the skaters, arms flailing in all directions. The kids whizzed by in a counterclockwise motion, scrambling to clear a path for him. Somehow, he wound up in the middle, feeling like a tornado was roaring around him. Moira was busy snapping pictures. If he survived this, he would personally—

"Smile, Clay!"

Just as he turned, the flash went off, blinding him for the one second that caused him to lose control of the skates. A split second later, airborne, he slammed into the concrete floor, pain shooting through his buttocks and up his spine. A slight groan escaped his lips. Probably wouldn't be able to sit for a week, and judging from the kids' reaction, he was sticking out like a zit on someone's nose.

"Oh Clay, I'm so sorry!" Moira shrilled, trying to get to him.

He motioned her back. "Don't risk it."

Tad skated up, excitement transforming his face. "Man, that was the best wipeout ever! You were like . . ." The boy mimicked Clay's flailing but stayed upright.

Lucas joined in, eyes glowing. "Yeah, like I wish we had a video!"

Clay shifted on his haunches. "Glad I could entertain you guys, but I need a little help here."

As they tried to heave-ho him to a standing position, Seth and Joaquin skated up and joined in the rescue. Moira looked fretful and hopeful as they maneuvered him back to the side.

"Oh Clay, I'm so sorry. So sorry. Are you alright?"

"I think I'll have to pass on the Chicken Dance."

Moira fussed over him for several more minutes and then patted his back, smiling, and left to take more pictures.

His phone vibrated. He unbuttoned the front pocket of his denim shirt. Well, well, well, Leila Stipes had finally decided to call.

CHAPTER SEVENTEEN

CLAY SAT IN THE CONFERENCE room of the agency, waiting. Why they had put him in a black padded office chair at the large oval table was anyone's guess. Perhaps Moira had informed her sister of his skating mishap. It still pinged when he moved too fast. Or perhaps Ms. Stipes was watching him through the security camera mounted on the ceiling by the window. He glanced at the clock. What was taking the woman so long? He got up and started pacing. The longer he waited, the more he felt like an experimental lab animal.

Finally, Ms. Stipes came in, clutching an attaché, her thin mouth a tight line. She stopped and scrutinized him. "Do you need a pillow?"

Great. Thanks, Moira. "No. Thank you."

"A hot beverage perhaps?"

He politely refused. Why was she suddenly so hospitable?

"Mr. Montes, I'd feel better if you sat."

He took a seat, gingerly. She sat across from him, hands folded around the case on her lap. She studied him for a moment. "You've done an exemplary job helping Moira. And now with your participation in the Big Brother program, well, let's just say, I'm plain tickled."

Leila Stipes tickled? Not a chance.

"Moira has told me everything. So, kudos to you, Mr. Montes."

Clay pasted on a smile. Just get on with it. "My pleasure, Ms. Stipes."

The woman cleared her throat. "I want you to understand that this case is not what we consider normal because of the extenuating circumstances. However, when I approached Judge Renfro, he was entirely sympathetic."

"Sympathetic?"

"Your son had a closed adoption. The records were sealed. There was no communication between the biological mother and the adoptive parents. Judge Renfro issued a court order to unseal the records. Otherwise, we would not be having this conversation."

She removed a file from the attaché. "When an adoption occurs, the original birth certificate with the birth parents' names is replaced by a new one with the adoptive parents' names. However, the biological mother of your son did not name the baby or you as the father, as you can see." She placed the certificate on the table.

He looked down at the white paper with blue scalloped edging, the print on the page jolting him. He hadn't really believed it until now when he saw Karis' name and the blank spaces. A baby with no name. And no father. A young girl, just barely twenty-one. Clay felt a sudden loathing for himself.

Ms. Stipes adjusted her glasses. "I'm sorry your son's story does not exactly have a positive outcome."

Dread squeezed his chest. He braced himself. "Is he . . . dead?"

"No, but his adoption was never finalized since the adoptive parents died in a car accident."

"Then, what—"

"No one stepped forward to take him. He became a ward of the state. I'm sorry."

"Ward of the state? For how long?"

"Most of his life, I'm afraid."

Clay felt a sledgehammer to his chest. "No one wanted him?"

She shook her head slightly, eyes averted.

"I've jumped through a lot of hoops for you, Ms. Stipes. Is this all I get?" The words came out sharp, but the woman didn't flinch.

"Mr. Montes—"

"You know after hearing this kind of news, it would actually be nice to meet him since—"

"Mr. Montes!" The woman raised her voice, then reclaimed her rigid demeanor once he stopped speaking. "You've already met him."

"What?"

She squared her shoulders. "He's on Moira's soccer team."

Clay stared at her, frustration rushing in. He struggled to tamp it down. "When were you going to tell me?"

The woman stiffened. "I didn't know if I was. Your son deserves better than the man who walked in here three months ago."

Clay could barely control himself. "So you put him right under my nose? Does Moira know?"

"Of course. I had to tell her."

"Of course."

A couple of conniving women, that's what they were. His mind raced through the team roster and settled on the most likely. The problem kid. The quick-tempered kid. The kid most like him. The kid he expected to be in prison someday. He'd always thought the boy resembled him with his Latino features. Now he knew why. "Lucas."

"No, it's not Lucas."

That brought small comfort. His mouth went dry. "Then who?"

"This is his current birth certificate."

Clay took the certificate, holding his breath, shock and heartache colliding. No wonder he gravitated toward the boy—he was a little version of Karis. He swallowed, feeling sick. "So who is Sharon Waters to him?"

"His foster mom."

"And the Lawtons?"

"I already told you. They died in an accident." Her voice seemed to soften as she handed him the file. "The whole story is in here, but I'll need it back."

He stared at the orderly stack of reports, his thoughts churning. What would this do to Karis?

*****

He drove like a possessed man back to his trailer, the damning file on the seat beside him. The campsite was almost deserted with only a few fools like himself occupying the tree-studded pull-in lots. He shivered when he stepped into the frosty air of the trailer, but he wouldn't turn on the heater. He deserved the darkness and the cold. Buttoning his jacket up to his throat, he sat down at the table and lit a kerosene lantern.

The words on the pages blurred as he read about the tragic accident that killed Brian and Sarah Lawton and injured six-month-old baby Seth, the children's home Seth lived in for the first seven years of his life, and the Waters family who had taken him in three years ago.

The file contained yearly pictures of Seth. As a baby, he was a spitting image of Clay, but as he grew, his hair lightened, probably like the hair Karis had as a child. He was a cute kid but rarely smiled in any of the pictures, and that fact bothered Clay more than anything.

He was average in school. Most of his report cards contained C's with an occasional B. But behavior-wise, he didn't cause anyone any trouble. The file also contained some school papers. His handwriting was practically chicken scratch, but given the fact that Karis was left-handed, Clay wondered if Seth might have been too.

His cell phone rang. Clay grabbed it.

"Do I need to call the police? Pull you out of some ravine?"

"What is it, Moira?"

"Leila called me. She saw you storm out of the parking lot. I was just wondering . . ." She was silent a moment and then added, " . . . if you're okay."

"I told you I wasn't a positive role model."

"That's where you're wrong, Clay. I know this must all come as a shock, but—"

"Why can't I adopt Seth? I'm not named anywhere, but with DNA testing . . ."

The silence hung for a moment and then Moira sighed. "I guess Leila didn't tell you everything."

"No surprise there."

"There's a really nice couple trying to adopt Seth. His story has been online for the past year. These days, more disabled kids are getting adopted. The couple's had one home visit, and Leila thinks they're perfect."

"So end of story. I lose the son I just found."

"You live in a trailer, Clay, and you travel a lot. You're a good guy, but I can't imagine any judge in his right mind giving you custody of a child."

"So there's no hope."

"Just call Leila."

*****

He'd been on hold for twenty-seven minutes. At this rate, he could have started laundry at *Loads of Fun.* He pushed his jeans and sweatshirts into a garbage bag and began rummaging for the detergent in the overhead cabinet.

The mind-numbing harp music finally stopped. "Yes, Mr. Montes?"

"What would it take for me to adopt Seth?"

Eight seconds of pinched silence followed. He could just see her sitting there, eyebrows raised, fanning herself. "You?"

Who did she think? "Yes, me."

She cleared her throat. "For starters, a stable home, a stable job, and a mother in the picture would be nice."

"Two out of three?"

"I'd choose someone else."

"Which is what you didn't tell me, right?"

"Mr. Montes, kindly remember that I will always put a child's best interest before yours."

"Then I guess I need a miracle."

"And a haircut."

"Should I buy a black suit too? Trade in my truck for a minivan?" The sarcasm spewed out like lava.

"I'm attempting to assist you, Mr. Montes. Ponytails are most frequently found on teenage girls, not thirty-something men."

"Anything else while you're on a roll?"

"I would prefer that you not share your identity with Seth."

"Why not?"

"Mr. Montes, try to think of someone besides yourself for a change."

*****

There it was again. His selfish preoccupation. The conversation replayed itself as Clay drove Seth home from kicking practice at the park. They'd been the only ones out on the chilly day. He tried not to stare but found himself studying the boy. He was absolutely incredible.

A wellspring of regret churned.

Seth turned to the passenger window and tried to write his name in cursive on the condensation. Clay swallowed the lump in his throat at the boy's empty left sleeve. If only things had been different, he might still have . . . but there was no sense in going there. The past with all its misery was long gone. And the present was slipping away. Could he ever make a difference in this boy's life, or would he simply slip away too?

Clay exited the interstate and turned onto a residential street. Almost every house had twinkle lights. It was magical. Seth gawked as an idea hit Clay.

"Hey big guy, what do you want for Christmas?" He would move heaven and earth if he had to, regardless of what Leila Stipes said.

Seth turned soulful eyes his way. "A dog."

"No kidding, what kind?"

Seth looked back out the window and sighed. "It doesn't matter. I can't have one."

"Why is that?"

"Sharon's allergic."

"Well, say you could get a dog. What kind would you pick?"

Seth's head swiveled back, a sudden smile on his face. "A big one."

"You're not hard to please." But Clay had been. His throat constricted as he imagined how meager the boy's holidays had been compared to his own exorbitant ones—unending toys, video game systems, big screen TVs, motorcycles, new cars. It was pathetic.

Unexpectedly, Seth's voice broke the stillness. "What do you want for Christmas?"

He noted the boy's face shadowed in the dim light, thinking his own situation was similar. It didn't matter—he couldn't have it. But that didn't mean he wouldn't try. "Well, I've been thinking, I'm getting tired of living in my camper, and it's kind of cold in the winter. A house might be nice."

"But your camper is so cool."

Clay had to smile. "Not everybody thinks so." He put on his right blinker.

"You should live out in the country. Then you could keep your camper."

"Sounds like a good idea."

"It wouldn't be crowded either."

"No?"

Clay pulled alongside the curb of the Waters' house, chewing on the boy's last comment. Ms. Stipes had told him the family had six foster children, and judging from the size of the house, the kids probably shared everything. Again, the disparity between his childhood and Seth's.

"Hey, buddy, have a good night."

When Seth reached the front porch, he turned and waved and then disappeared from view. Clay clutched the steering wheel, a thought gnawing at him. Someday he would have to ask. He couldn't live with himself if he didn't.

CHAPTER EIGHTEEN

A LIGHT SNOW FELL ON the roadway, the tiny flakes glistening. Karis drove slowly. The temperature hovered around the freezing mark. Her Spyder had slid all over the road. There were few cars in the parking lot. Why would there be more on such a dreary night? She parked in a secluded space away from the entrance and sat in the dark, watching the door. If she did go in, what would she do? Sign the guestbook, glance in the casket, and pay her respects. Respects for what exactly? Cruelty, treachery, deceit?

Part of her wanted to see the woman's remains, see her dead and cold. It would be a sort of triumph. But the other part of her was still afraid, still terrified. Still hurting.

Micah and his pregnant wife exited the funeral home. Her brother kept a protective hand around Clara. She was petite and pretty. They looked "wholesome." Karis watched them drive off, her mind made up. Visitation would be over in twelve minutes, the Celebration of Life service tomorrow at eleven o'clock, followed by a light lunch. Friends of the family were welcome, encouraged to share stories and fond memories of the deceased. That's what the newspaper had said at the end of Earnestine Judith Henry's obituary.

Karis turned the ignition and pulled away, leaving all the "fond memories" to rot with Aunt Ernie.

*****

Clay had stared at the square overhead light fixture most of the night, his thoughts spinning in a hundred different directions. He could just envision Lou, ready to thunk him on the head with another Bible verse. He was going crazy. After a quick breakfast, he set out on a hike to clear his mind.

Feather Lake had gone dormant. The new snow blanketed the woods in a pristine white while departing geese honked and flapped overhead, disappearing into the stony sky. Clay watched his breath in the cold crisp air, relishing the quietness of the morning. Nature, as always, continued to minister to his troubled soul. As he trudged down the path, he noticed two sets of tracks heading toward the lake.

A dog and owner had recently been in the area. He looked west and discerned two dark figures weaving among the bare trees along the shoreline. Since the temperature had dropped below freezing only in the past week, he knew the ice would be thin and dangerous and further compromised by the heavy snowfall.

In the next second, rabid barking filled the air as a squirrel scampered out on the lake. Breaking free, the dog gave chase. Realization slammed into Clay's brain at the sight of the familiar black dog and its trailing owner. A sharp crack split the air one second before the dog yelped and fell through. In the next instant, Clay watched horrified as Karis ran out and plunged in after the dog.

Reflexes kicked in. He scrambled down the hill, dodging branches and boulders, wildly looking for anything to aid a rescue attempt. Spotting a fallen limb, he dragged it to the shore, yelling. "Forget the dog!" He was already stripping off his jacket, kicking off his boots. In her flailing, crazed state, he doubted Karis even heard him.

A moment later, she managed to push the dog out where it hobbled for the bank, but she continued to struggle, shards of ice breaking off as she clawed.

"Quit thrashing, Karis!"

Her head went under and then reappeared. Clay jammed the limb under a boulder near the water, went down on all fours and inched toward her. She was twenty feet out. He tried to still the panic inside. She was moving wildly, shaking, turning blue. She no longer responded to his pleas. He lost patience and moved too quickly. The ice below his knees cracked and gave way. His body reeled at the shock of the frigid water. He began swimming toward Karis, horrified that she had slipped beneath the surface. He dove down. Three quick, powerful strokes took him to the bottom. In the brown murkiness, he could only grasp blindly, praying and searching. He ran out of air and resurfaced only long enough to fill his lungs and dive again. *Please, God, please.* His arm raked a solid object. He grabbed for it. An arm tethered to a body. He quickly clasped her to his chest and pushed upward, stroking with one arm.

He gasped for air as they broke the surface and then started swimming toward the tree limb, reaching for it slowly and then praying the ice would hold while he adjusted his grip. With one hand around Karis, he worked his way out and eased her to the bank.

She wasn't breathing. He checked her neck for a pulse. Nothing. *Oh God.* He ripped her coat open and began chest compressions. Two breaths. More compressions. *Oh God, please. Not now, not when there's a small ray of hope.* Two more breaths. He listened again, checked her pulse. Still nothing.

"Karis, come on!" He started the cycle again. On his second breath, he heard it. A shallow intake. She coughed as water began streaming out her mouth. He gently turned her sideways, watching her eyes flutter open and then close again. Her pulse was weak. She was starting to shake. He peeled off the waterlogged coat and then covered her with his jacket, slogging into his boots. In the next moment, he was climbing toward his campsite, stumbling over rocks, cradling Karis to his chest, the dog at his heels. He pulled an old blanket from the back of his truck, wrapped her up, and settled her in the front seat, still unconscious, but breathing. He threw the shivering dog in the back cab and sped toward the hospital.

*****

"Mr. Montes, here's some dry clothes and towels. If you'll follow me, I'll show you where you can shower." Clay looked up from his chair in the ER waiting room to see a nurse approaching.

"Any word on Dr. Henry?"

"Dr. Rhodes is still in with her. Nothing yet."

He followed the nurse to an empty patient room on the second floor where he showered quickly and changed into green scrubs. He left off his sopping wet socks and put his boots on his bare feet. Using the liner of the trashcan, he deposited his wet clothes in the bag and returned downstairs.

The place was almost deserted. One young family huddled around the registration desk, the father cradling a tiny girl who coughed intermittently. Clay sat down and fidgeted with a *Motor Trends* magazine but didn't see a word on the page. Karis weighed next to nothing, her body so slight he was hardly winded from his jaunt through the woods. But why was he shaking? From fear or exposure?

He had left her coat by the lake, thinking he would go back for it later, but now he never wanted to see it again. Not after what had almost happened. Ditto for the ugly blue cap. He checked on her dog and turned on the heater to dry him off and then went back inside.

An hour later, steps echoed down the hospital corridor. Clay looked up to see the baby-faced doctor who was treating Karis striding purposefully toward him. His white coat hung on his shoulders. He wore a blue bow tie. Clay tried to dispel a sudden lack of confidence. The guy probably didn't even own a razor.

"Mr. Montes, your quick response made all the difference, but I'd like to monitor Dr. Henry overnight. Most complications following a near drowning occur within twenty-four to forty-eight hours. We're giving warm fluids through an IV now to see if that helps her core temperature. She's drifting in and out. You can come on back for a short while."

Clay had told the check-in person he was a close friend—anything to get his foot in the door, but it was clearly a stretch of the truth. He followed the doctor. Thankfully, Karis was sleeping when he entered. Multiple layers of blankets encased her in a warm cocoon, and her color was returning to normal—still pale, but not gray-blue, thank God. He pulled up a chair, out of her line of vision, as the doctor left. Hopefully when Sleeping Beauty awakened, she wouldn't throw something.

*****

Six hours later, he'd eaten a stale sandwich from a vending machine, watched all four quarters of the Lions-Bears game on ESPN, and checked on the dog seven times. On his eighth trip in from the parking lot, Dr. Babyface, clearly agitated, caught him in the waiting area.

"Mr. Montes, we've had a situation with Dr. Henry."

Fear stabbed at Clay's heart. "Is she—"

"She refuses to stay overnight."

Inwardly, Clay breathed a sigh of relief.

Hands on hips, the man looked away, his face reddening. "She knows it's too early for discharge. I still need to assess her mental status, do a follow-up chest x-ray, check her O2 sats, and a few other things.

Clay wasn't sure what all that was, but it sounded important.

"I was hoping you could reason with her." The man tugged on his bowtie, perhaps trying to get more air?

Clay knew he was the last person Karis Henry would ever reason with. "I'll give it a try."

The man seemed to breathe easier.

*****

She was sitting up when he walked in.

"Where's Buddy?" Panic tinged her voice.

He'd just risked his life to save her, and all she could think about was her dog? "In my truck."

Fear flashed across her face. She swallowed. "Is he . . . okay?"

"Cold and miserable, but okay. I've been running the heater every hour or so."

Her eyes narrowed for a moment as if she doubted him.

He cleared his throat. "So Dr. Rhodes thinks you should stay overnight, and personally, I think—"

"You are not a doctor."

"Karis . . ."

She rang for the nurse. "I'm fine. I'm going home."

An hour later, Clay stood in the hall, listening to her argue with the soon-to-be-defeated Dr. Rhodes. The man stormed out and, seeing Clay, motioned him out of earshot and view.

He spoke through tight lips. "She needs to take it easy for a couple of days—that means getting plenty of rest, drinking lots of fluids, and especially *eating*."

Clay straightened to his full height, a good six inches above the younger man. "I'll see to it myself."

"And if she has any problems—breathing, fever, confusion, anything—you get her here immediately."

"Will do."

The doctor's phone rang. He walked off as the nurse came out and handed Clay a hospital folder and a bag with Karis' personal effects. She would have Karis at the ER entrance in about fifteen minutes.

He slipped on his jacket and headed for the parking lot. He got an earful of barking when he opened the door. "Relax, she's coming." He started to pet the dog, but then thought better when his gloved hand barely escaped the mutt's teeth. While he waited for the truck to warm, he glanced through the hospital folder, noting the discharge papers. No doubt Karis would throw a fit when he tried to enforce them.

When he arrived at the covered loading zone, Karis glared at him from the wheelchair. "My car's at the lake." More steel to the voice now. She was definitely coming back to life.

"We'll get it later." He attempted to help her out of the wheelchair. She threw off his hand. "Karis, I am taking you home. Now please get in."

A slight pink tinged her cheeks. Good. She looked healthier when she was angry. She settled into the seat, avoiding his eyes. He shut her door and went around to the driver's side, sliding in and grabbing his seatbelt in one motion.

He turned up the heat. "Still on Waverly Drive?"

Her head jerked sideways. "Still stalking me?"

There was no way he'd ever tell her about Grayson. He put the truck in gear. "I just hope your keys aren't on the bottom of Feather Lake."

Another glare, but then her lips quivered, and she swiped at her eyes. Opening the plastic bag on the floorboard, she removed a ring of keys. "They were in my jeans."

They rode in silence. Clay snuck in a few glances when she looked out the window, wondering what she was thinking, but he wouldn't dare ask. Her body language said one thing: *keep away*. If she was upset now, she would be livid at his next revelation, which happened twenty minutes later when he pulled into her driveway.

"I can make it in myself."

Clay shifted into park and fixed her with a steady gaze. "Let's just get this out now. I'm not leaving. I gave my word I would take care of you."

Now her cheeks were splotchy red. "I don't want you in my house."

He studied her wary expression. Was she afraid of him? Angry? He couldn't tell. "That's too bad." He killed the engine, let himself out, and came around to the passenger side where she had already opened the rear door and was attempting to grab Buddy.

He reached past her and scooped up the dog before she could argue. Then he took her bag and folder and pushed the door closed with his elbow. Motioning toward the house, he stood to one side. "After you."

She looked ready to blow or cry or something, but walked to the porch, back stiff and put her key in the lock. Clay kept a safe distance.

The house was small and old and in violation of multiple codes, judging from the electrical outlets, not to mention the sagging hardwood floor. The floral wallpaper in the living room looked like a giant bird had left claw marks and then pecked away at the injured drywall. Clay set the dog down. It scampered toward the back.

A Thomasville clock hung on the wall of the steps leading off to the right. Had it been just eight hours since he'd pulled her from the frigid waters? It seemed like an eternity.

Karis held the blanket tightly around her shoulders, eyes darting anywhere but on him. He casually walked through the dining area that opened to an orderly kitchen in the back. Only a powder room by the basement steps. "Where's your bathtub?"

"What? Why—"

"You're going to have a soak in the tub, Karis. Go get some pajamas or sweats or whatever you need to stay warm."

Now the eyes were flashing. "How dare—"

"Arguing will get you nowhere. You could have died this morning. Besides, a warm bath was on your discharge papers." He stepped past her and headed up the stairs, discovering a full bath and two small bedrooms at the top, one furnished, the other serving as storage for boxes, totes, and a kayak of all things. How in the world did she get that up here? As he turned on the water, he heard her close her bedroom door and lock it.

He felt like he was in a time warp from the seventies. The shower tile, toilet, and sink were a hideous mustard color while the floor was a plaid-patterned linoleum. But it was the wallpaper in brown, orange, and yellow flowers that screamed "groovy." Thankfully, two white towels and a white shower curtain tempered the space, and the brass mirror, hanging above the vanity, didn't look too bad. He rummaged through the basket on top of the toilet, discovering apricot bath gel among the soaps and lotions. A few squirts created billowing bubbles and a fruity scent. That should help her unwind and . . . He pulled his thoughts back suddenly. He was here as nursemaid. Nothing more. He shut off the water and then rapped on her door. "I'm going to fix some dinner. Tub's ready."

After he went downstairs, he heard the bathroom door close and lock. Good. She wasn't totally beyond reason.

He opened every cabinet, the fridge and freezer. No wonder the woman was a stick. There was hardly any food in the house. Besides some apples, a package of organic lettuce, and some natural peanut butter, he found crackers and a container of oatmeal. She must be starving herself. Clay grabbed the keys from off the counter and headed out. Karis Henry was in for a rude awakening.

CHAPTER NINETEEN

THERE WAS NO WAY she was soaking in the tub. Was the man insane? She had almost drowned. The bubbly water looked inviting, and she loved the scent, but the memory of the morning was too raw. She let the water out and took a quick shower.

She tried not to think of Clay in her house. He had bulldozed his way into her life again, catching her in a weak moment. But as soon as her strength returned, she'd get rid of him, even if she had to call the police.

The slam of the front door brought her back to full alert. Was he gone? She tried to shut out the nightmare of the water, pulling her down to a cold, dark silence, her throat searing with pain. She'd never been so terrified. She flipped on the heat lamp and let it beat down on her upturned face. Once dressed, she found Buddy waiting outside the door. She picked him up, shut and locked her bedroom door, and then slipped under the covers. Buddy snuggled next to her. He was so soft . . .

Somewhere in the drowsy fog, a door opened and closed. Buddy jumped up, growling. The front door? Footsteps. She came to partial consciousness and listened, fearful as she remembered. The lake. Clay. Was it a nightmare? She turned over, but her mind refused to relax.

Half an hour later, a rap on the door told her she was not dreaming. "Dinner's ready."

Her stomach growled. "I'm not hungry."

"Karis, this is non-negotiable. I'd prefer not to break this door, but I will if I have to."

She could easily see him doing just that. "I don't need your drama."

"Hey, I can bring you a tray or you can eat downstairs, but you are eating. Doctor's orders."

What choice was there? She unlocked the door. "I hope you're enjoying yourself."

He didn't say anything but gestured for her to proceed. She trudged down the stairs, noticing a pile of bags at the bottom. The man had actually entered Wal-Mart? She was surprised to find a candle burning on the small dining table and a vase filled with fresh cut flowers. Her old harvest gold plates occupied two settings. Embarrassment settled over her at their shabbiness. One had dishwasher burns, the other a chip. It was a far cry from the handcrafted stoneware at his lakefront home.

The plates were each filled with scrambled eggs, two slices of cinnamon toast, and a wedge of melon. Beside one plate sat a glass of milk and orange juice, beside the other, a lone glass of water. He pulled out a chair and she sat down, wondering if he would manhandle her if she refused.

After seating himself, he offered a simple prayer. She stole a glance at his bowed head, her eyes traveling to the ponytail, the coarse black whiskers, and the firm jawline. Her stomach churned.

When he caught her looking at him, she picked up her fork, perturbed, and stuffed a bite of eggs in her mouth.

"How are they?" He looked pensive.

"They're fine."

"I tend to overcook eggs."

"I said they're fine."

He reached for a bottle on the countertop. After opening it, he placed a pill on her plate. "Multivitamins with iron, formulated especially for women. I got the petite size. The others were horse pills."

"I don't think any of this is necessary."

"What you think and what is actually true are two separate realities. I'm curious how much you weigh these days."

She seethed at the impertinent statement, so like him, and could feel the heat creeping up her face. Her hand unsteady, she banged her glass against the plate after a sip of juice. "That will never be your business."

"Not according to Dr. Rhodes." He stuck his fork in the mound of eggs. "So in response, yes, this is all necessary. Vitamins were also on your discharge papers."

She tore a piece of toast. "I suppose you feel bad, missing church this morning."

Clay fixed her with such ferocity that she had to look away. "I don't think God wanted me in church this morning."

She shivered, the nightmare erupting again. If not for this troublesome man, she would be lying on the bottom of Feather Lake.

No telling when someone would have found her body. She wiped her mouth.

Clay retrieved a pan from the stovetop. "I assume you don't want coffee since it's late." He poured the boiling water into a mug and then plopped in a chamomile tea bag. "Honey or sugar?"

"Why not check the discharge papers?"

He didn't respond to her sarcasm but placed the honey container and sugar packets next to her mug. Sitting down, he cut even pieces of the melon with his fork and chewed quietly. "What about your family? Have you called them yet?"

The man continued to overstep his bounds.

"I would think your parents would—"

"What? Come running?"

He studied her for a moment. "Want to know."

She was on the edge, about to lose control, and the last thing she wanted was for Clay Montes to see her vulnerable. She moved her chair back, but Clay clasped her arm. "You haven't finished yet."

She jerked her arm away. "Oh yes I have."

*****

He'd underestimated her stubbornness, but sooner or later, he would uncover the real Karis, the one buried under the frigid veneer. The coldness must be a defense mechanism, something to hide the pain or at least keep it tolerable. He frightened her. That much was obvious.

As he hauled the Christmas tree from the truck, he had to admit his plans had changed the minute he pulled her from the icy waters.

If only God in his mercy might put all the fragmented pieces back together.

He opened the front door quietly, hoping he wouldn't disturb her. She'd locked herself away in her bedroom again. Thankfully, he'd finally made peace with the dog. He petted Buddy's shaggy head and set to work securing the tree to the plastic stand.

His mother had always hired someone to decorate a sixteen-foot white fir every year. The tree was perfection, holding crystal ornaments and hundreds of tiny white lights. One year the tree might showcase golden beads, the next year silver garland. After the tree came the house—greenery and bows on the balustrade, seasonal drapes for the windows, and Christmas pillows on every upholstered surface. The whole house was totally transformed. Saddest of all, his mother had no idea of the purpose behind the celebration. He prayed for his parents constantly.

But now he found Christmas humbling. The Christ child, incarnate God, born to die for the sins of mankind, for his own black heart—the idea was unfathomable. He celebrated the holidays simply, but with deep thanksgiving.

The tree would naturally look best in front of the living room window. He'd bought white lights and a brilliant gold star, but he would leave the ornaments to Karis. He'd laid the groundwork. He'd also taken a chance and bought a few other things to give her house a little festivity and hopefully cheer—some candles, two red poinsettia plants, and a small nativity scene.

He turned off the lamp by the couch, plugged in the lights, and lit the candles, giving the room a soft glow.

"I don't celebrate Christmas anymore." She stood midway on the staircase, her mouth a tight line. "Buddy will probably pee on that tree."

"Then I'll go back to Wal-Mart for carpet cleaner since they stock everything."

She continued down the steps and passed him on the way to the kitchen. He heard her rustling in the pantry and watched Buddy scurry toward the sound. He stepped to the threshold as she put a cup of dry dog food in a silver bowl and moistened it. The dog fairly danced as she sat the bowl by the back door and filled up another bowl with water.

"Did you sleep?"

"No." She looked at him as if it was his fault.

"Why not? Was I being too loud?"

"No."

She walked past him back to the stairs. He followed her. "We need to talk business. Why don't you have a seat?" He motioned toward the couch.

She seemed to weigh her options and then sat at one end of the sofa. He sat at the other end and turned toward her.

"By taking it easy, I assume Dr. Rhodes meant no working for the next few days. Who should we call? Belinda? Lauren?"

"I have thirty-nine patients scheduled tomorrow."

"Sorry."

"You don't seem to understand. I am legally responsible for my patients."

"You're not leaving this house tomorrow."

She was clearly angry. She huffed and crossed her arms, turning away from him. In the candlelight, her profile made a perfect silhouette. It would be so easy to pull her into his arms, drink in the sweet scent of her skin. But he wouldn't dare. Instead, he left for the kitchen to retrieve her cordless phone. He'd discovered her section of Harbor, at the foot of the bluffs, had spotty cellphone service. "Lauren gave me her number, by the way. Twice." He threw over his shoulder.

She was by his side in an instant. "I will call her myself." She grabbed the phone and stormed back into the living room. He picked up a dining chair and straddled it backward, across from the couch and away from her. He rested his arms on the back and listened as she made the call.

When she punched the phone off, her eyes flashed at him. "So basically I'm a prisoner in my own house."

"Karis, after this morning—"

"What's in it for you?"

She still didn't trust him. Not even after saving her life. "I've been celibate for two years, if that's what you're worried about."

She blushed and looked away, agitated.

He let out a long breath. "I give you my word, I won't try anything."

Buddy finished eating and padded into the living room and then jumped up and burrowed under Karis' leg. She stroked his furry black head. "Don't you have more houses to build? More money to throw around?"

She was doing it again, flipping the conversation away from herself. "Nothing that can't wait. Can I get you something else to eat?"

As he'd ambled through the store that afternoon, he began to realize how little he knew about her. He tried to pick out things he hoped she would like, but everything he put in the cart was a big guess. VHS tapes were getting harder and harder to come by, but since she still had a VCR, he threw a few old movies in the cart. And microwave popcorn with butter. She could use the extra calories. And what woman didn't like chocolate?

"There's dessert." The defenses came down when he mentioned the French Silk pie.

After placing a piece on the side table next to her, he brought the kitchen chair back to its former place across from the couch, hoping the distance would ease her discomfort. They ate their pie as Buddy slept peacefully beside her. When the Thomasville clock chimed eight, the dog repositioned himself on her leg. Karis returned her empty plate to the side table and started fiddling with the cuff of her warm-up jacket. The silence became awkward.

Clay watched her, wishing he could go back. The words slipped out before he could stop them. "I didn't marry her. Marcella . . . my fiancée."

Her eyes snapped to his. "You don't owe me an explanation."

"I wanted you to know."

She looked down. "It doesn't really matter now."

"Karis . . ." It was on the tip of his tongue. But she was so fragile, so lost, and yet how much longer could they ignore the yawning creature in the room? She seemed willing to talk about anything, but *that*.

Her hands had gone limp in her lap. She looked at the Christmas tree as if lost in another world. "She called it off then? Your fiancée?"

Were her lips quivering? Clay wished he could at least sit next to her, but with the darkened room and the lights glowing in her eyes, he didn't trust himself. He took a deep breath. "No, I did."

Her eyes found his. "What did you say?"

"I called it off."

She stared at him. "Why?"

"Isn't it obvious?"

She stood abruptly, hugging herself. "I'm tired."

Clay watched her disappear up the stairs, the weight on his soul bearing down. Always, she was running from him. *What now, Lord?*

CHAPTER TWENTY

WHAT WAS THAT NOISE?

Karis blinked several times, the outline of her room coming into view, consciousness returning. Then fear. Who was in her house?

"Breakfast is ready."

The memories of yesterday came flooding back. Clay banged on the door again. She shrugged on her robe, but felt dizzy as she tried to get off the bed. "Just a minute."

"Are you alright?"

Across the room, she noticed her reflection in the dresser mirror. "I'm not feeling well."

A pause and then. "I'll bring you a tray."

Had she ever had breakfast in bed? "That would be nice."

After his footsteps retreated, she unlocked the door and stumbled into the bathroom, brushing her teeth first and then splashing cold water on her face. Her hair was beyond help. She spritzed and combed it. When she opened the door, he was putting food on her nightstand—muffins, hot cereal, jam, milk, juice, tea, and a vitamin.

"You must want a good tip."

He didn't respond but backed away as she got into bed and pulled the covers over her flannel pajamas. He looked like a caveman with his whiskered jaw and unbound hair but acted like Florence Nightingale. The idea was almost absurd.

For a fleeting moment, she thought of the contents inside her little jeweler's box. Was it the same as . . .

Clay sat down across from her on the floor, legs outstretched, crossed at the ankles, a book by his side. He laced his fingers, bowed his head, and prayed out loud. "Dear Jesus, thank you again for your provisions. We are in your debt forever. Amen."

His prayers were beginning to get on her nerves.

"Aren't you going to eat?" She picked up the bowl of oatmeal with brown sugar swirls and let the steam warm her face. A small chunk of butter floated in the middle.

"I already did."

She glanced at the clock then, surprised. She had never slept until eleven.

"I woke you up so I can make sure you get three square meals today." Clay forked his fingers through his hair. "About last night, I didn't mean to make you—"

"Let's just forget it."

"Karis." He seemed disappointed. He shifted uncomfortably. "How did you sleep?"

"Fine." She had stared at the ceiling for three hours, but he didn't need to know that. She picked up a banana muffin and took a bite.

From the first floor, Buddy suddenly barked as a car roared down the street. She almost spilled her juice as she struggled to get out of bed. "Oh, Buddy!"

Clay didn't move. "I took care of Buddy. He's been fed, watered, and let out to pee twice, so finish your breakfast."

Last night in her disturbed state, she had completely forgotten about her little dog. They normally slept together, Buddy's head occupying the space between her chin and neck. She glanced at Clay. He had made a ridiculous promise to take care of her, but not her dog. She smoothed the blanket over her legs. "Thanks."

"You're welcome."

He picked up the black book beside him.

"I don't want to hear the Bible."

He ignored her, flipped to a certain page, and cleared his voice. She sat amused as he embellished the lines of *Ode to a Grecian Urn* with a British accent. After the fourth ode, he looked up. "More?"

"You remembered." On a single occasion, she had mentioned her love of John Keats.

He set the book down and stood up.

She looked at her empty bowl, the two muffin wrappers, and her still unfinished tea. "That was very good. Thanks."

He leaned in close to take her dishes, maybe a little too close. She felt herself flush. It was becoming more and more difficult to treat him poorly. He was doing his best to keep things businesslike and impersonal, but she still . . .

"By the way, a man called this morning, around five-thirty. Said he had the wrong number."

"You answered my phone?"

Clay sighed. "I was barely awake."

Fear pecked at her throat. "What did he sound like?"

"Soft-spoken. Older."

"It was my father." She felt the blood leave her face and panic nest in her stomach. "He'll think the worst. He always does."

"You haven't done anything wrong, Karis."

"I told you I didn't want you here."

Clay spread his hands. "I'm sorry. What can I do?"

"Just . . . leave."

Clay moved toward her bed. "I'll do that for a little while, but only to run a few errands. Will you be okay?"

"Worried I might run away?"

He rested his hand on the footboard. "Do I need to be?"

"Where would I go?"

He gazed at her and then looked down, brushing his hand over her feet. "Things will work out. Try to believe that."

If only she could.

*****

Clay had wondered if she was dead. How many adults slept so late? It was all he could do not to pound on her door every hour.

After answering the phone, he had gone back to sleep only to be awakened a short while later by her infernal dog jumping on top of him. Her couch wasn't terribly uncomfortable. It just wasn't big enough to accommodate his large frame, and the throw pillows didn't offer much neck support. He woke up stiff and achy.

As he drove around downtown Harbor, he scoured Main Street for a vacant parking space that his truck could fit into—no small task given the long bed. About a block away from the Bullfrog Bar, he pulled into a spot as a large conversion van pulled out. The roads weren't in bad shape, but several snowbanks spilled over from the sidewalks, making it difficult to park.

He'd grabbed a clean Blues sweatshirt from his trailer, but this afternoon, he'd need to do some laundry. He wondered what kind of fuss Karis would make. He strode into Nelda's Fashion Boutique, hoping they might have the kind of coat he had in mind. Karis' frayed gray coat was still at Feather Lake for all he knew, but come Wednesday, she would need something warm.

A mousy older woman with brown hair approached him. She scrunched up her nose while looking over silver-framed glasses. "What can I do for you?"

"I need a coat."

The woman drew herself up and clasped her hands behind her. "This is a woman's store, sir."

"Not for me, for—"

"Your wife, of course." The woman threw a hand up and spun on her heels. "Right this way."

Clay decided not to correct her—the woman gave an air of omniscience. She bustled over to a rack beside the large display window and gestured toward a row of coats. "This is all we have left from our big weekend sale which you missed by one day. They are full price now."

The woman looked like she expected him to argue, but he just smiled and nodded his thanks.

"I'll leave you to browse then." And off she scurried.

The long black wool coat would look great with her blond hair and her apparent wardrobe, or at least what he'd happened to see in her closet. At two hundred dollars, he was probably paying too much, but Harbor had few options. He paid for the coat and left.

When he let himself into the apartment, he knew something was wrong. He heard the toilet flush, but the retching didn't stop. He threw the coat on the couch and took the steps two at a time, thankful she'd had enough common sense to leave the bathroom door unlocked. She vomited again. He moistened a hand towel from the sink, squeezed it, and then tried to give it to her.

"Get out!" She batted his hand away. "I don't want you in here."

He didn't say anything as she sat back on her feet, gripping her midsection. He sat down next to her and held out the towel again.

She finally took it, burying her face in the folds.

He flushed the toilet. "I always feel better after I puke. How about you?"

"A little."

"What happened?"

"That is a stupid question."

"Do you need to see Dr. Rhodes? Is this a of complication from—"

"No!" That was pretty emphatic.

He wanted to ask her flat out if she was bulimic, but their relationship was already on shaky ground. "Was it my cooking? Something you ate?"

She wiped her brow. "The only time I get this sick is when I eat Brazilian nuts or have food poisoning or . . ." She closed her mouth abruptly.

Clay stood up. "I'll be right back." He ran downstairs and dug the muffin box out of the garbage. He had assumed the nuts in banana muffins were pecans. At least, that was what his mother's maid always used. He took the box upstairs.

Karis was standing by the sink, brushing her teeth. When she saw him, she spit and quickly wiped her mouth.

He held the box up. "This is probably the culprit. No Brazilians, but mixed nuts are listed in the ingredients."

"I never eat mixed nuts for that reason."

"I'm really sorry. Any other allergies I need to know about?"

She shook her head.

"What about other side effects? Diarrhea? Do I need to get some Imodium? Kaopectate? The pink stuff?"

She almost smiled. "Is there anything you won't talk about?"

He felt the pressure in his gut and swallowed. Sooner or later. "Karis . . ."

Her face paled even more. "No. Don't say another word."

Clay sighed. "Let's get you back in bed."

She let him guide her into the bedroom and help her into bed. As she straightened the covers over her feet, he jammed his hands in his pockets. "Guess you won't want any lunch for a while?"

She covered her stomach. "Tea?

"I'll be right back."

*****

Pity. It must be pity. Karis had looked at her sallow reflection in the dresser mirror when Clay had run downstairs and wondered how he could hang around with the smell. Even her own mother could hardly stand to be in the same room when her children had vomited. She patted her stubborn cowlick. As soon as the dizziness passed, she would shower. But for now, she felt too weak.

His hands were warm and firm when he guided her to bed, and she didn't have the energy to shake them off. Sometimes, the whole idea of Clay Montes in her house, taking care of her, felt like the Twilight Zone. When he brought up a steaming cup and placed it on her nightstand, she caught his strong, soapy scent.

He backed up and looked down at her. "Ready for another fight? I'm doing laundry. Dirty clothes?"

"Absolutely not."

He was already halfway to her closet, swinging open the door before the cry escaped her lips. "No!"

He turned around and looked at her. "It's just underwear, Karis. What's the big deal?"

The state of said apparel was the big deal, and she found herself caring desperately what he would think of her personal belongings. With her exhausting schedule, she hadn't shopped in ages. But their relationship was changing. He was becoming a persistent cough that she couldn't get rid of. And what about the personal nature of the whole domestic chore? The thought brought a fresh flush to her cheeks.

He picked up the laundry basket while she gauged its contents— a few blouses, her jeans, several pairs of socks, and the plain white Hanes hip huggers. He gave her a disarming grin. "Don't worry. I know how to sort."

She fell asleep while he was gone and didn't know when he left a plate with toast and applesauce by the side of her bed. When she woke up around two, she felt ravenous. After eating the simple offering, she headed into the bathroom for a shower. Maybe she could set things back in order once she was dressed and felt better about her appearance.

She pulled on the black warm-up pants and a lavender hoodie her mother had sent last year on her birthday. Comfortable and warm, she wore it every weekend during the winter. She decided not to mess with makeup since the day was half gone anyway, and Clay had already seen her at her absolute worst. Anything was an improvement over this morning.

She heard Clay whistling when he came up from the basement. She eased down the steps and watched him dump two loads of laundry on the couch. Sure enough, a dark pile and a light pile. For a moment, she just watched him. He was fastidious. Picking up a towel, he folded it in half, the corners matching perfectly. Then he folded it in half again and finished with a tri-fold for a tidy bundle.

When he started to pick up her panties, she quickly came down the rest of the stairs. "I can fold my own."

He looked her over, scanning her appearance. "You feeling okay?"

"Better now." She gathered her underwear quickly, deftly folded them in half and then picked up various shirts and blouses.

"Any thoughts on dinner?"

"I'm fully capable of cooking."

"I'm sure you are, but I'm making shepherd's pie. Got a radio handy? I cook better with music."

That he cooked at all came as a continual surprise to her. The same man had dined at expensive restaurants or paid exorbitant prices for catered food. She had wondered if he'd ever been in a grocery store.

In the spare bedroom, she found her old black-faced clock radio in a box marked "College Stuff." It was a faux wood-grain dinosaur with red LED numbers, four silver clock function switches, and a massive snooze bar. It had been her only Christmas present in 1991 and she had loved it.

He rapped on the doorframe an hour later, realizing she hadn't even closed her door. She put down the *New England Journal of Medicine* and followed him downstairs. As they neared the kitchen, she detected strains of classic Christmas carols in another language. She listened closely. "Who's singing?"

"Jose Aiolia, an up-and-coming opera singer."

"And you like that? What happened to your heavy metal?" She would never forget riding in his Corvette on a hot summer night, the radio blasting, the bass vibrating against her chest, and Clay beating the dashboard in sync with the drums.

"I discovered something better."

"You continue to surprise me."

He poured her a large glass of milk. "Hopefully in a good way."

She placed a napkin in her lap. "You don't drink anymore. Why is that?"

He sat down next to her. "Same reason I have a ponytail."

She pondered his enigmatic answer over his bowed head. He blessed the food and then picked up a fork and ate with gusto. She followed suit, thankful for the music that drowned out the need for conversation.

*****

Clay almost felt like patting himself on the back. Under his care for a mere twenty-four hours, Karis' color was better, she looked healthier, and to top things off, they were actually having a pleasant meal without her stomping off to her bedroom. He wanted the evening to be low-key, so he'd steered clear of controversial topics.

When he suggested that they watch a movie after dinner, he watched her eyes spark with interest. How long had it been since she had any fun?

After he finished the dishes, he sat the bag of movies on her lap and waited for her to pick one.

"*Top Gun*?" He tried to hide a smile. "So you like Tom Cruise. Now I know."

"No, I just think it's fascinating that planes can take off and land on aircraft carriers."

"Uh-huh. Maybe I should have bought a military documentary instead. On F-14s."

She rolled her eyes. It was a good sign, a very minor thaw in their icy, tenuous relationship. He savored the moment.

Clay worried about the movie's love scene, and since he didn't want to make her uncomfortable and he personally didn't want to see it, he grabbed the remote and fast-forwarded to another part when it came up. She had looked puzzled, but he shrugged his shoulders at her. "I'm a PG guy now."

Who would have thought that she was a pig when it came to popcorn? She polished off three bags.

It was almost nine o'clock when the movie ended. Clay turned from his end of the sofa to find her playing with the zipper on her jacket. "I guess you don't want any pie?"

She shook her head and looked at him, her eyes soft and warm. "Dinner was really good. Thanks. I haven't eaten this well in months."

For a brief moment, he saw the girl from yesteryear. She picked up the empty popcorn bags. "I'll get you a blanket. There's one in my closet."

Clay let her words sink in, realizing for the first time since they'd reconnected that she was trying to do something for him, not because she had to, but seemingly because she wanted to. For a brief moment, he let himself hope.

CHAPTER TWENTY-ONE

THE SKY WAS GRAY AND OVERCAST on Tuesday morning. Clay worked the kink out of his neck, folded the thermal blanket, and switched on the Christmas tree lights, hoping to brighten the living room. Since Karis kept her house toasty, he hadn't really needed the blanket—instead he'd just slept in his sweatpants. He padded into the kitchen in bare feet, rummaged around for a skillet, and then set out the ingredients for buttermilk pancakes.

The opening of the front door surprised him. He heard Karis murmur to Buddy. A moment later, the front door opened again, and the little black dog scurried in, rubbing against his leg. He turned as Karis entered the kitchen. She flinched at his bare chest and then averted her gaze. He must look like an untamed grizzly. "Sorry." He walked past her and plucked his T-shirt from the couch. Returning, he broke two eggs in a bowl. "How'd you sleep?"

With his back turned, he heard the chair scuff as she sat down at the table. "Good."

He beat the eggs with more vigor than was necessary. "Feeling okay?"

"Just hungry."

"Glad to hear that. This recipe makes about ten pancakes." He looked over his shoulder. She was fingering the petals of the flowers, her mind off somewhere.

He began measuring dry ingredients and then heard her stand and move to his side. He glanced at her. She looked well-rested, somehow less haunted, and . . .beautiful.

"Where'd you learn to cook?"

He dumped in the flour, alternating it with the buttermilk, and stirred. "Our maid. She spoiled me. Probably since my parents were gone a lot, she cooked whatever I wanted. Can you find the syrup in that lower cabinet?"

As she looked for the syrup, he poured the batter into the skillet. It sizzled in the hot butter and soon bubbled on top. She set the syrup on the table and stood near again. "I was always terrible at flipping pancakes."

"It's all in the wrists." He demonstrated with a spatula. After the three pancakes were browned on the second side, he slid them onto a plate for her. "Go ahead and eat while they're hot."

"Thank you."

"Butter's on the table."

While she ate, he made seven more pancakes. After putting five on his plate, he sat down next to her. "What do you want to do today, besides your follow-up with Dr. Rhodes at 1:30?"

"I get a choice?"

"If you're good." He almost winked.

"Buddy needs a walk."

"Can I drive you somewhere later? Say, when it gets dark?"

She turned with a questioning look.

"I'd like to show you something."

She offered to help with the dishes, but he sent her into the living room instead with a cup of tea. He was going to make sure she had every opportunity to rest up. When he finished cleaning, he found her with the book of poetry he had picked up at the used bookstore.

"I'm going to grab a shower while you're reading."

She glanced up with a hint of a smile. "Good idea."

"That bad, huh?"

"You know what they say, cleanliness is next to godliness."

"Whoever 'they' is."

After Clay finished up in the bathroom, he came downstairs, noticing Karis had changed into jeans and boots. While she went into the kitchen for the dog's leash, Clay took the black coat from the front closet.

She came into the living room with Buddy happily pulling toward the front door. He held up the coat. "Here, you need this."

She looked puzzled. "What happened to my coat?"

"I left it at the lake."

"On purpose?" The hackles were up.

"More or less. I wasn't exactly thinking about your personal belongings at the time."

She stepped back. "I can't afford that."

"You're not going outside without a coat on." The words came out harsh, and he instantly regretted them. "Look, I lost your coat. I'm taking full responsibility for my actions, okay?"

"The last time you gave me something, it ruined my life."

He could have kicked himself for thinking she wouldn't remember the bathing suit. "It's not like that now."

Her voice hardened. "I don't want to be indebted to you."

"Karis, it's just a coat."

She hesitated a moment and then took it from him, her face set. "I will do your follow-up appointments for gratis."

He sighed. "Whatever." Had he ever met a more stubborn woman?

*****

Fully lined, the coat fit perfectly, but she sensed Clay's frustration. He'd kept himself polite, almost brotherly, but now he seemed pensive as he lagged behind. Karis almost wished she hadn't brought up the past. As much as she hated to admit it, she had begun to enjoy the noise he made in the kitchen, the way he hummed under his breath, the lingering musk scent in the living room . . .

At the end of the walk, she opened her mailbox to find a yellow postcard on top of the mail. She'd missed a postal delivery that required a signature. She removed the stack of envelopes and tucked the card in her pocket. Clay stood a few feet away. "Sorry, I forgot about your mail. What's that?"

"Probably something from my mom."

"You want to pick it up?"

"Is that allowed?"

He took out his keys and pressed the fob to unlock his truck.

"What about Buddy?"

"Bring him."

She followed Clay to his truck. He opened the door for her, picked up Buddy, set the dog in her lap, and gave the door a resounding slam.

Opening the driver's door, he slid in and fixed her with a sharp gaze. "I would give away my soul to change the past."

She looked away from him. "I shouldn't have said anything."

He slammed his door. "We have to talk about him sometime, Karis."

She tried to swallow, blink away the tears that threatened. "No."

Clay sighed and backed the truck out. They rode in silence to the post office. She reached for the handle before he was fully parked in the lot. She could hardly breathe around him.

Already the post office was crowded. She stood behind an elderly man with four small packages. As they moved forward, he turned her way and smiled. "Homemade fudge for the grandkids." She nodded politely.

When her turn came at the counter, she was surprised to see a larger-sized rectangular box with her parents' return address. Probably another random care package from her mother. She would take the home-baked goods to the office and try to find a use for the little whatnots her mother had probably picked up from the myriad of craft shows in southwest Missouri.

Clay was standing by the truck when she came out. Without a word, he opened the door for her. She wished he would stop acting like such a gentleman. It just made the whole situation more difficult. She slid in next to Buddy and propped the box on her lap.

Clay told her he had arranged with a friend to pick up her car at the lake. She had argued that she could drive, but he wouldn't hear of it. He took her keys and deposited her curbside at her house. She took the box to the kitchen table and found a pair of scissors in the basket on top of the microwave. Buddy camped out under the table. When she cut through the tape and opened the box, he pounced on the packing peanuts that escaped.

Her breath caught suddenly. He hadn't thrown it away after all.

She gently lifted the molded black case and switched open the locks. Just as she remembered, the warm amber-colored violin lay nestled in the burgundy velvet. She touched the smooth wood and picked up the note that was tucked within the strings. *Play for us at Christmas? Dad.*

It was another way he'd punished her, forbidding her mother from sending the violin, and never mind that she had paid for it with her own money. Another vestige of her childhood lost, she had longed for the therapy the instrument afforded. She unsnapped the clasps and slid the wooden bow out and then the violin. It would be sorely out of tune. She plucked the strings, listening, adjusting the pegs. A friendship restored, she tucked the instrument below her chin, lifted the bow and stroked the strings. The passion returned as sweet melodies danced between her fingers, song after song—the masters, the classic hymns, and then her favorite, rife with the deep groundswells:

> *Amazing grace, how sweet the sound,*
> *that saved a wretch like me.*
> *I once was lost but now am found,*
> *was blind but now I see.*

She didn't hear him come in but felt his presence. A rich baritone, he sang softly, his voice intertwining with the notes of the violin in a tender caress.

She stopped, embarrassed where her thoughts had led. His voice tapered off.

"I didn't know that you played." He stood behind her.

She lowered the violin. "I didn't know that you sang."

"If you'll just give me a chance, Karis."

His breath warmed her neck as his hands gently touched her shoulders. Her breathing stopped. "Don't."

He backed off. "I'm sorry." His voice was ragged.

She closed the case. "I need to call my office."

*****

Of all the dumb things to do. She'd retreated into her fortress again. He'd scared her to death with one foolish gesture, but he sensed she had felt the connection too. Lunch was a quiet affair. She hardly said a word but dutifully ate her chicken sandwich and fruit salad and then removed herself to her bedroom until they left for her doctor's appointment. Thank God, everything was normal. When they returned, she shut herself off again. They could have had a pleasant time, playing Scrabble or something. But now it was like talking to stone, and the weight of his words tonight might break her into a hundred pieces.

He'd planned an ethnic meal—enchiladas and homemade tortillas, not as good as Rapheala's, but much better than the rubber stuff from the grocery store. The salsa would be fresh, too. He would tell her about his grandfather's immigration, his Spanish heritage, his family, and find out her thoughts about the future and then somehow turn the conversation to Seth.

When he set the meal out, she told him that onions upset her stomach. He frowned as she dismembered the enchiladas, putting the onions in a neat pile and only eating the shredded chicken. And the tortillas were too dry. He could tell on the first bite. Wordlessly, she plucked the butter tub from the fridge and coated a piece of bread as if to spite him. Bad food. Bad company. Served him right.

When she'd finished her glass of iced raspberry tea, she stood and gave him a cursory glance. "Are we still going somewhere?"

He looked out the kitchen window into the darkness of the early evening. "I'll clean up first."

She nodded and went into the living room with Buddy. He washed the dishes and dumped the ill-fated entrée down the disposal, wondering if she was prejudiced against him specifically or anything remotely Hispanic.

When he came into the room, she pulled the new coat out of the closet, her face set. She gave Buddy a rawhide and watched him scurry behind the couch.

The roads were pretty much deserted for a Tuesday evening. He drove carefully since the recent drop in temperature had turned the slushy streets to treacherous ice. Karis looked out the window, her expression unreadable.

He found the access road in fairly good condition and headed for the northern edge of the county. Though he'd driven the road scores of times during the last six months, he hadn't seen this part of the countryside in winter. The snowdrifts and frosted forests shimmering in the moonlight gave off an ethereal quality against the black velvet sky. Karis seemed spellbound. When they rounded the last turn of the road, he heard her breath catch. Hundreds of luminaria candles softly glowed along the drive and steps leading up to the monastery complex. As they approached, warm light filtered through the arched windows of the unpretentious chapel as if in welcome. Behind, a lit path beckoned. Would it be too much for her?

Clay looked over. "Do you want to get out?"

She didn't answer.

Clay parked the truck and came around to open her door. He held out his hand. She wiped at her cheek. How he wished he could read her mind. She looked at him then, eyes moist and tortured. What kind of war waged within her heart? The despair was almost palpable. He started praying. She finally slid out but ignored his hand.

They walked in silence, the flickering candles of the luminaries beckoning to the path's end. Clay knew what would be there. Would Karis be angry? He didn't want to push.

The path became an icy rock-hewn staircase leading down a ledge, a weathered handrail to the right. He took the lead, bracing himself with each step. At the bottom, just yards from the cave, she stopped. "Why did you bring me here?"

He turned. "I thought you might find it therapeutic."

She moved away abruptly, her ten-foot wall securely in place. He felt like shaking her. The answer was so obvious. Why couldn't she see it? Or maybe she saw it but wouldn't accept it. He kept a safe distance and stopped at the cave's entrance as she stepped inside. Sheltered in the alcove from the night wind, candles burned in every crevice, bathing the life-size limestone statues in soft light. A labor of love from a long dead monk, they stood primitive, stark, and silent. A dirt floor. White against gray against black. Karis seemed paralyzed, her eyes staring at the statue. Little more than a girl herself, the young mother cradled the baby against her breast. The father hovered, his hand cupping the infant's head. The place felt holy. Raw. Had it been like this the night He was born?

"What are you thinking?"

Karis continued to stare, hugging herself. Finally, feather light, her words floated through the stillness. "She was so young." Her fingers touched the infant's cheek. "I didn't even get to say goodbye to him."

"Karis—"

"He was beautiful." She choked back a sob.

It was now or never. Clay's heart slammed against his chest. "He still is."

Her head jerked sideways, her blue eyes wide and wild, her voice unnatural. "You've *seen* him?"

He breathed deeply and gave one slow nod, suddenly feeling unprepared for the fallout he had detonated.

Her voice continued to climb, accusing, the words knotted together. "I've been looking for years. How did you find him?"

He glanced toward the cave's entrance. What had possessed him? "I'd rather not say."

She was suddenly animated, her voice strained to the point of snapping. "Why didn't you tell me?"

He balked inside, but anger wouldn't win this round. He searched for the path of least resistance, knowing he was walking a minefield. "Karis, it's . . . complicated."

Peace and good will suddenly dissipated.

"Life is always complicated with you." Her face twisted in anger. "How could you not tell me? You have no idea what I went through, no—"

"How could I know?" So much for patience. The words shot out. He was way in over his head. "You shut me out. Continually."

She turned on heel and rushed past him. He caught up, grabbing her arm. "See what I mean?"

She struggled to get away, but he held her shoulders. "You're starting to shiver."

"Let go of me!" She fought against him.

What choice did he have? He released her. "I'm taking you home now."

"No." Her breathing was becoming uneven.

"Karis, please."

She whipped around suddenly, her face contorted. "You want to know what I went through? I was sent away so I wouldn't bring shame to my family. My aunt treated me like trash, and then she stole my son. That is what I went through!"

A primal cry escaped. She hid her face.

It was more than he could stand. He grabbed her tightly. "I just found out a few days ago." He meshed his words in between her sobs. "I wasn't trying to keep anything from you." He wiped at her wet face with both hands and then crushed her to his chest as she spent herself.

The wind cajoled the nearby pines. After a few minutes, she raised her head and stared at him, each breath seemingly a struggle. "Is he . . . well?"

The truth sat like a semi on his chest. How to tell her?

"All things considered, he's well."

The moonlight touched her questioning face. Why did it have to be here in the cold?

She searched his eyes. "What does that mean?"

He breathed in deeply, fishing for a good lie, but coming up empty. "I wish . . . Karis, he was never adopted. He's in foster care."

She shrank away, despair moving in for a second assault. "Foster care? No one wanted him?" Both hands came to her head, fingers dragging through the short strands, a crazed look on her face. "Why?"

Clay swallowed hard. "He's . . . disabled."

Her head jerked up. "But I saw him. I held him." Her voice accused. "He was perfect."

Hearing her torment, Clay hated himself even more. If only things had been different, if only he'd done the right thing. "If only" was another name for hell. "Karis, he doesn't have a left hand."

*****

The cold swallowed her. Clutching her stomach, she slid to the ground, wanting to melt into nothingness. The night seemed to close in as the memories played again—living with her aunt, the long days, the even longer nights, the labor pains, pushing him out, the sheer joy when she held him, and the blackness when he was gone. She buried her head in her hands. Only one thing had kept her going all these years—that Aunt Ernie really had found a good home, that her son was well cared for, that he wasn't paying for her mistakes . . . that he was happy.

Clay sat down next to her, but she drew herself away from him.

He blew out his breath. "When would you like to see him?"

Was he out of his mind? She looked at his profile, the fierce jaw, the deep-set eyes, and strong nose. The man continued to torment. "See him?" Something cried inside. "He'll hate me."

"He's not like that."

"And how would I know?" Fresh anguish.

"His name is Seth. He—"

"Stop it!"

"I'm taking you home now."

When she resisted his hand, he hauled her up. They had a chilly ride back. She got out of the truck and stormed inside. A few minutes later, he was at her bedroom door, his fist pounding.

She yelled above the noise. "What?"

"I'm leaving now. I'll be calling every day to harass you, so get ready."

She pulled open the door, seething. "I am a grown woman. I don't need to be checked on."

"Sorry, but I'm your new 'thorn in the flesh.' Here's your keys."

*****

Clay stared at the computer screen, wondering if he was imagining the words, but the town had only three listings for the last name Henry. And it couldn't be Ora or Nathan. One was too old, the other too young. It had to be Paul. He did a quick search to see if any additional information popped up. Spouse: Lorna. Both in their sixties, Paul seven years Lorna's senior. That seemed right. Unfortunately. When he entered the data on the secure website, three children were listed. He suddenly felt ill.

Now it made sense. Karis Henry was a preacher's daughter.

CHAPTER TWENTY-TWO

LONG-HANDLED TONGS IN one hand, Lou swung open the door with the other. The RV reeked. Lou grinned. "Just in time for breakfast."

Clay stepped inside. "That's not turkey bacon."

Lou's face soured. "Not in the mood, Clay."

"Did you fill the prescription?"

Lou's doctor had put him on blood pressure medicine, his first ever. He wasn't too happy about it.

"Shut the door. Yes, I filled it." Lou added four more pieces of thick-sliced, applewood-smoked bacon to the hot skillet, grease popping, crackling, and splattering the compact cooktop.

Clay eased onto the dinette bench. "Well, did you take it?"

Another sour look. "What are you, my mother?" And with the next breath. "Want some eggs?"

Clay hid a smile and opened his water bottle. "I already ate, but thanks." The protein bar had been quick.

"So what's up?" The great bacon master flipped all four pieces in one fluid motion. Small grease specks had already stained his flannel shirt.

Clay noted the egg carton, white bread, raspberry jam, and stick of butter by the kitchen sink. Obviously, the Mediterranean diet recommendation had fallen on deaf ears. He shifted uncomfortably, the results of his recent computer search coming to mind. He'd argued with himself all night. "I need some advice."

Lou plopped the bacon on a paper-toweled plate, laden with six other pieces, and started cracking eggs. Hopefully his meds could handle the load. "Shoot."

"I guess I'm wondering if I should let a dead dog lie."

Lou beat the four eggs and poured a yellow stream into the skillet where they were instantly married to the bacon fat. "Depends."

"On what?"

"On how smelly it is."

"Next to rotten, I'd say."

"Then maybe you need to bury it proper-like. What does He think?" Lou glanced upward.

"I have no idea. One thought keeps eating at me."

"That might be your answer."

"I'd rather stab myself." Clay moved the blue plaid curtains by the dinette table. The sun was just starting to cast a peachy glow on the Saturday morning's horizon.

"We're made for the hard stuff, Clay." While the eggs cooked, Lou punched two pieces of bread into the toaster.

Clay expelled his breath, expecting something spiritual to pour out of Lou's mouth any minute. As he leaned back, his eye caught a brightly colored package on Lou's back nightstand. The tangle of shiny silver and gold spiraling ribbon cascaded down the decorative polka-dot gift bag. It definitely wasn't something Lou would rig up.

"Looks like Santa came early. I guess you were a good boy."

Lou dumped the eggs onto a plate and then started slathering the toast with butter. Next came suffocation with jam. Lou glanced his way. "What're you talking about?"

Clay pointed to the back. "Your present."

Lou suddenly turned red and coated the second piece of toast with even more jam. "You want some coffee?"

"What's in it, Lou?"

Still ignoring him, the man showered his eggs with salt. "You can at least have some bacon." Lou banged the plate on the table.

Clay selected a less-charred piece and watched Lou sit down opposite, fork in hand, coffee spilling on the Formica tabletop. Clearly, he'd struck a nerve.

"Well?"

"Well what?" Lou grabbed five pieces of bacon, his voice strained.

"If I didn't know better, I'd say you were stress eating."

Lou slurped his coffee. "Ridiculous."

"So you're not going to tell me?"

More coffee doused the table as Lou's cup came down. "There's nothing to tell."

"You haven't opened it, have you?"

Lou stabbed his eggs. "What is this, CSI?"

There was only one thing that would jerk Lou's chain. Clay smiled to himself. "So when did she come by?"

Lou's eyes nearly popped out. He quickly looked down and shoved half a piece of toast in his mouth, washing it down with several gulps of coffee. "No comment."

"You should at least see what's in there. If I know Moira, she's gonna want to know how you *feel* about it."

Lou tore a piece of bacon in half with his teeth and chewed like a starving man. Poor guy. Clay rested his elbows on the table, unable to resist one last jab. "You know, a wise man recently told me that we're made for the hard stuff."

If looks could kill . . .

*****

He'd practically done backward somersaults, but four hours later, Clay picked up Seth at ten o'clock and headed toward Fenton in search of the Huppenbauer's farm. A family of eight, they bred Labrador retrievers. After a long discussion with Mr. Huppenbauer, an extensive Internet search, and a good deal of research at the local library, Clay had concluded that a Lab would be a good choice for Seth.

"Hey, you missed the turn." Seth sat buckled in the front of the truck in his Packers jacket. A single black glove hung out the side pocket. He whipped his head around to Clay as they passed the soccer complex.

"I've got a surprise for you."

Seth's eyes brightened. "You do?"

"Yep."

"What is it?"

"You'll have to wait and see."

As they pulled onto the interstate, Seth talked about the upcoming Christmas program at his church. He'd been cast as a shepherd and was relieved he didn't have to sing.

"Do you have any lines?"

"Just one." He lowered his voice. "'Let us go and find the babe.'"

Clay smiled. "Sounds like you've got it down. When's your program?"

"Next Sunday night. When it's over, there's lots of food."

"And that's why you're in the program, right? For the food?"

Seth nodded happily.

"That's my man." Clay exited and followed the country road through a series of rolling hills.

Seth was bug-eyed. "I've never been out here. Are those buffalo?"

A snow-covered field came into view with four ponderous beasts. Clay stopped the truck and squinted out the side window. "Looks like it."

"Wow, what are they doing out here?"

"I'd say they're having lunch." The bison were gathered around a six-foot hay roll.

"Wow! They're huge."

Clay could not help but enjoy the boy's exuberance. They watched the creatures for a moment. After pulling back on the road,

Clay spotted a barn board sign, announcing the Huppenbauer Farm two miles down a plowed gravel road. He made the turn and noted rows of bare apple trees lining both sides of the drive. A white clapboard house stood at the end, an impressive barn to the right, and an odd collection of vehicles and tractors to the left. Clay parked behind a burnt orange Volkswagen van.

Seth gave him a puzzled look as they got out of the truck and walked up the front steps to the house. Clay rang the doorbell and smiled down at Seth who seemed intrigued by a tree trunk carved into the shape of a bear.

A woman appeared at the door with a bright smile. "Clay Montes?"

"We're here to see the puppies."

Seth turned large eyes his way. "Puppies? You're getting a puppy?"

"No, you are."

The woman smiled again. "Let me grab a coat, and we'll go out to the barn. My son's out there now."

As the woman closed the door, Seth turned to him. "But Sharon said—"

"No pets at your house, but she was fine with me keeping a dog for you in my camper."

Clay could tell Seth wanted to run ahead, the way he fairly jumped off the front porch and almost tripped up the woman on their trek to the barn. This would be a Christmas he would never forget.

There were seven in the litter. Two males and one female had already been sold. That left two yellow females and two black males. The mother, a yellow mid-sized dog, lay peacefully on her side as six of the pups nursed energetically in a wire pen. A smaller yellow puppy sat off to the side on its haunches.

Clay thought one of the black male puppies would be perfect for Seth. "What do you think, Seth?"

Seth hadn't said a word since they entered the barn, but as he watched the woman's teenage son pick up a puppy and hold it gently on his palm, he tried to scoop one up. The black puppy squirmed out of his grasp, but Seth tried again.

"Do you like this black one?" Clay knelt down.

The puppy popped out of his hand again and trotted back to his mother. Seth picked up the lone yellow female.

The teenage boy petted the nursing mother. "That one's the runt," he said, indicating the puppy Seth was now holding with some success.

Seth stroked the soft golden fur with the stub of his hand. "She's soft. How come she's the runt?"

The woman stepped up. "She had trouble nursing, so we've had to bottle feed her. Part of her tongue is missing, but she's very sweet."

Seth held the puppy to his cheek. "I think she likes me. Can I have her?"

Clay wondered if he should try to persuade Seth to reconsider. What if the dog had problems down the road? But how could he say no? "You bet."

The woman smiled at Seth. "We thought about keeping her. She's our favorite, but as you can see, we have a lot of animals. She'll be ready to go home with you in about two more weeks. Can you wait that long?"

Seth nodded enthusiastically.

After Clay paid for the puppy, he guided Seth back to the truck.

"You've got to pick out a name for her."

Seth climbed in the cab. "I get to name her too?"

"She's your dog."

Seth sat spellbound. "I've never got to name anything before."

"Well, then you'll have to come up with something special." The boy looked out the rear window until the farm disappeared from sight.

"You hungry?" Clay already knew the answer.

"Uh-huh."

"Tell you what, I've got a friend who lives pretty close by. Let's pick her up and then find a place to eat."

*****

Nothing seemed normal. Her mind, a jumbled mass of fear, swirled around thoughts of her father, her son, her mother, and Clay. Always Clay. Sleep proved elusive. She struggled through patients, drank excessive coffee to where her hands shook every morning. She was a wreck and 'her thorn in the flesh' didn't help. True to his word, he called her the day after he left, several times, and every day since, making sure she was eating and breathing. He was like a mosquito, buzzing around her every move. But his message last night scared her senseless.

"I'm bringing Seth by around noon tomorrow."

She listened to the words again and again and panicked and paced and tossed all night long.

Seth. She whispered his name and then spoke it aloud, trying to imagine him as she had done thousands of times.

She stared at the blue veins protruding from the backs of her hands and thought she'd never been so nervous in her life. She'd tried watching TV, reading, answering email, even scrubbing the kitchen sink, but nothing worked. She hadn't wanted to worry about Buddy, so she put him in the bedroom. Now she debated with herself. Part of her wanted to run away. She could tape a note to the front door, telling Clay she'd been called to the hospital, but knowing him, he'd come looking for her. The other part of her could hardly stand the waiting. Every time a car passed by, she held her breath.

11:48 a.m. The familiar rev of his truck. Footsteps on the driveway. Clay's low laugh, a child's exclamation. Her child. Could it really be? Her very own. It sounded so right, but scared her to death. Her heart pounded as the steps grew closer and the doorbell rang. Somehow she walked to the door. Somehow she turned the knob.

Unbidden, a prayer slipped out. *Dear God, please, please let him like me.*

Her eyes met Clay's steady gaze and then traveled downward. She was almost afraid to look at the cropped blond hair, spiking in all directions. Or the tanned brow or the dark chocolate eyes so much like the man standing behind him. Or the freckles sprinkled generously across an upturned nose, a long scar on the right temple. He was absolutely breathtaking. She forced herself to exhale.

"Karis, this is Seth."

Not knowing what else to do, she put out her hand, hoping he didn't see the shakiness. The boy grasped it with his right. Sweet warmth. Was she really holding *his* hand, barely smaller than her own? "Hello, Seth." But her doctor's instincts kicked in as her thumb brushed rough, dry skin. Her eyes flew down to his knuckles. Eczema. She would tell Clay later. She carefully kept her gaze from his other arm, but even in her peripheral vision, she could see his coat sleeve hanging. Lifeless. Empty. *Oh God*.

"Hi." He looked up at her. "Which do you like better, pizza or burgers?"

The question took her by surprise. "Um. Pizza." She released his hand reluctantly.

"Yes!"

"You win. Pizza it is." Clay tousled his hair and then searched her eyes with an intensity she could hardly stand. "Come with us."

Lunch? As in eating and not choking? How would she do that? Clay hadn't mentioned anything about food. How could she ever get anything past the lump in her throat? Any minute she might break down.

Her eyes returned to Seth. He would be tall someday. Already he came to her chest. She drank in the sight of him.

"What about Mario's?" Clay's eyes seemed to twinkle at her discomfort.

She had a hard time tearing her gaze from the boy. "I've never been there."

"Grab your coat." A command, but Karis wouldn't argue. Not this time.

She joined the two of them outside. They walked to Clay's truck where Seth bounced into the back as Clay held the door for Karis to slide into the front passenger's seat. How different this time was in Clay's truck. Last Tuesday, she'd been heartbroken and sick. All week her mind had conjured up images of a little boy who would turn away from her in disgust if he knew who she was. She buckled her seatbelt, hardly believing what was happening now.

Clay let Seth pick the booth. Not surprisingly, he chose one adjacent to the arcade. After they'd ordered, Clay emptied his pocket and slid a handful of quarters to Seth. "I see a Grand Prix game. Why don't you give it a try?"

Seth was on his feet in a second. "Really? You want to play too?"

"I'll let you have all the fun this time."

A quick nod and he was gone.

Karis gazed after him. "Can he actually play those games?" She turned back around and found Clay studying her, an easy smile on his face.

"You'd be surprised what that little guy can do."

"I just can't believe . . . how did you . . ." Suddenly at a loss for words, she felt relief when the waitress delivered the sodas to their table.

Clay peeled back the paper covering of his straw. "At some point, you're going to have to acknowledge God's hand in all this."

She still couldn't go there, and Clay always swung the conversation back in *that* direction. She took a sip of the frosty root beer and looked away.

Clay caught her hand. "I haven't got all the details figured out, but I'm going to get him back. I've filed adoption papers."

For a brief moment, she could see the old Clay, the man who always got what he wanted. He looked big and rugged and invincible in the black sweatshirt. "I've started looking at land. I don't want to raise a son in a camper, although he actually likes that idea."

Karis could hardly believe what he had just said. Did he think he could just gallop in and claim some happily-ever-after ending? She felt the old anger come to life. "Does he even know who you are?"

Her question seemed to break his concentration. He blinked, distracted. "I'm praying for the right time to tell him."

How could it always be God with this man now? "What about me? Are you ready for all the questions he's going to ask?"

"I won't lie, Karis, if that's what you mean."

"I don't want him to know about me."

Clay frowned. "Why? You are a wonderful, beautiful person."

"I couldn't keep him. I couldn't protect him. I couldn't stop—"

"Can't God work things out for good?"

"Do you call that good?" She choked the words out, barely able to stomach the sight of the boy's empty sleeve.

"Karis, why can't you believe—"

"Don't start."

"Have it your way." Clearly angry, Clay abruptly slid out of the booth and joined Seth. Karis dropped her head into her hands and felt the familiar gnashing.

*****

Clay smiled at Seth, but inwardly mourned. Guilt was eating her alive. He hadn't counted on that. She felt responsible for the boy's loss. How could he make her see that it wasn't her fault, that just the miracle of finding Seth with the possibility of getting him back was something to celebrate? If anything, the blame belonged squarely on him. In the few months he'd known Seth, the boy hardly gave any thought to his missing hand. In fact, he totally compensated. Should he remind that bull-headed woman that their son could have been killed, but God had spared his life?

Clay peered over the video game and saw the waitress picking up three plates and a large pan. "Looks like our pizza is almost ready."

Seth kept his eyes locked forward, his right hand clutching the steering wheel. "Two more laps."

The machine made a loud whirring noise and flashed Seth's score. "Aww! Only twenty points away from the record."

"Next time, big guy. Come on, let's eat, but wash up first." He guided Seth to the men's room.

When they sat down, Karis kept her eyes averted as the waitress delivered the pizza. They'd ordered a large thin crust with extra pepperoni and cheese. Seth was about to dig in, but Clay reminded him of the blessing. The boy suddenly stopped and put out his hands.

Clay watched Karis flinch as he slid his left stub across the table to her, tearing up as she gently grasped it.

Seth looked to Clay. "I'll pray."

"Have at it."

"Dear God, thank you for this food, the snow, Sharon and Rick, Jeremy, Scott, Maddie, Sarah, and Amy. Thank you for Clay and . . ." Clay raised a lid to find Seth looking at Karis.

"Karis." He told the boy.

"Karis," Seth repeated. "And thank you for Pumpkin. Please help her eat good. Amen." Seth was already pushing his plate out, pointing to the pan. "Can I have that one?"

Clay noticed it was the biggest piece. "You bet. And by the way, who's Pumpkin?"

Seth bit into his pizza enthusiastically and then slurped his Mountain Dew. "My new dog."

"You're going to call her Pumpkin?" Clay put a large slice on Karis' plate even though she obviously didn't want it, judging by the severe look she gave him.

The boy nodded.

"How'd you come up with Pumpkin?"

"She's kind of orangey, and pumpkins are orange, and I really, *really* like pumpkin pie." His eyes grew bigger.

Clay laughed, and even Karis smiled. "Sounds like you've got it all figured out, Seth."

"Yep." Seth eyed another piece.

As Karis nibbled on her pizza, Clay noticed her gaze lingering on Seth, and he couldn't help looking at her, wondering what she was thinking.

The pizza disappeared within twenty minutes, and even though Clay felt the strain between himself and Karis, Seth didn't seem to notice.

On the way out, Karis asked him to stop by her office. She ran in quickly and came back out with a small plastic bag. Clay decided not to pry. She was already on a short fuse.

They drove to her house, listening to a country radio station that Seth requested. As they pulled in the drive, Karis turned abruptly and looked at Seth. She seemed to be fighting for control as she reached over, picking up Seth's right hand and perusing the splotchy patches on his knuckles.

"Do these spots bother you?"

"Sometimes."

She took a small tube out of the bag. "This cream should help. I'm going to give it to Clay to give to your—"

Clay finished. "To Sharon."

She blinked several times, her eyes moist. "To Sharon. I want her to put it on this rash twice a day for two weeks. Do you have any other areas that look like this?"

Seth was wide-eyed. "Right here." He pointed to the inside of his elbow.

"Then put the cream there too. Okay?" Her eyes traveled back to meet Clay's.

"Will it hurt?" Seth seemed to be bracing himself.

She looked again at Seth. "Just a little at first, but the cream should clear up the rash. If it doesn't, have ..." She swallowed. "Sharon call me. Here's my card." She handed the card to Clay.

He gazed into her eyes and wished he could assure her that somehow God would create something beautiful out of this painful mess. Instead, he just nodded. Waiting on the Lord was not something he did well.

On the ride back to St. Louis, Seth kept glancing at him. Clay turned to him. "Something bothering you?"

Seth's eyes were big and serious. "What if you don't like Pumpkin?"

"Hey, I told you Pumpkin can stay with me no matter what, okay?"

The boy nodded and looked out the window. "I might get adopted."

"Yeah, I heard that too." A stone lodged in Clay's throat. "You ever think of your real parents?"

The boy's arms rested in his lap, his eyes fixed on a Mack truck fifty feet ahead. "Yeah, someday I'm gonna find 'em."

"Yeah?"

"I'm gonna tell 'em about Jesus."

Wow. "That's good, Seth. That's very good."

The boy turned suddenly. "I hope my new family likes dogs."

Clay tightened his grip on the steering wheel. "Me too, big guy."

*****

She would not cry again in front of Clay. After shutting the door and hearing the gunning of his truck, she collapsed on the couch with a box of tissues, terrified and exhausted. Buddy barked upstairs for some time before she let him out.

She had continued drinking tea each day and picking through the food Clay had left for her to eat. And she had been eating, not because she was really hungry, but because a small strand of hope had tied itself around her heart. Seeing her child felt like an impossible dream come true. At first, she doubted. How could he be her child? And how would she know? Maybe Clay was making it all up. But the moment she saw him, she knew. She just knew. But his hand . . . *Oh God, why?*

The telephone interrupted her reverie. She picked up the handset reflexively.

"Karis, did you get the violin?" Her mother's voice caught her off guard.

Her mind jumped back to her present reality. "Sorry I didn't call, Mom. It came on Tuesday."

"Your father sent it."

"I guessed that."

"Honey, you sound funny. Are you sick again?"

Just the least little inflection and her mother knew something was amiss. She had managed to keep her near drowning confidential, but she couldn't hold back the news of Seth. She released her breath, needing to shed the heaviness crushing her heart. "No, I was . . . crying."

"Honey, what's the matter?"

She felt herself losing control. "I saw someone today."

She could envision her mother's mind trying to grasp her meaning. "Yes?"

Her throat barely worked, the words coming out in a ragged whisper. "I saw my little boy today." Another deep breath. "His name is Seth."

Ten seconds of long-distance silence.

"He's . . . Mom, he's . . . incredible. All boy. So full of energy . . . I just couldn't believe . . . but . . ." She cried again as she told her mother the heartbreaking details of his hand and the accident and the foster care.

"But Karis, how? I mean . . ."

"Remember that guy at the restaurant?"

More silence and then a slow intake of breath. "Your 'friend,' right?'" Mom could have been a police detective. "When Dad called your landline last week, a man answered. It was 5:30 in the morning, Karis."

"His name is Clay Montes." She took a deep breath. Maybe the truth deserved a chance. "He's Seth's father."

The silence morphed into a black hole and then her mother's strained voice. "Do you want to tell me what is going on?"

The shame returned suddenly, broadsiding her. She had been so young, so naive that day she came home, and she would never forget her mother's face in the aftermath. There was no anger, only sorrow and heartbreak.

"Mom, he slept on the couch. I promise."

"Overnight in your house?"

It sounded horrible. She hadn't been raised that way.

"But why was he there in the first place?"

"Because . . . he was taking care of me." She launched into a brief description of her lake experience and explained how Clay had pulled her from the icy waters. She even found herself defending him.

The phone was silent for what seemed an eternity. "Karis, why didn't you tell us? Losing a child is my worst nightmare. Are you okay? Do I need to come?"

"No, Mom, really. I'm feeling better than I've felt in a long time."

"I'm relieved to hear that, but . . . are you sure this is a good idea after what happened?"

"I've been asking myself the same thing." She wiped her nose with a tissue.

"So what now?"

She released a long breath. It was ludicrous. "Clay wants to adopt Seth."

More silence and then, "What does that mean for you?"

"I don't know. It's been a strange week."

"And Christmas, Karis?"

"I'm still thinking."

"And I'm still praying."

CHAPTER TWENTY-THREE

IF ONLY HE'D DONE THIS years ago, but he was a different person then.

Clay punched off his phone and set it on the dinette table, wondering at the awkward but strangely positive conversation he had just experienced. He almost hadn't called. He wasn't normally the nervous type, but for some reason, the thought of talking to Reverend Paul Henry had set him on edge, especially given Karis' past account of her father. But the man he'd just talked to didn't square at all with his mental image. In fact, he found himself hopeful for the first time since last June, almost like he'd met a fellow team member, someone who was equally ready to bury the old dead dog of the past.

Now to convince Karis.

*****

"Before you say no or slam the door in my face, just hear me out, okay?" Clay hoped she would invite him in. He had just picked up Seth's puppy and made an irrational decision to ask Karis in person. The weather had dipped into the teens, and a nasty wind-chill made the temperature feel even lower. Buddy crowded around his feet, smelling his pant legs.

She was still in her doctor clothes but wore house slippers. Must have just come home.

"You might as well come in. My electric bill is already high enough."

Not exactly the warm welcome he was hoping for, but he'd take anything at this point. He stepped inside and removed his jacket. She took it without ceremony and hung it in the closet. As he looked around the living room, he noticed she had placed a few crystal ornaments on the Christmas tree. "Those are nice."

She smiled wryly. "My staff gave them to me."

"Oh." At least she didn't throw them away. He decided to make himself at home. He sat on one end of the couch. "I was sort of in your neighborhood and thought I'd stop by."

She gave him a wary look and crossed her arms. The deep purple of her blazer contrasted sharply with her blond hair. If he wasn't mistaken, it was longer.

"Is this a house call then? Let's see—I ate a bowl of cereal for breakfast, a tuna sandwich and apple for lunch, and I was thinking of chili for supper, unless you have a problem with that."

She was as feisty as ever. Good. Maybe his little nursing stint had made a difference. "Look, about last week, I'm sorry."

"How is he?"

Clay wished he could just hold her hand, for once. "He's fine."

"And the rash?"

"Clearing up."

"That's good." She stared at her hands, clasped in her lap.

"I just picked up his puppy. She's out in the truck."

Her head jerked up. "You left his puppy in your truck? In this weather? Alone?" Mother bear had apparently come out of her den.

"Karis, they come with fur."

She was already at the closet door, reaching for her coat. "Give me your keys."

"Hang on. I'll go get the little thing."

She followed him out the door, house slippers and all. When he unlocked the truck and opened the kennel, Karis was right behind him with outstretched hands. She tucked the puppy in her coat and padded back inside.

Carrying the small bundle to the couch, she sat down, coat still on, cradling it against her chest. "She's little for a Lab."

Clay shut the door. "She's the runt."

Buddy looked suspicious from his perch on the couch. He nosed his way over and sniffed the puppy thoroughly. Karis patted his head. "You're not jealous are you, Bud? This is Pumpkin. Isn't she sweet?"

Buddy continued to stand next to Karis until the puppy turned his way, and then he jumped from the couch and sat by Clay's legs. Clay rubbed his head. "Don't worry, we're not staying."

The woman was complete mush with a puppy in hand. Next time Clay anticipated another showdown with her, he'd wave Pumpkin in the air like a white flag. "Any chance you're going home for Christmas?"

She looked up suddenly. "Why do you ask?"

"My folks are in Aruba and they wanted me to check on their house in Springfield. We could ride together."

She glanced away, no doubt formulating several excuses. "I would need my car."

"We could take yours, split the gas, and you could drop me off at their house."

"I wouldn't be staying long. Maybe two days, three max."

"Perfect."

She gave him a pointed look. "What are you not telling me?"

Clay glanced down. He'd been dreading this moment. "The agency rejected my application. Turns out I'm not exactly 'quality father material.'"

She didn't look up or speak but stroked the squirmy puppy. "Does Seth know you applied?"

Clay shook his head.

"That's good."

Clay felt the old self-serving anger resurface. "Why is that good?" In his warped view of thinking, he'd rationalized that if Seth had known he was his real father, this whole thing would have turned out differently.

"Hasn't he had enough disappointment?" Karis' voice quivered.

He looked into her eyes and found a mother's tender compassion. Ms. Stipes was right. He was vain and egocentric. No wonder God had said no. Chastised, Clay nodded. "I've been told a nice couple is adopting him."

Had she wiped at her eyes? The puppy nuzzled Karis' cheek. "I can leave Friday after my last patient, but on two conditions. I drive, and I pick the music."

Clay was dumbfounded. She'd actually agreed.

CHAPTER TWENTY-FOUR

IF HE HEARD ANOTHER twangy song, he'd personally pull the radio from the dashboard and throw it out the window. How she could enjoy that crooning was beyond his comprehension. She had played Mozart on her violin for crying out loud. Who would have guessed country was flowing through her veins at the same time?

He repositioned his long legs, wishing again they'd taken his truck. If they ran into bad weather, her car would be worthless.

She glanced his way. "It was good of your friend to keep Pumpkin."

Clay let out an exasperated sigh. "Yeah, I just hope Moira doesn't sue me over that dog. No telling what he'll chew up. I've already lost three shoes and part of a mattress."

"Will Seth get to see Pumpkin over Christmas?"

Clay let his eyes wander over her profile, illuminated by the green glow of the dashboard lights. Every time he saw her, he could feel her hunger, though restrained, to know more about Seth. "Moira's picking him up Sunday afternoon." How sad that they were discussing their own son, not as parents, but like window shoppers viewing a live display.

"So why did you want to drive with me?"

Her question sliced through his thoughts and brought him back to the present. "Environmental consciousness and all that, you know." She gave him a skeptical look, but he couldn't very well blurt out the truth. She would know soon enough, and hopefully there wouldn't be fireworks.

"I don't believe you."

"No surprise there."

She tightened her hold on the steering wheel and concentrated on the red taillights of the thick holiday traffic. The Friday before Christmas was a rotten time to travel. As expected, I-44 was packed. Buddy snored soundly in the back seat.

An hour later, she ordered a supersized hamburger, fries, and diet soda. When he stared at her, she looked defiant and quickly exited the fast food joint. He followed, chuckling, with his grilled chicken sandwich. Back in the car, he offered to drive so she could properly consume her man-size portions. She wasn't amused. Turning the key, she glanced his way. "It's been years since I had French fries."

Clay raised his palms. "Hey, no judgment. You're an American. Personally, I'm glad to see you with a healthy appetite."

She slurped her soda and pulled onto the interstate. "Don't you get tired of water all the time?"

"Not really."

She chomped on a French fry. "So why only water?"

Clay didn't answer right away. The whole endeavor had seemed right, given the severity of his past, but still he wondered. Finally, letting out a deep breath, he admitted, "I'm just trying to be a man of my word."

"So it's a spiritual thing, not some new California diet."

"Right."

She probably had a hunch. Raised in a minister's home, knowing the Bible inside and out—how could she not? Big man. Big sin. Big repentance. He spoke quietly. "I know what you said before, but . . . any chance you'll ever forgive me?"

She didn't take her eyes off the road. "Maybe."

It was the most hopeful thing she'd ever said to him.

*****

A brick guardhouse, gates, security sensors—Karis stared at the massive houses beyond the dim glow of the streetlights of Clay's neighborhood. It was almost midnight. As they pulled into the entryway, she lowered her window and swiped the card Clay gave her. The gate opened. He directed her toward the end of the subdivision. She took one look at the columned three-story brick home and felt like hired help. Clay directed her to follow the automatic lamps illuminating the driveway to the back. As she passed the garage, lights flickered on. Buddy woke up, but thankfully remained quiet.

Just before opening his door, Clay reached inside the pocket of his jacket and removed a small wrapped box. He set it on the center console. "This is for you."

Her voice caught in her throat. "Clay, I—"

"Merry Christmas." He let himself out, retrieved his bag from the backseat, and walked to the door of his house, turning briefly to wave before he disappeared inside. She swallowed, suddenly feeling alone and lonely.

She rubbed her finger over the smooth silver wrapping paper that reflected the dashboard lights. What had he done now? Fear welled up inside, commingled with loss. If she gave in and admitted the truth, there was no way she'd survive a second round with him. She put the box in her purse and then turned around and drove down the quiet streets toward the highway that would take her "home." But did she even know what that meant anymore? At the intersection, she paused. A right hand turn would lead to Harbor, a left-hand turn to Mandalay. Six months ago the choice would have been easy. But now? What would Clay do if she left him stranded? She imagined his parents' four-car garage full of expensive cars. And he was more than capable of fending for himself. But what would he think? It was starting to matter. Would he forgive her for running? Leaving him? Deep down, she knew he would. He had become an incredibly generous person.

The car continued to idle while she debated. The real issue wasn't leaving. The real issue was staying and what that meant, what a left-hand turn meant, and what awaited her. The decision was terrifying as past memories grazed her mind. But wasn't ten years long enough? It had been an eternity since she knew any kind of real peace.

Come home.

That gentle voice again, the One she could barely hear anymore. The One she tried to ignore. What to do? A deep breath and then another. She put on her left blinker, hand shaking, and looked up. The star-peppered sky hovered above, vast and unfathomable. Just like the future.

When she reached the deserted road outside of Mandalay, a full moon exposed the remnants of a recent snowfall. Barren, gnarly trees cast fingerlike shadows on the road's edge. She shut off the headlights just short of the drive, hoping to sneak in, but a dark figure stood on the porch. Her heart began to race. She quickly checked the locks and braked. The figure began moving toward her, causing a stab of fear. A few feet away, she discerned the familiar form. He reached for the door handle. Her heart lurched wildly against her chest, panic setting in. She wasn't ready for this. *O God, help me.* Of its own volition, her left index finger unlocked the door, and in the next moment she felt her father's arms, his voice a choked whisper by her ear. "I never thought you'd come home again. I'm so sorry, Peanut. Shutting you away was the worst mistake of my life."

Peanut. Her childhood nickname. Something welled up inside when she heard it. They both stood there crying, clinging to each other as light poured into the dark places. The prison door opened. Freedom fluttered out.

She tightened her grip. "I'm sorry too, Dad." And she really meant it.

With his arm around her, they went inside together.

*****

Karis awoke with Buddy's head wedged between her jaw and neck. The dog had apparently forgotten her mother's rules and jumped on the bed during the night. But oh how she loved the soft, warm fur. After saying good night to her dad, she'd finally fallen into a semi-conscious state. A train whistled at three o'clock, the newspaperman came at four, and someone used the bathroom twenty minutes later. Karis had been awake ever since.

Eden slept soundly across the room in the matching twin bed, her hair splayed against the tie-dyed pillow, the pink plaid comforter pulled up to her chin. It was odd sleeping in the same room she had shared with her sister so long ago. Everything felt different and yet the same—from the tiny pink floral wallpaper to the stain on the beige carpet by the window. Eden had spilled the contents of Karis' chemistry set on one occasion, and no amount of Mom's scrubbing or concoctions could get it out. Over the years, it had darkened to a mustard brown.

The sound of Mom's cooking echoed down the hallway. There would be cinnamon rolls and egg casserole for breakfast, the damask red tablecloth covering the trestle table in the kitchen. Mom's favorite decoration, a trio of white ceramic angels—Karis, Micah, and Eden— would be nestled in a puff of white tulle, left over from Mom's wedding veil. Karis' heart ached. How she had missed these simple touches from her childhood.

She looked at her baby sister again. No more secrets. No more hiding the past. She would tell her this morning. Eden deserved the truth. Hopefully, it would somehow guide her to a better path.

The golden head moved. Two blue eyes blinked open. "Hey, when did you get here?"

"Late."

"We should go for a run." The girl was already throwing off the covers, revealing her beloved blue and green frog pajamas. She gave Karis a sleepy hug.

"The roads are icy. I don't know—"

"Okay, what about sledding then?" Her sister stretched and yawned loudly.

"Eden, can I tell you—"

"In a sec. Be right back." She disappeared into the hall.

Karis heard the bathroom door slam. She unzipped the pouch inside her suitcase to reveal the little velvet jeweler's box. Her hand closed around it, her heart thrumming as the moment neared. What would Eden think? She could envision the subtle shift, the fallen look on Eden's face as her big sister's pedestal crumbled to the ground. The faucet was running and then a whirring sound. The door opened and her sister appeared, her mouth jiggling around the red electric toothbrush.

"What did you want to tell me?" She grabbed a tissue just as a dollop of foamy toothpaste ran down her chin.

"Oh, um . . ." Karis tucked the box back in its hiding place, her heart pounding. She just couldn't do it. "We're getting an outlet mall by the interstate."

Eden pulled the toothbrush out. "Seriously?"

Karis nodded weakly. "Opens next month."

Her eyes brightened even more. "I could come some weekend."

"Sure. That'd be great." She placed her suitcase behind the bed, out of the way, her best intentions dropping into a puddle of failure.

Strains of a familiar hymn filled the hallway. Mom always had a song on her lips.

> *Are we weak and heavy-laden,*
> *cumbered with a load of care?*
> *Precious Savior, still our Refuge;*
> *take it to the Lord in prayer.*
> *Do thy friends despise, forsake thee?*
> *Take it to the Lord in prayer.*

Mom clanged a skillet on top of the stove.

In His arms He'll take and shield thee;
thou wilt find a solace there.

But would He do that now?

*****

Still a formidable figure, her father seemed older and now strangely domestic. He helped wash the breakfast dishes and fold a load of towels. Throughout the day, he asked about the community clinic, her house, the town of Harbor, and even tolerated Buddy. It was as though he couldn't hear enough. When Eden ran off to visit her old high school girlfriends in the early afternoon, he sought out her company, questioning if she would like to help with a difficult puzzle. For two hours, they pieced the outer border of the Grand Canyon. Her mother interrupted midafternoon with Christmas cookies and hot tea and words to fill any awkward lulls. Eden returned soon after.

At four o'clock, Micah and his wife came, and her mom, true to form, had a veritable feast laid out on the dining room table by five o'clock—roast turkey, mashed potatoes, gravy, green bean casserole, yams, corn, cranberry salad, yeast rolls, and ham for her daughter-in-law who didn't like turkey. She'd even embroidered each family member's name in gold on deep crimson napkins that were folded neatly beside the white china placed around the table. An arrangement of silk magnolias and red roses adorned the center of the table, and two red tapers glowed in crystal holders at either end.

Lorna dimmed the overhead light and summoned the family together. Her father took his seat at the end of the table while her mother sat to his right nearest the kitchen, Eden alongside her. Karis found herself in her old place to her father's left, with Clara to her left and Micah at the end. She had dreaded this meal, but as the food circled the table and silverware chinked against china, she began to relax. Clara offered a few pregnancy stories, and Micah interrupted with his own version. Eden told jokes, and soon they all laughed. Just like old times. It was music. It was therapy.

Following supper, they assembled around the Christmas tree for gifts. Karis hadn't really planned on participating. For the past several years, she had not been included in any type of exchange although her mother always sent her a box with cookies, fudge, and a nice gift. But this year, after deciding to come home for Christmas and not wanting to hurt her mother's feelings, she had purchased Cardinal's baseball tickets for her brother, a gift certificate to Babies R Us for her sister-in-law, running gear for Eden, a friendship tablecloth for her mother, and a tie for her father.

She tried not to care as she watched the members of her family open her gifts, but deep inside she desperately wanted their approval and acceptance. Her mother fairly gushed over the tablecloth, declaring that she had always wanted one. Her father's eyes moistened when he opened the small box. "I'll wear this tomorrow. Thank you." She nodded and looked away, uncomfortable. She had merely grabbed the first Christmas tie she saw on the rack at Wal-Mart. Next time would be different.

Karis looked at her own presents—a new cookbook, a book of British poetry, a basket of gourmet coffees and teas, and a homemade afghan in varying shades of blue. She looked at her mother, whose face said it all. It was a labor of love in honor of Seth, even though he would never use it. Deeply touched, and unable to speak, she held it to her chest.

Mom jumped up. "Let's have cake."

Karis gently refolded the treasure, wrapped it back in the tissue paper, and then followed her mother to the kitchen.

"Can you believe I forgot to add the vanilla?" Her mother removed the three layer red cake from the refrigerator.

"I'm sure it will be wonderful, Mom."

"Could you make coffee, honey?" Lorna sliced the cake. "And did I tell you we don't have Sunday school in the morning? Just regular service at eleven."

Karis removed a coffee filter. More dread. "I'd rather not go to church."

Peripherally, Karis could see the stricken look on her mother's face. "But Micah and Clara are coming. I thought we'd all sit together. It's been so long."

"I didn't bring a dress."

"You don't have to wear a dress." Her father stood at the doorway with a garbage bag full of wrapping paper.

Karis' eyes darted his way. Never in a million years did she expect to hear such words from her father. "Dad, I—"

"Just come. Please."

She looked back at Mom, her eyes glistening with hope and agony.

*****

Karis took off her coat and hung it in the hall closet, relieved to be home again. She had gone to the church service, wary of the deacons, especially Calvin Springer, the head deacon for decades. Mom must have sensed her unease, leaning over during the offertory and randomly saying that Calvin had died of pancreatic cancer two years prior. Her father had hovered nearby during the greeting, at times resting a light hand on her shoulder in a protective sort of way. He had made a point of introducing her to new faces and emphasizing her medical title. Karis struggled with his sermon— gentle words of hope, reassuring promises, and God's unconditional love, manifested through a baby in a manger. It sounded so good. If only her faith were stronger.

While Eden ducked into the bedroom to chat with a friend, her mother beamed as she bustled into the kitchen. "I was in heaven when Rosetta hit that last note of 'O Holy Night.'"

"Need any help, Mom?"

Micah was spending the rest of the day with his in-laws, so it would just be the four of them for lunch. "Would you butter the bread?"

Karis had to smile inwardly. Mom had trouble sharing her kitchen with anyone. She had planned an extravagant luncheon though the refrigerator bulged with last night's leftovers. The choice of barbecue brisket and twice stuffed potatoes seemed a bit odd, but Lorna Henry had declared that she wanted a "Cowboy Christmas— something to hang their hats on." Along with the meat, she served up ranch-style beans, coleslaw, and pumpernickel bread. Between the four of them, they would hardly make a dent in so much food. Karis removed a stick of butter as the doorbell rang. Lorna rushed to the front foyer. Who would interrupt on a Sunday?

"Oh do come in. It's so nice to officially meet you, and such a wonderful service, don't you think?"

Karis stopped and listened incredulously as her mother welcomed the last person she ever wanted to see in her parents' house.

"What did you think of the choir special?"

Clay's deep voice answered. He must have sat in the balcony. In disbelief, she heard her mother ask if she could call him by his given name.

Karis stepped to the doorway. "What are you doing here?"

Her mother's head jerked around. "Honey, we *invited* him."

Karis knew that tone. It was a reprimand. Guests were next to royalty in Lorna Henry's book. Her mother plucked a hanger from the front closet and took Clay's black leather jacket. "Actually your father did. I'm afraid he's been held up at the church but should be along shortly. We're almost ready to eat."

"He's staying for lunch?"

Her mother shot her a warning look followed by *the tone*. "Yes, Karis."

"Don't you think I should have been consulted?"

A buzzer sounded. "That's the meat." Her mother, lips firm, disappeared around the corner, giving her one last *look*.

Clay's face had lapsed into wariness.

She lowered her voice, fighting for control. "You talked to my father? Behind my back?"

"What do you want me to say? No? Yes, Karis, it was the next step."

"The next step for what?"

He lowered his voice. "Can we talk about this later?"

"I don't like surprises."

The front door opened suddenly, admitting Reverend Paul Henry. Karis' pulse quickened as she watched her father step in and the two men size each other up. Clay was one inch taller, twenty pounds meatier. They shook hands. Karis held her breath, a sudden feeling of doom gnawing at her stomach.

"Mr. Montes, welcome. Glad you could make it."

"Thank you again for the invitation." A perfect and polite response, but what was really going on?

Her mother appeared with a platter of potatoes, setting them on the table as she glanced toward Karis. "The bread?" And after a quick survey, "Where's Eden?"

"Where she always is. Preoccupied." Karis marched past the washed and freshly ironed rose and ivy friendship tablecloth that her mother had draped across the dining room table. She knew her mother's frown followed her as she disappeared into the kitchen.

Her father made small talk with Clay in the living room. Eden's voice suddenly interrupted. "Oh, hi!" Clearly, her sister had just caught sight of the unexpected guest. "Clay, right?"

"Eden, take drink orders, please. Your father wants water." Her mother's voice was polite but firm.

Karis dropped the butter knife on the floor. Just what she needed—her younger sister drooling over Clay, and her parents thinking the worst. Thank heavens she hadn't told Eden everything.

She suddenly felt exposed, even naked. Had anything really changed? All earlier peaceful thoughts vaporized. Eden babbled before finally extracting a drink order from Clay. Water, of course. The girl fluttered in and made a big to-do about putting four ice cubes in Clay's goblet. Her mother came in and sliced the meat while Eden flitted out, forgetting to ask what her older sister or mother wanted to drink.

"Karis, the beans are almost done," her mother said without looking up. It was as if the last ten years had not happened. She dutifully removed a white serving bowl.

"And the slaw is in the refrigerator."

Karis took the beans to the table, noting Eden's proximity to Clay on the couch. The men were discussing the new addition to the church, Clay's interest perked by the size of the beams in the sanctuary. Karis returned for the coleslaw.

"What do you want to drink, Mom?"

"Honey, I'm sorry I didn't tell you." Her mother drizzled the warmed barbecue sauce across neat rows of thinly sliced brisket. "After our earlier conversation, I thought—"

"It's just so awkward, Mom. I wasn't ready for this." She shut the cabinet door a little too hard, rattling the additional goblets on the counter. "It feels like an invasion of privacy. I don't want you and Dad looking at me and him and remembering."

Her mother fixed her cobalt blue eyes on Karis. "Honey, he saved your life. Can't we show our gratitude? No one is focused on the past except you."

When they were seated, Karis found herself next to her father again, at the head, but this time Clay to her left. Eden seemed enraptured to be across from Clay while her mother sat pensive and decidedly in charge to her father's right. Before her father said grace, her mother encouraged Clay to sign the tablecloth. Karis watched as he took the marker and scribbled his name, writing Romans 8:37 by a blood red rose. She had forgotten the verse, but her father quickly reminded everyone at the table.

"'No, in all these things, we are more than conquerors through Him who loved us.' Good choice."

She had often dreamed of coming home again, sitting around the table again, just like it had been, but not under these circumstances. Her stomach churned as Eden babbled and her father looked on. What were her parents *really* thinking? She dreaded the day when she would tell Eden.

When her left arm bumped Clay's right arm, a forkful of coleslaw landed on his black slacks. She apologized, feeling her cheeks redden. He smiled good-naturedly and collected the remnants with his spoon. Her mother was quick to supply him with a fresh napkin and more food.

The conversation turned to Clay's work. Karis remained silent and uncomfortable as he discussed his job with her father who seemed particularly impressed with the scope of *Sanctuary Homes*, homes for seniors, the disabled, and those without financial resources. It was a magnanimous ministry. Eden interrupted with silly questions. Later her father mentioned his love of photography. Clay responded that his mother was an avid photographer, and he'd always wanted to learn more. Lorna asked if anyone cared for dessert.

While they continued talking, she brought in slices of cake, a coffee pot, and cups. Clay declined the coffee but requested more water.

At the conclusion of the meal her father folded his napkin and invited Clay to his studio. They left for the basement while Lorna directed the clean up. Eden loaded a few glasses in the dishwasher just before her phone went off. Lara, one of her high school friends, had just received an engagement ring from her boyfriend for Christmas. And would Eden be her maid of honor? Ecstatic, her sister quickly left the kitchen.

Karis finished loading the dishes, feeling her mother's disappointment. "What?"

"You hardly said a word all through lunch."

"I didn't know what to say."

"Do you want to know what I think of Clay?"

Karis started scrubbing the roasting pan. "Not really, but I'm sure you'll tell me."

"He's a fine man, Karis. It's not hard to see the Lord in him." Lorna covered the coleslaw with plastic wrap. "Who knows? Maybe—"

"Don't go there, Mom." She hefted the garbage bag by the back door. "I'll run this out."

*****

Clay could not get past the chill that came over him when Karis' father showed him the picture of the little girl with long blond curls lying on her stomach on a porch swing. In her chubby fingers, she clutched a handful of wilted dandelions. The little girl could easily have been Seth's twin. It was clearly Karis.

Karis' father sighed deeply. "I still don't know how to thank you for saving our girl."

"I'm glad she told you."

"She told Lorna." The older man straightened and then looked him in the eye. "I haven't been the best father. I failed my daughter horribly before, but I won't fail her again. What exactly are your intentions toward Karis now?"

Clay shoved his hands in his pockets. He should have been better prepared. "That's a complicated question. At first I just wanted to set things right, apologize, let her know how sorry I was, but now . . . I want a lot more."

"I won't see her hurt again. Not by you, not by anybody. Understand?"

"You have my word, Reverend Henry."

"And I will hold you to that." A steel edge rimmed his words.

Clay swallowed and gave a brief nod.

"And what about Seth? We heard you were trying to adopt him."

Clay shook his head. "Not anymore."

Visibly saddened, the older man looked back at the picture. "So much lost."

"I wish you could have met Seth."

"One of my biggest regrets." He turned toward the stairs. "And let's forget this 'Reverend Henry' nonsense. Call me Paul."

*****

Karis sat in the darkened living room. Everyone had gone to bed hours ago. She had tolerated an afternoon of Scrabble and card games, avoiding a conversation with Clay at all costs. She sensed his disappointment, but at least Eden had kept things lively. He was gone by five. Her mother soon had leftovers out, declaring she had a headache and was going to bed early. She would be up to fix waffles and chocolate syrup in the morning.

Eden had loaded *It's A Wonderful Life* with Jimmy Stewart in the old VHS player. They watched it with Dad as a light snow fell outside, dusting the night in winter white. Poor George Bailey. Karis had always felt bad for him. He never got what he wanted, but in the end, it didn't seem to matter. Something changed inside. He changed.

Karis rubbed her forehead. Would the ache ever go away for the child she lost and for the lost child she had become? She suddenly felt tired. Bitterness and sorrow had turned her into an older woman, or so it seemed. She took out the small wrapped box. What had Clay bought now? She sensed that something was about to change, and it scared her to death.

*****

"And don't take Missouri 43. The road construction is terrible. I nearly hit one of those big concrete dividers."

"What do you mean you 'nearly hit' one? Since when are you driving?" Karis looked at her mother, standing in her purple winter robe on the front porch. Not wanting her to leave, her mother had kept up a constant flow of conversation since the last cup of coffee, but with more snow now in the forecast, she hoped to be home by midafternoon before the storm arrived.

Her father put his arm around her mother's shoulders. "Since I've been teaching her."

They both seemed very pleased with themselves.

"How's she doing, Dad?"

"A regular hot rod."

"You will call when you get back to Harbor?" Her mother pushed her bangs aside. Once a mother, always a mother.

Karis smiled at her mom. "Of course."

"Oh honey, I'm so glad you came. Now remember, we'll plan on coming the first week in March, if that's okay?"

"Of course it's okay."

"And we can stay in a motel."

At this rate, she would never be able to leave. "Mom, we'll all stay together. Now give me one more hug, and then I really need to go."

She felt herself squeezed, and then her father's arms were around her. He whispered in her ear. She suddenly felt herself tearing up. "Thanks, Dad."

By the time she extracted herself from her mother's arms and slid into the car where she had already deposited Buddy, another ten minutes had passed. Her mother waved furiously as she pulled away. Smiling, she waved back until she could no longer see them and then turned to face the road and her next stop, The Oaks at Barrington Place. Unfortunately.

*****

By the time she pulled into his driveway, a hundred thoughts had run through her head. Four hours in the car with him. Why had she ever agreed to this torturous trip?

Clay came out of his house whistling, a to-go mug in one hand and his duffel in the other. He threw it in the back seat, petted Buddy's head, climbed in the front, and then handed her the mug. "My folks have an espresso machine. These beans are from Tanzania. I did add some sugar."

She wasn't exactly in the mood for a peace offering. She took it and set it in the cup holder. "Thank you."

He buckled his seat belt. "Sleep well?"

She took his gift out of her purse. "I can't keep this."

His eyes narrowed. "It's engraved, Karis."

"It's too expensive. I assume it's real."

A slight edge tinged his words. "Of course it's real. I would never give you a fake emerald."

"Why did you give it to me in the first place?"

He blew out a big breath. "Can't I celebrate Seth? Can't I affirm you?"

"It'll just remind me." Tears threatened. "Every time I see it, I'll remember."

"That's the point!" Clay ran fingers through his unbound hair. "Honestly, Karis—"

"I don't deserve such a—"

"And that's the problem, isn't it?" He slapped the dashboard with his palm. "You keep beating yourself up, refusing to believe God can forgive you, like it's beyond Him or something. Good heavens, Karis, what does He have to do? Smack you in the face? In case you hadn't noticed, we're all screw-ups!"

"You have no right—"

"I have every right! I caused this." Clay grasped her hand. "Look at me! It was my fault, not yours."

She wrestled out of his grip. "But I should have known better. I should have been better. I should have—"

"You've forgotten who you are, Karis. A daughter. *His* daughter." He motioned upward. "And He loves you."

She put the Spyder in gear, refusing to answer. He didn't understand. He couldn't understand. Buddy whimpered in the back seat. She drove to the interstate.

As she picked up speed and merged onto I-44, Clay sighed heavily. "Look, I know things are complicated, but we'll figure it out."

He still didn't get it. "There is no 'we.'"

He took her hand again. "Hey, this isn't ending just because—"

"I'm not that girl you met at the lake!" She pulled her hand back.

"You're a thousand times better."

"Stop endorsing me."

Clay's jaw tightened. "Have it your way then."

He started tapping the dashboard, annoyingly. He looked ready to explode. They rode in silence for the next hour, Clay frowning out the window, she gripping the steering wheel and pretending he wasn't there.

A sudden impatient sigh. He turned toward her. "I'm sorry. I just . . ."

"What did you talk to my dad about?"

He angled toward her. "You."

She swallowed, afraid to ask more.

"And me."

A car honked from behind. She had drifted over to the passing lane. She jerked to the right and nearly hit another car. Clay grabbed the steering wheel, correcting.

Her heart was racing now, panic rising. She pushed his hand away. "We can only be friends. Nothing more."

He glared at her. "So glad to have your permission."

"This was a bad idea. This whole trip. We can't even have a normal conversation." She tried to breathe deeply.

"There you go again, running away and hiding. You're so good at it, Karis."

The tension in the air was suffocating. "I am not hiding."

Clay flipped open the jeweler's box to reveal the mother's necklace. She glanced down. The emerald little boy charm sparkled against the white satin. She felt Clay's eyes on her.

"Yes, you are. You're hiding from the truth. The truth that God is crazy about you, forgives you, wants to bless you, is doing *everything* for you. Face it, Karis, you're a coward."

"How dare you say that?" She wished she could slap him without threatening their lives.

"Then prove me wrong. Grow up. Love hurts. Get used to it."

Did he think she didn't know that? Her heart had been bleeding for ten long years.

She refused to speak to him the rest of the drive. When she pulled into her driveway, she grabbed Buddy, gathered her bag from the trunk, and purposefully strode to her door. Clay was right behind her. Before she could put her key in the lock, he grabbed her shoulders and whipped her around, trapping her against the door. He was inches away, his breath warming her face, his eyes on fire. Buddy squirmed out of her arms.

"I refuse to just be friends." His lips closed over hers. "And I don't think you want that either. I'm coming for you Friday. Be ready at six."

He let her go. She threw her bag down. "You can't tell me what to do!"

The roar of his truck was the only response.

CHAPTER TWENTY-FIVE

SHE WAS RIGHT ABOUT ONE THING—they did have a lousy track record when it came to having regular conversations. If only the woman wasn't so bull-headed, Clay mused on his drive back to Moira's house. Tomorrow he would review the land survey for the new construction in Ashland, since things were wrapping up in Harbor. Lou had met with the Board of Trustees and gained approval for the blueprints of the senior housing project. The land had already been purchased.

Clay didn't especially like the thought of being over two hours from St. Louis and even farther from Harbor, but he still planned on seeing Seth on weekends and palling around with Tad and Lucas as long as he could. As for Karis, he would hound her until she accepted the truth. Maybe things never would work out between them, but he'd die trying. He slowed as the land he'd recently purchased near Feather Lake came into view. It was a perfect site for a house—sturdy, ancient oaks along the ridgeline, a meadow to the west, wildlife, birds, an incredible view of the lake. But he no longer needed a house. Seth was leaving. That dream was gone. He'd call the real estate office on Monday.

Moira practically pulled the door off its hinges when he rang her doorbell. "At last, my salvation. Sophie may need therapy."

The diabetic cat did look a bit traumatized.

"That bad?"

"Shall I run through the casualties?" She motioned him in, and then quickly closed the door before the puppy could run out. Muddy pawprints peppered the foyer. Sophie hid under a chair. At least Pumpkin seemed happy to see him. The dog jumped up on hind legs and licked him thoroughly when he bent down to scratch her head.

"I'll just take her and go. It's been a long day." He scooped the puppy up.

"Next time you feel the need to buy a pet for a child, I suggest a turtle. By the way, thank you very much for my jacket. I love it."

Moira was very frugal and would never have considered a personalized jacket for herself, but Clay had learned she bought jerseys for every one of her soccer players, paying out of her own pocket when families or the children's home couldn't afford the expense. In light of her sacrifice, he felt the red jacket with "Coach Kandar" on the back was perfect. Besides, she was gaga over the color red.

"You're welcome, and thank you for the work gloves."

"Lou helped me pick them out."

Clay tried not to look surprised. "Lou? Went shopping?"

She beamed. "Of course I wouldn't take no for an answer. He does know a lot about work gloves, and then I suggested dinner at Mecca's, the organic diner."

"Uh-huh. And how was that?" Oh, to be a fly on the wall.

"Fabulous. I ordered Lou falafel."

Oh boy. "What did he think?"

"He loved it." Moira clasped her hands together. "He kept smiling and motioning for more water."

No doubt. "I guess I'd better keep an eye on you two.

"Maybe you'd better." Moira chuckled, her dimples practically dancing.

He repositioned the wiggling puppy. "So how was Seth?"

"He hasn't come down to earth yet. He insisted on holding Pumpkin in his lap while he ate supper. I think the dog got more food than he did."

"I can just imagine."

"I told him you'd call. He's off from school all week."

"You can bet on it."

"How was your Christmas?"

Clay thought back to his visit at the Henry's home. He had enjoyed his time with her family, which was so different than his own, even though Karis had been about as comfortable as Sophie hiding under the chair. "It was good. Enlightening."

When Moira sneezed suddenly and ran for a tissue, he slipped a wad of money into her purse. He heard a loud honk from the bathroom and then the water running.

"I'd better get going. Thanks again, Moira." He called out.

But before he could get out the door, Moira rushed after him, drying her hands on a Christmas towel. "Clay, Leila called."

His pulse quickened.

"A court date's been set for Seth's adoption."

"When?"

"The first part of February."

He breathed in, trying to ignore the wrecking ball in his chest. "That's only about a month away."

"I'm sorry, Clay."

*****

Clay found himself hanging onto every moment he spent with Seth, noting the way he tilted his head when he asked a question, the way his eyes never rested long in one place. His feet were large, and Clay suspected he would be every inch as tall as his grandfathers and father one day.

Seth had wanted to take Pumpkin to a park to see if she would fetch a toy ball he had found in his backyard. They wound up at Winkler Park after Clay bugged out early on Wednesday afternoon. The day was crisp, the sky a pale blue, and the young maples around the playground bare and spindly. A few inches of snow from the latest storm covered the ground, but boy and dog didn't seem to notice.

Seth held the orange rubber ball to Pumpkin's nose and then threw it a short distance. The puppy lolloped after it, happily carrying it back to her young master. They continued until Seth's cheeks and nose were a bright red, and a soda bottle blew across Pumpkin's path, diverting her attention.

After catching her, Seth cuddled her closely and slid down the slide, laughing at the way she tried to wiggle out of his hands.

Only one more month.

"Hey, big guy, you hungry?" Food was one thing that always got Seth's attention.

"Yeah! Can we have ice cream?"

Clay laughed. "Aren't you cold enough?"

"I'm not cold."

"Tough guy, huh? Well, come on."

They sat in the truck, swirling double dipped chocolate cones with their tongues. A drop of chocolate fell on Seth's jeans, but he quickly wiped it up before Pumpkin could lick it. "That'll make you sick, Pumpkin. No."

Clay looked over at him. "Where'd you hear that?"

"My library book. Chocolate is bad for dogs." He turned somber eyes on Clay. "You better remember that." His lower lip quivered. "My new family doesn't like dogs."

Clay swallowed. "I'll remember, Seth."

Only one more month.

*****

Karis was thankful for the final flurry of year-end patient appointments to keep her mind occupied. She still seethed over Clay's parting words. She could just envision sharing an icy cold dinner with him and letting him pay. Of course it would be a complete waste of his time. That's what he deserved, the jerk. But even as the thought crossed her mind, guilt swelled. A quiet voice reminded her of all he had done.

When she wasn't consumed with anger toward Clay, she obsessed over Seth, wondering what he was doing, wondering when she could see him again, if he'd had a good Christmas, if he knew how much she . . . oh, but her heart ached. She used up a lot of tissue and tears but tried to stay sane. Her father's words for cleansing, healing, and renewal had touched her deeply, but she still held back.

You're a coward, Karis.

On Monday, in between patients, Belinda slipped her a message from Clay. He had a conflict Friday night—some meeting. Would she please return his call and reschedule? Fat chance. She spent the rest of the afternoon working through patients, lab results, and dictation. By the end of the day, she was on the verge of throwing her shoes away.

A knock on the door. Lauren handed her the day's mail. Near the bottom of the stack, she found a photo mailer and an invitation to a surprise birthday party for Clay on Friday, December 31 at 7 p.m. When he'd made his demand for Friday night, he hadn't said anything about his birthday. She felt ashamed of her earlier tantrum. Why did she always assume the worst of him? Of course, she wouldn't go to his party. She didn't even know Moira Kandar, the woman who had watched Seth's puppy. She would just send Clay a card. Putting the invitation aside, she eyed the anonymous mailer. She wasn't expecting anything.

But her breath caught when she found the 5x7 picture between two pieces of cardboard. There was Seth, her little boy, in a bright red jersey, one foot on top of a soccer ball, smiling up at her. She cradled the picture. There was only one person who would have sent this treasure. She picked up the phone.

*****

Karis eyed the row of simple ranch houses on Sunrise Avenue in Kirkwood, a southwest municipality of St. Louis. When she spotted a house with an assortment of inflatable Christmas lawn ornaments, she felt certain that Moira lived there. Clay had once mentioned that the woman was a bit quirky. Her suspicions were confirmed as she pulled alongside the teapot mailbox bearing the numbers 821. Finding a side street as Moira had requested, she parked the car and zipped up her coat.

The evening air was frosty, the sky a sheer black canvas for the myriad of twinkling stars. She walked the short distance to the house and rang the doorbell, nervous about seeing Clay and conversing with strangers.

The door opened to reveal Seth. She suddenly felt lightheaded as yearning grew. His warm eyes traveled up to meet hers.

"Hi." A simple greeting, but it melted her heart.

"Hi there." She swallowed. "Is this where the big party is?"

"Yep. Do you want me to take that?" He indicated the gift bag she was carrying.

"Are you in charge of gifts?"

"Uh-huh."

As he reached out for the bag, she found herself freshly shocked. His sweatshirt was knotted where a hand should have been. She quickly looked away and followed him inside. Why had no one arranged for a prosthesis? But even as the thought crossed her mind, she knew the answer. The devices could cost thousands of dollars.

The small living area was noisy and chaotic with boys squirming on the pink furniture, darting into the kitchen. An exuberant voice suddenly burst out, followed by the entrance of a short, round woman with silver curls and John Denver glasses. When she saw

Karis, she laid a hand on her arm. "Dr. Henry, right? So glad you made it. Hopefully, Clay won't shoot me. He didn't want anyone to know. Let me introduce you to some folks."

There were several men, most from *Sanctuary Homes.* An older man named Lou seemed familiar. When he talked about fishing at Feather Lake, she knew she'd seen him before. And then all the boys. She and Moira were the only females. It was a large, happy gathering, and despite being a newcomer, Karis had to admit that she enjoyed the effervescent energy.

When seven o'clock neared, Moira shepherded everyone to the two back bedrooms. She had told Clay that Lou would be at her house, so he could pick him up for "the meeting."

Karis' eyes found Seth bouncing on his feet in Moira's floral bedroom, his excitement barely contained. After the doorbell rang, they heard a flurry of movement in the next bedroom and soon joined the small wave of well-wishers pouring into the front of the house. Clay's face registered complete surprise, and Moira seemed beside herself for pulling off the stunt. She instantly started serving up sloppy joes. Mini corn on the cob came next, followed by a spoonful of fruit salad. Karis stepped in to help with the drinks. Lou directed people to the garage, which Moira had turned into a cozy party room housing three round tables decorated with assorted balloon centerpieces and small party favors. Purple streamers hung from the ceiling.

Karis wound up at the quietest table with Lou and men from the work crew. Between bites, she looked across the room and found Clay looking her way, an unreadable expression in his eyes. The boys sat at the other two tables, Clay in the midst of them, Seth at Clay's right. Watching the two of them, Karis could see unmistakable similarities—they had the same broad forehead and the same small ears—and when they both laughed, she felt a longing for something she couldn't even put into words.

When the meal ended, Moira asked the boys to help collect the disposable plates and cups while she brought out a large chocolate sheet cake. Thirty-five candles lined the edge. After the group sang to Clay, he blew out every candle. Karis received a large piece of cake with confetti ice cream. Afterward, Clay opened cards and gifts. Karis squirmed when he picked up the plain blue gift bag.

She touched her mother's necklace, which she had been wearing inside her shirt. When he took out the tissue paper, her heart started thumping erratically. Clay was a master at giving, but she really had no idea what to give him.

*****

Nerf guns, a Whoopee cushion, bubble gum, a rocket launcher—what more could a guy ask for? The boys hooted every time he opened a gift. The simple white envelope was next—a card with a lake scene, geese flying overhead. *Have a Happy Birthday. Karis.* Innocuous. Inside the gift bag, he found a forest green sweater, extra large.

It was clearly a "just friends" gift, but he'd give her a hard time later, maybe pull off his shirt and try on the sweater right in front of everyone. That would get a rise out of her, whether she liked it or not. He glanced across the room just in time to see her look away. He still couldn't believe she had come. He found himself impatient to get the party over with so that he could talk to her. She had never returned his phone call, and he'd left several messages on her machine. He could only imagine how angry she must have been, but apparently the picture of Seth had worked some magic.

The guys began to leave by nine. When he saw her trying to slip away unnoticed, he cornered her in the living room. "You didn't call me back. Still mad?"

"Yes."

"But you came. Does that mean—"

"It means I'm grateful. Thank you." She looked uncomfortable.

"And thanks for the sweater. By the way, what are you doing later in January?"

She pulled her coat from the front closet. "Even if I knew, I wouldn't tell you."

He did love to perturb her. "I've got two tickets to the opera. I want you to go with me."

She struggled with the left arm of her coat. "And why would I do that?"

He helped angle the coat, enjoying the exasperation on her flawless face. "Because you've never seen me in a tux."

Steam was practically coming out her ears.

"Am I interrupting something?" Moira stood in the doorway with a foil-covered pan.

"Not at all." He backed away from a very flustered and red-faced Karis.

"Here's what's left of the cake. I thought if it's alright with you, I'd send it home with Seth."

"Great idea."

"Maybe you and Dr. Henry could take him home now."

"We sure can." Clay grabbed Karis' hand. "Where is the little rascal?"

After Seth found his coat, the three of them set off for the short walk to the Waters' house. Clay couldn't help but think that this was the way it was meant to be, even if Karis refused to hold his hand. She marched beside him, hands in her pockets, and kept her attention solely on Seth, who was picking out constellations.

When they arrived at Seth's house, she was visibly saddened. She seemed to wilt as they climbed the front steps. The front light was on, but the door was locked. They knocked and waited. Sharon came to the door with three little children huddled around her legs. Karis was pale and rigid under the fluorescent glow of the porch light. Clay put his arm around her as Seth said good night, and the door closed.

She shrugged off his arm and took off walking at a brisk clip. Clay easily matched her stride. "Tell me what you're thinking."

She refused to look at him. "I'm trying to decide if it was better not knowing."

"And?"

Deflated, she slowed and spoke quietly. "No. I'm grateful for this small taste."

"And I'm sorry I can't give you more."

A car passed by on the left, its headlights causing their shadow to elongate across the sidewalk. She pressed the remote on her keys, but Clay stopped her from getting into her car.

"I'm packing up this weekend for the project over in Ashland."

"For how long?" It was an apparent attempt at stoicism, but he detected a slight quiver in her voice.

"Probably a good three months, but I'll be coming back up here on the weekends. I promised Seth he could see Pumpkin every Saturday until his adoption goes through, which is . . . soon."

Her breath caught. "When?"

He reached out and touched her cheek lightly. For once, she didn't back away. He hated that he had to tell her. "February fourth. Do you want to meet us this Saturday?" He didn't want to pressure her, but felt she should have the option.

She finally breathed in and looked down. "Won't that just make it harder?"

He lifted her chin. "Love hurts, remember?"

"I'll have to think about it."

He wanted to brush his lips across her brow, but he held himself back. "Be careful driving back."

She could only nod.

*****

If only she had more courage. If only she could find the faith she had embraced as a little girl. If only she could just believe. But Clay was right. She was a coward, her life a tapestry of anger and fear with emptiness and hurt knotted in the ugly underside. What would it take to unravel such a hideous piece of work? She stepped into her darkened living room, despair swirling at her feet, threatening to pull her under.

CHAPTER TWENTY-SIX

WITH THE WEATHER CLEAR and warmer than average, the local carpenters showed up a week early in Ashland. The day before, Clay had scrambled to finish the basement dimensions. Underneath the topsoil, the backhoes had run into stubborn clay, which had retained some moisture from the last snow. When Clay received the call from Shale Concrete Company, they were knee deep in gray sludge, but with Lou's expertise and pep talks, the guys came through.

It was good to be working with Lou again and living a few spaces down from him in the campground near Ford's Park. After the Harbor project, Lou had taken a couple weeks off to visit his brother in Florida, but he drove into Ashland ready to attack the ground for the senior housing complex.

Moira had become a regular visitor, often dropping by with another healthy snack or low-fat dinner option. Lou took it in stride and even shared that his cholesterol was a healthy 135 when she'd badgered him one evening. Come spring, she was to learn how to fish.

The digging was hard, and Clay was thankful for the workout. He hadn't been able to exercise during the month of December. The soreness and exhaustion felt good. It also kept him from dreading the coming month when he would have to say goodbye to Seth. Seth's adoptive parents were from New Mexico. Leila had told him on the phone last night when he called for a progress report.

Karis hadn't accompanied them to the park last Saturday. She had been congested with a slight fever and croaked on the phone. But Clay also worried about her mental state. She had told him that she struggled with depression during the darkness of winter and, with the heavy news that Seth would soon be lost to them, he wondered if she might hide herself away more. He'd kept in touch with Paul Henry. Every Saturday morning, they prayed over the phone together for Karis. She didn't know about it, and he would never tell her. She'd probably just get angry and accuse him of meddling, and she would be absolutely right. Maybe someday, she would be whole again enough to . . .

But he didn't want to go there. He thought back to the single kiss he had stolen from her and how much more he wanted. The thought of having her all to himself was particularly tantalizing. He would have to be very careful. Mourning for Seth and yearning for Karis were driving him insane, not to mention the blankety-blank puppy who was slowly chewing up all of his socks. He picked up a shovel and stabbed a mound of dirt.

*****

"Look! Pumpkin's trying to catch the football."

Clay stood, hands on hips. "Finally, something she can't put in her mouth."

Even though the day was windy and cold, Seth had wanted to go to the park. As he watched the boy run after the puppy, he tried to freeze the image in his mind. Only one more Saturday, and that would be it. He thought about Karis, how she had seemed fragile and reserved last week when they had met. She could only stay an hour. Her phone went off and she had to leave to check on a patient. Today they had agreed to meet at a McDonald's in Caney Creek, a town halfway between Seth's house and Harbor. Of course she was coming for Seth and putting up with him.

As they walked to Clay's truck, Seth looked up. "Karis is your girlfriend, isn't she?"

Clay tousled the boy's hair. "Well, she is a girl, and she is my friend, so I guess you're right. How'd you figure that out?"

"You've got dopey eyes."

"What are you talking about?"

"When you look at her, you get all dopey and dumb."

"Out of the mouths of babes." Clay rolled his eyes.

"She's got dopey eyes too."

"Alright, Mr. Know-It-All, hop in the truck."

Clay found a classical radio station just to gauge Seth's reaction to opera. The boy scrunched up his face. "What is that?"

"That is *musica robusta*." Clay couldn't help laughing at Seth's sour apple expression.

The boy repositioned Pumpkin in his lap. "I don't know what they're saying."

"Neither do I, but it's passionate, deep, and soul-searching."

"It's dopey."

Karis was waiting for them in the crowded parking lot. Seth declared he was too big to play in the tunnels and slides that occupied half the interior of the fast food restaurant. And he didn't want a kid's meal either.

Clay ordered their food while Karis found napkins and straws, and Seth volunteered to get the ketchup. After dispensing ketchup into six small cups, Clay told him that was plenty. A table near the restrooms opened, and they scrambled for it, then went back to get their drinks. When they were all seated, Seth announced that he wanted to pray.

"Dear God, thank you for these French fries and for my root beer and thank you for the person who invented Big Macs. Please help Pumpkin not to get too cold in the truck. In Jesus' name, amen."

When Clay opened his eyes, Karis was smiling at a very hungry Seth who had already crammed a big bite of hamburger in his mouth. She squirted ranch dressing on her salad and started mixing the greens with a plastic fork and knife. "Didn't you guys freeze at the park today?"

Seth dunked three French fries in ketchup. "It wasn't cold."

Clay picked up his chicken sandwich. "We were moving the whole time."

"Did Pumpkin have fun?"

Seth's eyes grew big. "Oh yeah, you should have seen her run. She's almost as fast as me."

"Maybe I can see her next week."

Seth noisily slurped his soda. Taking another bite of his burger, he noticed Karis' necklace hanging within the V-neck of her navy sweater. "What's that?"

She swallowed and reached for the charm, lifting it up. "This is . . . a mother's necklace . . . and this . . . is my son's birthstone. See, it looks like a little boy with arms and legs, and in the center is an emerald.

"Cool. What's his name?" Seth chomped on four more fries at once.

Karis paled and then cleared her throat. "His name is Seth."

"Just like me. Cool."

A winsome smile crossed her face, her voice trailing off. "Just like you."

A loud clunk and then a wail. The baby at the table next to them dropped her bottle. It rolled under Clay's feet. Seth jumped out of his seat and crawled under the table to retrieve it, handing it to the weary mother who was also dealing with two other squirming preschoolers.

Clay rescued the conversation. "Seth, do you need more ketchup?" The boy was on the last sampler.

"Nah, I'm good."

"That was nice of you to help that mother." Karis looked over at him, her face falling when her eyes fell to the stump of his left arm.

"Yeah."

Given his circumstances, Clay knew it was second nature for Seth to help out when small children were underfoot, but how would he do in a home as an only child? Would he want to be the center of attention? Would he miss the Waters family? His brief time with Seth would gradually fade to nothing in the boy's memory, but he shook off the thoughts. Better to enjoy the time remaining. "Anybody want ice cream?"

Karis raised her eyebrows. "Are you crazy?"

Seth bobbed his head. "I do."

Clay laughed. "What will it be?"

"Chocolate sundae."

"You got it."

As they walked out of the restaurant, Seth ran ahead and put his right hand next to the window as Pumpkin licked the glass, and then he moved it in a circular motion. The dog's tongue followed. They both laughed. Joy in the midst of sorrow. If only . . .

*****

A soft, wet tongue licked her cheek. Buddy was awake and saying good morning. Karis petted the furry head with her eyes still closed. "Just a minute. I know. I know. I'm getting up." She shrugged on her robe.

The little dog ran down the steps ahead of her. While he was outside, she went into the kitchen and set the kettle on to boil. After Clay's nursing stint, every morning started with a cup of tea. She left the front door slightly ajar, knowing Buddy would return when he was finished. Shortly, she heard him race toward the kitchen, anxious for his breakfast, which she had already scooped up and set by the window. While he chomped on the crunchy tidbits, she shut the door and picked up the small leather attaché she had purchased yesterday from the Christian bookstore on her way home from lunch with Seth and Clay. She had driven by the store many times, pretending it wasn't there, but yesterday, something pulled her inside.

An older woman with shiny red hair, reading glasses perched on her nose, had stood behind the counter studying a computer screen. When Karis had walked in, she looked up and asked if she could be of service.

"I'm looking for a Bible."

The woman smiled warmly and indicated the opposite wall. "If you don't see what you want, I can certainly order you one. We've got lots of catalogs."

As she looked at the wall of Bibles, the memory returned of *that* night—the night she told her parents she was pregnant and all the nights in between. Aunt Ernie's ghost swelled and then faded away with her baby. With empty arms and heart in pieces, her faith had withered to almost nothing. Oh how she had longed for her little boy, dreaming of him, obsessed with him, the feathers to mark his life as she counted off ten long years. But even more she realized now, she had missed the One who knew when she sat or stood, the One who understood her thoughts from afar, the One who knew her ways, the One who put her tears in a bottle . . . how full was it now?

Her fingers skimmed the firm leather spines along the wall while her eyes searched for the same Bible she had thrown away in the bus station. And there it sat on the bottom shelf—a brown leather Thompson Chain Reference. She picked it up and let it fall open. The smell of ink wafted up from the crisp pages. She let her eyes descend, suddenly afraid of what lay beneath. *Have mercy on me, O God, according to your unfailing love; according to your great compassion, blot out my transgressions.* She couldn't stop. The words of the Psalm ran over her, touching her deepest hurt, ministering to the emptiness of her soul. She wanted more. *You do not delight in sacrifice, or I would bring it; you do not take pleasure in burnt offerings. My sacrifice, O God, is a broken spirit; a broken and contrite heart you, God, will not despise.* She drank in what her heart already knew. Her fingers flipped to the book of Isaiah: *I have swept away your offenses like a cloud, your sins like the morning mist. Return to me, for I have redeemed you.*

She almost got a speeding ticket driving back to Harbor, anxious to get home and read. She stayed up past midnight, needing the healing words like an addict craving a drug, and finally, the peace that passed all understanding seeped into her heart and caressed her soul — loved, forgiven, redeemed — back to its Lover.

She poured her tea and then settled into a chair. Unzipping the leather covering, she opened the Bible, knowing she needed a "fix" daily. She had a long way to go to complete restoration. Post-operative care and time made all the difference toward the healing of a physical wound. Was it any different for the human heart? She would obey the instructions of the Great Physician. The old had passed away. The new was here. Buddy jumped up on the couch and sat next to her as she read the book of John. A thought passed through her mind. It was Sunday after all and long overdue.

*****

More than shocked, Clay still couldn't believe the phone conversation he had just had. Karis wanted to know where he went to church. He spouted off the address, never expecting to see her Spyder pull into the parking lot, but an hour later, she gave him a timid wave. She looked tired, but her eyes held a peace he had not seen in the past seven months.

He somehow convinced her to have lunch with him afterward, and they found a barbeque restaurant near the I-270 loop. With a table next to the fireplace, they ate a meal of pulled pork, coleslaw, and fresh rolls, but neither he nor Karis brought up the subject of

Seth's approaching adoption. Instead, he asked about her new Bible, and she told him about her visit to the Christian bookstore. The sparkle was back, the light nearly flooding her eyes. *Thank you, Lord.* He couldn't wait to tell Paul, but maybe he should hold off. Such happy news should be personally shared.

He had to leave early to get back to Ashland. The crew was scheduled to frame the walls of the three-story complex in the upcoming week with the roof tresses arriving Friday. He explained all of this to Karis while she ordered a piece of chocolate cake.

"So, about the opera, you still haven't given me an answer."

"Does it really matter what I say?"

"It would be nice if you would just agree to go, so I wouldn't have to hogtie you and drag you downtown." He stole a bite of her cake. "People might stare, you know."

"Does this arrangement include dinner?"

"Actually I would love that, but I won't have time."

"So you want me to just show up there? At the theater?"

He matched her sarcasm with his own. "Like I would let you wait alone in downtown St. Louis at night. Do I look that stupid?" He could almost see her hackles come up.

"I'm just trying to make it easy for you."

"Don't say that, Karis."

She blushed, seemingly both angered and embarrassed. "I didn't mean that."

He captured her hand. "You have always been my greatest temptation."

Frustrated, she pulled her hand away. "Is this outing really necessary?"

"I'm trying to prove my gentleman status. Meet me at Moira's house at six-thirty."

They would have to drive half an hour, park, and find their seats, but Clay thought if he left early and arrived in St. Louis after rush hour, they could make it by eight o'clock.

When the waitress arrived, Karis insisted on paying for her own meal, spouting her "just friends" mantra again. It would seem the Lord and everyone else except him had been restored to her good graces. He said goodbye with a certain amount of angst, thinking January 21 might hold great promise, but possibly even greater heartache as time slipped away and Seth was gone.

CHAPTER TWENTY-SEVEN

"EDEN, SLOW DOWN!"

The parking lot was pure ice. Her sister turned briefly and waited for Karis to catch up. Hordes of customers were flooding the front entrance of the new mall, oblivious to the subzero temperatures.

Eden's eyes darted about. The girl had refused a coat, striking a defiant pose in her jeans and lightweight hoodie. "If I miss the free T-shirt at Boosters, I'll never—"

"Would you prefer a broken leg?"

"Would you lighten up? This is supposed to be fun." Her sister slipped through the automatic glass doors without a backward glance.

Karis rushed after her. The neon lights of the department store sign blinked furiously, reflecting a myriad of colors on a countdown clock. It was beyond ridiculous. A line had already formed outside. Eden planted herself behind two teenage girls who were gulping large caffeinated beverages. Karis eased in with her, wishing she'd never mentioned the grand opening to Eden.

When the countdown clock pulsed zero, the crowd went wild. A second later, the massive steel barn doors slid apart. Music blared. A trap door above suddenly opened, spilling red tickets like confetti onto the writhing ocean of bodies below. Shrieks, cursing, jostling.

Karis hugged the wall next to a pyramid of purses. Eden disappeared below the swarm, then resurfaced, then disappeared again. Several minutes later, she emerged, clutching a coveted red ticket to her chest. Hopefully she hadn't drawn blood to get it. When she spotted Karis, she waved victoriously and pointed toward the vintage boxcar that had been placed in the middle of the store. There, frantic store clerks were handing out the red and white T-shirts to piranha-like ticketholders.

Eden was all smiles as she rejoined Karis and proudly displayed her prize. "You can't touch this online for less than a hundred bucks. Where to now?"

Eden was apparently finished with Boosters. "You mentioned shoes."

Her sister's eyes lit up. "We passed Light Steps on the way up here."

"Lead the way."

Eden practically danced up the escalator. As they browsed the incomprehensible rows of every type of women's shoes, Karis noted the strappy sandals on sale. With a three-inch heel, she would only be a few inches shorter than Clay and better able to look him in the eye. She slipped off her shoes. The sandals were reasonably comfortable. She tucked the box under her arm as Eden popped out from behind a display of flats, a pair of purple tennis shoes on her feet.

"These are 40 percent off. What do you think?"

"Don't you have enough tennis shoes?" The girl was flying through her Christmas money.

"But they're purple. Hey, what'd you find?"

Before she could stop her, Eden grabbed the shoebox, intertwining her fingers in the straps. "Wow, these are beautiful, but they're so not you. What are you not telling me?"

Karis felt her pulse quicken, the untold story still weighing heavy. She had hoped to avoid any talk of Clay until a more opportune time, but Eden was like a bloodhound.

"I'm going to the opera, if you must know."

"As in a date?" Eden's eyes widened, her voice entertaining a sultry tone. "With Tarzan, by chance?"

"I told you not to call him that."

"You are so prickly, Karis." Eden tossed the tennis shoes back in the box. "What are you wearing?" It was more of a demand than a question.

"I haven't decided."

"Well, you need a dress. Something nice."

I wasn't born yesterday, little sister. Karis bit back the retort. Her head was starting to throb.

"Did you see the dresses at Bianca's? The ones in the window? They're perfect." Eden spoke with an air of loftiness. "I'll scope 'em out while you pay."

Karis decided not to argue.

Bianca's was just as packed as every other store. Karis glanced at the faceless mannequins in the window. The dresses were striking, but not exactly what she would select and definitely not in her price range. Eden seemed preoccupied with a rack of floral maxi-skirts, obviously not opera-worthy, but more in line with her upcoming spring break trip to South Padre Island.

"I'll be along the back." Karis inched by her sister who nodded absently.

The clearance section had several mid-calf suits that seemed reasonable. She removed a black one with a velvet lapel. Her maroon blouse would coordinate well, the price was right, and it was classy. She headed toward the dressing rooms only to be intercepted by Eden.

Karis held out the suit. "I can wear it to work too. What do you think?"

"I think it's hideous. Something Mom would wear to a funeral."

"Eden—"

"You know I'm right."

Before she could respond, her sister plucked the suit from her hand and hung it on a random rack, then grabbed her arm and dragged her to the front of the store.

"If I was going to the opera, I would wear this." Eden's eyes practically glowed when she handed her a teal one-shoulder gown. It *was* beautiful, but the price and the neckline . . . Eden pushed her toward the waiting room and beamed like a triumphant athlete when Karis stood before the triple view mirror.

"Now *that* is what you wear for Tarzan." The seductive lilt was hard to ignore.

"I told you to stop, Eden!" The words came out loud and harsh as the old memory played through her mind—what Clay had taken, what she had given, what she had lost, and what she was losing now.

The hurt skittered across Eden's face. She wiped at her eyes, turned quickly, and walked away. Heart sinking, Karis rushed after her. How could she treat her sister that way? She caught up to her. "Eden, please. I'm sorry. Let's get some coffee and talk. I need to explain."

Eden pulled back and crossed her arms, defiant. "I will if you get the dress."

"I'll freeze to death."

"That's not the reason."

"No, but after we talk, you'll understand. At least, I hope you will."

Karis cringed as she signed the sales ticket and followed Eden out of the store. They drove to the small coffee shop in downtown Harbor. As she watched her sister dump in sugar and cream, Karis remembered their tea party one Saturday morning long ago. Mom and Dad had been out visiting hospitalized church members. With a sugar high, there had been no naptime that afternoon for three-year-old Eden, but it had been so much fun.

Oh, how she wanted that back with Eden.

As her sister blew on her coffee, Karis removed the black velvet jeweler's box from her purse. This time she would do it. She placed it on the table. "No other person has ever seen inside this."

"The box in your drawer?"

She nodded. Opening the box, she held it out for her sister. Eden's face registered confusion. "I thought it was your lost love or something."

"It was. Is."

Her sister reflexively touched the silky black hair, her face asking the question her lips had not yet formed.

Karis breathed in deeply, willing the dread away. "There's no easy way to say this." Another intake. "I had a baby when I was your age. A little boy. And that's why it's been . . . the way it's been."

"And why you left?"

Karis nodded. "So now you know. And I'm sorry. We've all suffered for it." The rest of the story came tumbling out before she could stop it.

Eden cried. She cried. By the time Karis finished telling her all about Clay and Seth, they were both beautiful messes, but the colossal weight was gone.

*****

Wearing strappy sandals in the middle of winter seemed the height of stupidity, even with nylons. Karis wiggled her toes, trying to keep them warm with the heater going full blast. She sat outside Moira's darkened house, her coat buttoned over the teal gown. Clay's truck was nowhere to be seen and no vehicle sat in the driveway. Karis looked at her watch. 6:45 p.m.

You've never seen me in a tux. The nerve of the man. He was always good at marketing himself. She could just imagine the swiveling female heads tonight when he entered. Those same women would scrutinize her too, wondering what a man like Clay Montes saw in her and why she was so special. She should just leave and forget all of this nonsense.

With each passing minute, she grew more and more incensed. Past memories started niggling. Was he standing her up? How could she be so gullible? So hopeful? She couldn't decide if she was more angry or hurt. She shut off the car at 7:00 p.m. Now she was freezing, her toes were numb, and there was still no sight of the man. She checked her cell phone for messages, called his. Nothing.

When 7:30 p.m. came, she turned the ignition and jerked the car onto the road. Clay Montes was out of chances.

One hour later, she arrived at her apartment with a headache and a speeding ticket. She kicked off the sandals, peeled off the dress, and threw both of them in the closet. What had possessed her to agree to a night out with him and then spend a fortune on a dress? She was acting like the complete idiot she had been eleven years ago, and look where that had landed her. To think he would actually keep his word—for all his Christian rhetoric. She dialed his cell phone again and left a cold message.

CHAPTER TWENTY-EIGHT

SATURDAY WAS DEADLY QUIET. Sunday began much the same way until the phone rang, but she refused to answer. She listened as the answering machine picked up, fully expecting some well-thought-out excuse. But the deep voice was not Clay's. It was Clay's friend, Lou, who, with a distinct southern accent, stumbled over the words—crane malfunction, roof trusses, broken ribs, collapsed lung, lots of bleeding. She listened, horrified.

Clay had been flown by helicopter to Barnes Hospital where he had been in surgery for over five hours Friday night. He was in critical condition. After coming to coherence late Saturday night, he had insisted that his friend call the next morning.

How life could change in a hand's breadth of time. Karis sat still, numb, before the phone shrilled again. This time she answered reflexively.

"Dr. Henry, this is Moira Kandar. I'm afraid I have some bad news."

She somehow found her voice. "Mr. Barrows just called."

"Can you come? Clay really needs you."

Needs me? When did Clay ever need anyone? He was independent and self-sufficient and stubborn. "I'll be there as soon as I can."

She put away the phone, feeling as though she was standing on a cliff with the ground crumbling beneath her feet. If only she could put on her doctor glasses and think of his injuries in medical terms, then the fear wouldn't be so terrifying. But her heart thumped wildly as she drove to the hospital and peered in the window of his room.

Oh dear God, have mercy.

He was lying on his right side facing the wall, his back heavily bruised, his breathing labored, the chest tube protruding out from his left ribs. Blood seeped through the tubing to drain the pleural space. She eased into the chair by his bed, wishing she had the courage to just touch him, the confidence to bare her heart as he so easily exposed his.

Mercifully, he slept, while she stared at his face, swollen and bruised. Where would she be if he hadn't come to her office last summer? Had God, in His sovereignty, used this man, who had wounded her so deeply, to bring her back to Him? The very idea seemed crazy, but the Holy One was full of surprises, choosing to confound the wise with foolish things.

All Clay had asked for in the beginning was forgiveness. But forgiveness without love was impossible. She knew that now. The act required submission just as her Lord and Savior had so incredibly expressed on the cross. She could do no less. She slipped to her knees. His left hand rested on the sheet, chapped and cold. She covered it with her own and whispered the words he so desired. Maybe he heard.

He stirred slightly. His eyes fluttered open, trying to focus. The fear returned. She withdrew her hand and retreated to the chair.

He licked his lips. "Sorry about Friday." His throat was little more than a hushed rasp. "Guess I'm not Samson after all. Couldn't hold up that . . ." He breathed in slowly.

Her mind jumped to the story of the strong man. In the end, he triumphed over his enemies but lost his life. She shivered. "Don't talk."

"So bossy." He let out a long breath and shut his eyes briefly, and then opened them again. "You mad?"

"No."

"Liar."

"I'm not mad." Just scared to death. She looked around his room, wishing she didn't know what all the machines and tubes were for. "Do you need anything?"

"A kiss."

"Be serious."

"I am." A wobbly smile.

"All right." She leaned over and pecked his forehead.

"Coward."

She let out a harrumph. The man could be on death's door, and he still enjoyed harassing her.

Footsteps echoed behind her. She quickly turned to see an older Hispanic man beside an elegant blond-haired woman. They had to be Clay's parents. She introduced herself. Though visibly shaken, the woman greeted her, but quickly went to Clay's side. The man shook her hand and watched his wife with a sober expression. Karis left the room, surprised to find the older man trailing behind.

Once in the hallway, he turned his dark eyes on her. It was as though she was looking at Clay thirty years from now with the man's silver hair, dark features, and handsome looks. "I don't mean to be rude, but what exactly is the nature of your relationship with my son?"

For a moment, she was speechless. "We're just . . ."

The man crossed his arms. "He stands to inherit a considerable fortune someday. If anything happens to him and you suddenly announce that he has a child . . ."

The words were a slap in the face. What had Clay told his parents? "I lost that child years ago, and I certainly don't want your fortune."

"I'm just trying to anticipate any future complications."

As if Seth could be a complication. She spun on her heels, but the man's dogged words continued.

"Why is he just now getting adopted?"

She whirled around. "You overstep, sir."

"Dr. Henry!" Moira was getting off the elevator with one arm around Seth. Lou was close behind. Karis' heart started racing. The last thing she wanted was for Seth to get hurt, but how could she protect him now? Moira hurried over. "I'm so glad you're here. Have you been in? And you must be Clay's father?" Moira grabbed the man's hand. "And this is Seth. We are dreadfully sorry that this has happened."

Karis watched Mr. Montes study Seth, his eyes quickly taking in the boy's appearance, then traveling down to his left stub. The man exhibited more than an ordinary curiosity at Seth's disability. A growing fear gnawed. He must know.

"Dr. Henry, do you suppose Seth could go in? He made something for Clay." Moira indicated the box Seth was holding.

It was on the tip of her tongue to answer, but Mr. Montes spoke out. "Children under twelve are not allowed in the ICU."

Seth was visibly disappointed. Moira hugged him. "I think I'll ask anyway. Be right back."

Moira marched to the nurses' station. Karis had no doubt that if anyone could railroad their way in, it would be Moira Kandar. But what was the woman saying? The nurse looked pensive, then nodded. Moira smiled in victory and returned, putting her arm around Seth again. "Five minutes, but we need to wait until Clay's mother comes out. Shall we sit while we wait, Seth? My feet are killing me."

Lou offered to get coffee and left. Moira herded Seth to the row of chairs in a small alcove on the opposite side of the corridor. Karis followed them, anxious to get away from Clay's father, who gave her a cursory glance and then went into Clay's room. After they were seated, Karis drank in every detail of the boy in his jeans and bright yellow T-shirt. He held a Packer jacket over his left arm, a small box in his right, and was in desperate need of a haircut, as usual. He was talking about his dog.

"Who's watching Pumpkin?"

The boy's eyes swiftly turned her way, melting her heart. Such a warm brown, and dark lashes, almost as dark as Clay's. Oh, how she wished . . .

But Moira answered. "She's in Lou's RV. They're at the same campground."

"Is she okay?"

"She's fine. It's Lou's blood pressure I'm worried about."

Seth interrupted her thoughts. "I wish Pumpkin could get adopted with me."

Moira reached over and patted his leg. "I know, sweetie. I do too, but the Binghams thought that a dog might be a little too much. And don't worry. Pumpkin will be in very good hands."

The boy studied his scuffed white tennis shoes. "Yeah."

Karis' heart sank with his. She had missed their time together on Saturday even though she'd been furious with Clay. She didn't want to ask about the events of the upcoming week. The court date was looming, and if the judge agreed, the adoption would proceed. The thought brought searing pain.

When Clay's parents came out, Moira sprang up and made her way over. Seth and Karis followed behind. Mrs. Montes barely gave Seth a glance on her way to the restroom, and Karis, to her surprise, found herself angered.

Moira guided Seth into the room. Karis was left standing next to the glass window beside Mr. Montes. She found herself trapped again under the man's dark stare. "He looks like you."

"Excuse me?"

"The boy." The man turned back to the window. "I presume he's your son." Karis noticed how he didn't assign ownership to Clay, and heaven forbid that he would claim him as a grandson.

"The boy's name is Seth."

"Too bad about his arm."

Perhaps the man had some compassion. Looking through the glass, she couldn't help but smile when Seth presented Clay with a wooden red and blue birdhouse. He'd obviously made it himself—the boards were nailed haphazardly.

"Why don't you want him? Is it because of his arm?" The man's rudeness knew no bounds, but he was just as Clay had described.

Of course she wanted him! she felt like screaming as anger ripped through her chest. She wanted him more than life itself. But the pain quashed the anger. It always did. She rushed to the ladies' room, nearly colliding with Mrs. Montes. She locked herself into a stall, and her breathing grew shallow, the metal walls fuzzy. She clutched her head between her hands, the man's words echoing. *Why don't you want him?* She would never answer that question in public, never verbalize her fear to another human being. Only God knew the naked truth, the one fear she could never overcome. *How could she ever go on living if her son didn't want her?*

*****

"You made that all by yourself?" Clay watched Seth nod energetically. How he wished he could hug the kid. "That's awesome, Seth."

"You can hang it on your trailer when it gets warm. See, right here is a hook."

"I sure will. Some lucky bird is going to get a great house." It took all his energy to put words past the lump in his throat.

"Thanks for getting me a dog."

Clay could see the boy tearing up. "You're welcome. I'll take good care of Pumpkin. I promise."

"I don't have a picture of her."

"I'll get you one."

Moira kept her hands on Seth's shoulders. "Well, we better go before the nurse chases us out. Can you say goodbye now?"

Clay put out his hand. "Give me five."

"Won't that hurt?"

Not nearly as much as saying goodbye.

Seth touched his palm gently. "Bye."

Clay could only swallow.

*****

Any moment now, she would lose it. After Moira and Seth came out, Lou ducked in, and then it was her turn again. She slipped in for a brief moment, relieved that Mr. and Mrs. Montes had gone to the cafeteria for lunch. Clay's eyes were moist. She'd never seen him this way.

"I should probably be going. You need to rest."

"I'm so sorry, Karis."

"You don't need to be."

"Are you okay?"

"No, but I will be."

"Will you come back?"

"If you behave."

"One real kiss before you go."

She closed her eyes and tasted his lips, warm and soft. When she opened them, he had drifted off. She touched his cheek, hoping, praying that he would somehow survive, that they would all survive. Somehow.

Seth gulped from a drinking fountain near the ICU entrance. Moira told him to slow down. As she neared, Moira turned her way.

"Dr. Henry, did you know the Packers are in the playoffs tonight?

Suddenly animated, Seth whipped his head around. "Yeah, but they're not at Lambeau, where it's like, a hundred degrees below zero!"

Lou tousled Seth's hair. "Well not exactly, but it can be mighty chilly there.

Moira smiled. "I've invited Seth and Lou to watch the game. If you don't have any plans, you could join us at my house."

"But you can't be for the Bears!" Seth's eyes bulged.

Karis saw it for the gift that it was—an extraordinary gift of time. Probably the last time. She looked at Moira. "I would love to." Then, to Seth. "I'm actually a Chief's fan."

"They lost to the Ravens."

"I know, but you always stand by your team. That's what my dad says."

An hour later, the four of them sat in Moira's living room with large bowls of popcorn, warmed-up pizza, and sodas. The couch felt like a trampoline as Seth jumped up, and then fell back, over and over, throughout the game. By the end of the fourth quarter as the clock ticked down, he stood on a cushion, ecstatic. The Packers were going to the Super Bowl.

Soon the inevitable came. Moira started cleaning up. Seth's coat was in the chair next to Karis. She picked it up and helped him put it on, and then leaned over the zipper, realizing for one priceless moment, the Lord had let her be his mother again. If only she could have hugged him.

CHAPTER TWENTY-NINE

EACH DAY WAS AN ENDLESS repeat of the previous one. The weeks of February blurred together. Karis dressed every morning; diagnosed influenza, diabetes, shingles, and a few cases of appendicitis; treated warts, rashes, and rheumatoid arthritis; stitched up cuts and a terrible dog bite to a toddler; and prescribed lotions, creams, and pills. Her patient load had picked up as winter eased, and she gratefully buried herself under the pace—anything to forget a little boy, a big man, and a faceless couple. She forced herself to run five miles every morning, waking before dawn and stumbling back home by 7 a.m. She buried herself in God's word, prayed daily, witnessed to her staff, and cried a lot—for Seth, for Clay, for herself, for what might have been. Her appetite waned, her pants loosened, but she didn't give up. The Lord's gentle hand rested on her shoulder from morning through evening and into the night.

After a week in the hospital, Clay had been discharged, but he never called. He went home to recuperate at his parents' home. They had made a big stink about it, and when Karis had called their residence multiple times, his mother had been evasive. The same dead end came when she tried his cell phone. She wondered if Clay ever received her messages.

She started attending a small community church in Harbor, the older pastor much like a grandfather. With each passing Sunday, she felt herself growing, buoyed by the Lord's presence. But the ache of the past was slow in healing.

Clay's six-month follow-up for melanoma had come and gone. Her staff had sent a reminder card to his parents' address, but with no response.

*****

Karis hung up the white curtains and smiled to herself—mission accomplished. She had finally tamed the living room with a soft yellow paint color. Raspberry throw pillows, a floral rug, and a polka-dot lamp she picked up at a resale shop completed the cottage look. The end result was both soothing and inviting. As she put the stepstool away, the doorbell rang. Her parents were early.

"Honey, this is so cute." Lorna beamed as she stepped over the threshold, arms full, and surveyed the living room. Dad, gripping two suitcases, was close behind, a peaceful smile on his face.

Her mother set her bundles on the couch and gathered Karis in a hug. "Oh, it's so good to see you." Her dad followed suit.

Buddy jumped on the couch and began sniffing the brown paper. Her mother was already taking off her jacket. As she pulled off her scarf, Karis noticed the new hairstyle. Gone was the bun, and in its place, a short wavy cut. She was also wearing jeans. Had her mother ever owned jeans?

"Mom, what's gotten into you?"

Lorna smiled. "It was your dad's doing. He entered me in a makeover contest at Paulette's Salon, and I won. What do you think?"

"I think you look fantastic."

"With all that's happened, I feel like I have a new life. Oh, and wait until you see what I have in these bags."

Lorna began removing Ziploc bags from one shopping bag. "Banana bread, pumpkin bread, poppy seed bread. And here are some dishtowels for your kitchen. I crocheted the tops." Her mother held up six towels in varying patterns and designs. "And you must open this now." Looking jubilant, she held out a large brightly wrapped package.

"I don't know what to say." Karis sat down and fingered the ribbon on top of the floral wrapping paper. "What's the special occasion?"

She saw her dad wink at her mom, who smiled in response. "Perhaps we could call it a long-overdue housewarming present."

The paper was almost too pretty to tear. She eased a fingernail under the tape and slid back the paper, revealing Grandma Miller's double wedding ring quilt. Karis was speechless. She looked over at her mom. "Are you sure you want me to have this? I mean—"

"Of course, I do."

Karis touched the priceless heirloom, which had been passed down between mothers and daughters for four generations. "What about—"

"Eden gets the crazy quilt. It fits her perfectly. And since you have your own home now . . ."

Karis thought she might as well bring her mother back to reality. "Well, me and the mortgage company, anyway. I'm in debt up to my eyebrows." She had never discussed the college and medical school loans with her parents. "But I'm making progress. At my current rate, I will be free and clear in twelve years."

"We should have a garage sale!"

That would only make a small dent, but she didn't tell her mom.

Karis stood up. "Don't worry about me, Mom. God knows, and He's providing everything I need. But the roast is done, so let's eat."

After dinner, they enjoyed poppy seed bread and cups of hot chocolate. Lorna excused herself early and went up to bed. On his second slice, Dad turned her way. "Do you remember the first summer you came back from Camp Jubilee? You must have been ten or eleven."

Karis nodded. "Edward Stein was the guest missionary. He ran a medical clinic in Kenya."

Her dad wiped his mouth. "I believe that was the first time you mentioned medicine. Although, I thought you meant nursing. And here you are. I'm so proud of you, Karis."

The words felt like sweet rain from heaven. A large lump formed in her throat. "Thanks Dad."

"How is Clay?"

The lump wouldn't go away. "I honestly don't know."

"Haven't heard any more?"

She shook her head. "I feel like I've lost everything again."

"Your mother mentioned that your contract is almost up."

Karis hugged herself and pushed against the sadness. "With all that's happened, I can't stay here. I applied for a position in rural Iowa."

Her dad's arm came around her shoulders. "Keep the faith, Peanut. We don't know what's around the next corner, but God does. Make sure He's always number one. There is nothing more important."

She could only nod.

*****

"Don't look at me that way, Buddy." The dog was moping on the couch again. "I can't help the rain."

For a week now, the late March weather had dampened the ground and the dog's spirits, not to mention her own. No walks, and mud everywhere. If it warmed up, she'd have to mow. Karis peeled off the last of the bathroom wallpaper, tossed it in a garbage bag, and then collapsed next to Buddy.

"Don't ever let me do that again."

Buddy fixed her with his mournful brown eyes. She rubbed his head. "I know it's not fair. Maybe tomorrow."

The rain continued as she spackled the wall with joint compound, determined to complete the sanding by Sunday night. Then if time allowed, she'd apply the primer and paint before the real estate agent came on Tuesday evening. Hopefully, the dungeon-like basement wouldn't scare potential buyers away. She thought back to Clay's brief stay in the house before Christmas. He had filled every room in a comforting but exasperating way. It seemed like a lifetime ago. Where was he now? And Seth?

She got up abruptly and retrieved a couple of cardboard boxes from the attic. She might as well start packing.

*****

On a Wednesday in early April, Belinda brought her an envelope that required her signature. She glanced at the return address, her heart sinking simultaneously. Hartford Mortgage Company. Bad news. She could feel it. When the insurance companies had rolled out the latest fee schedule, her reimbursements had been cut by thirty percent. After she called customer service last month to report the change, the representative had assured her a partial payment would be acceptable under her circumstances. But a default on the loan would doom her credit. With pounding heart, she opened the envelope.

She sat down at her desk. Sliding out the bundled papers, her eyes immediately caught the red stamp on the promissory note. PAID IN FULL dated April 1, 2011. Five days ago. What on earth had happened? This was obviously a mistake. She called the company. No. The college loan was paid off. $37,000 just paid off? But how? The woman said she could not divulge any information. The benefactor was anonymous.

The next day, a similar letter arrived in the mail from Eastern Point, the company that managed her medical school loans. $92,000. PAID IN FULL. She almost fainted. She called the company and received the same information. There was no mistake. The loans were paid, her school debt totally wiped out. She called home and questioned her father, who seemed just as surprised. The next day she went to work in a state of shock.

Down the hall, Belinda joked with a patient. Her insides suddenly knotted at the timbre of the familiar voice. She grabbed the schedule, surprised to see a name scratched out and his name added. He must have called while she had dealt with the hospital consult.

But he had never bothered to call her. She'd practically wasted away, waiting to hear from him. But that wasn't entirely true. The Lord had seen her through the difficult days, and she had survived them all without Seth. And Clay. Besides, he had been very ill, near death even, but was that an excuse not to call? His mouth had worked fine in the hospital. *Dear Father, please help me. Part of me is dying to see him, and the other part of me wants to smack his jaw.* She pushed the exam door open brusquely. "You're two months—"

Her breath caught. Seth! He was sitting on the exam table, swinging his legs side to side, so like the man next to him. Clay grinned like an idiot. They were wearing matching T-shirts, burnt orange with a white fish outlined on the chest pocket. Clay's ponytail was gone, his short hair curling around his ears like it did years ago. He also sported a neatly trimmed beard. Drop dead gorgeous. She stared, dumbfounded. "What is going on?"

Clay sidled up and encircled her with his arms, clearly enjoying her shock. He whispered in her ear. "I know you hate surprises, but . . ." He gave her a loud smack on the cheek. His whiskers tickled. Belinda giggled from behind as she quietly closed the door.

Karis felt like punching him. "You are insufferable."

"Is that all you can say?" He wouldn't let her go. "Woman, I have missed you." His voice was ragged. "But I can tell you're not hearing a word I say." He released her and winked at Seth who was rolling his eyes at the PDA. "Shall we tell her?"

"Tell me what?" Her hands rested on her hips now.

Clay crossed his arms. "Nah, I don't want to tell her. Let's just show her, but after my check-up. I'm trying to be a good boy."

"Fat chance that will ever happen. Why didn't you come in for your follow-up? I was worried sick."

"I was still horizontal back then, but I'll explain later. Trust me."

"In your dreams."

He smiled and turned to Seth. "Hey buddy, while I visit with Karis, why don't you check out the TV in the waiting room."

Karis followed Seth into the hall and asked Lauren to show him where the remote was located. When she returned to the room, Clay was removing his shirt. He had lost some weight. His tattoo was even more noticeable, but now an inscription filled the length of the warrior's blade: *La espada del Espiritu es la palabra de Dios.* "What does this mean?"

"The Sword of the Spirit is the Word of God."

"Ephesians 6:17."

"That's my girl. It's the only way to fight."

At least they agreed on one thing. "Have you noticed any new spots anywhere?"

He took the chart out of her hands and laid it behind him on the exam table. "First things first." He placed his hands on her shoulders, pulled her close, and kissed her soundly. When she started to object, he put his finger against her lips. With Clay's bare chest only centimeters away, she could hardly think straight. He seemed to capitalize on her weakness. His arms came around. "Seth's adoption fell through. I don't know all the details, of course, but the adoptive parents had some type of misfortune, and then there was all the legal stuff to deal with."

The floor swayed. "Is he okay?" Karis felt herself wilt inside. Had her son suffered even more?

"Better than ever."

"But where has he been all this time? Is he back with the Waters family?"

Clay's fingers caressed her neck. "No. He's been living in a camper and loving it."

"You mean—" It all became clear.

"I have temporary custody."

"Why didn't you tell me?" Anguish seeped around her heart. She suddenly felt like someone who hadn't been invited to the party.

"I didn't want to until now." He brushed his nose against her cheek and she was powerless to push him away.

"Why not?"

"You'll see, but let's get this exam over with first."

She touched his back, felt the smoothness of his skin, and nearly died inside. How she had missed him. She took care to check him thoroughly. Thank the Lord there were no suspicious spots. "I have one more question."

"Guilty."

"You don't even know what I was going to ask."

"I just do what God tells me."

"Clay, you can't just go around paying off my debts!"

"I also have ulterior motives."

Thirty minutes later, they were driving north. Karis hadn't returned to Feather Lake since that chilly December day when she had plunged beneath the icy waters. But as they passed blooming dogwoods and redbuds and leafed out maple, elm, and oak trees, the memory receded in the beauty of the countryside.

Clay turned up a steep incline and pulled the truck off on the gravel road leading to the land that had been for sale.

"Close your eyes."

"You've got to be kidding."

"Nope. Seth and I will hold your hands. We're going for a walk."

Stumbling over uneven ground to the lake was not exactly inviting, but she obeyed and allowed the two of them to guide her, relishing the small hand on her left and the big hand on her right. The air was filled with the noisy call of magpies and finches, and a slight breeze lifted her hair. As they walked out of the shaded areas, the sun warmed her face.

"Okay, stop. Open your eyes."

A sage-green Craftsman-style bungalow stood stalwart at the top of a gentle incline with Clay's camper beside it. Karis studied the stone chimney, the honeyed timbers of the rustic porch, and the cobblestone walkway leading to an elaborately carved mahogany front door. She surmised Clay was back in construction. Probably another ministry project.

Seth pulled on Clay's arm. "I'd better check on Pumpkin."

Clay tousled his hair. "Alright, but don't let her eat any more frogs."

The boy sped off, yelling behind him, "I won't."

Clay turned back to her. "Last week she threw up for two days."

She couldn't help raising her voice. "Is he in school?"

Clay stepped closer and wrapped his arms around her waist, forcing her into another embrace. She tried to push him away, but his lips found hers. He kissed her hungrily. Her strength ran out. His fingers were in her hair, his mouth next to her ear. "Did you miss me?"

She finally found her will and pressed her hands against his chest. "No."

"That's not what your kiss just said." He drew back, but didn't let go. "Your hair looks really nice. How long are you going to let it grow?"

"Clay!"

"Yes, Seth is in school at Adams Elementary, just down the road."

Karis swallowed. Seth had been practically living under her nose.

Clay motioned with his head toward the house. "Want to see my latest work of art, although I'm not quite up to snuff yet? Lou and the guys have been helping me since the grunt work of the Ashland house is finished."

"Another worthy cause?" With the Lord's help, she'd been trying to curb her sarcasm, but the words slipped out. She would have to confess her jealousy.

Clay didn't seem to notice. "You might say that."

"I thought you sold this property."

He gave her his trademark dazzling smile. "I did, but I bought it back."

"So this house is—"

"Mine. And Seth's."

He grabbed her hand and pulled her toward the walkway. Removing a key, he opened the front door. The interior stud walls were half insulated and drywalled, the floor still plywood. Clay pointed out the foyer, dining room, stairs leading up to the second floor, and the four bedrooms. A powder room was situated underneath the staircase on the right. Next, he led her to the rear of the home where a spacious white kitchen overlooked the back meadow and opened into a great room with a custom-built fireplace. Two beanbags sat haphazardly in front of a small television set. A game system was connected to the television. Nearby, a box housed DVDs.

"We've still got a ways to go, obviously—paint, floors, light fixtures, plumbing, etc. Care for something to drink? I've got lots of water bottles and chocolate milk." He motioned to a dorm-size refrigerator.

It was all too perfect. The man needed a reality check. "This is all wonderful, but does Seth know who you really are?"

Clay shut the refrigerator door and turned toward her. "I cut my hair. Do you know why?"

She suspected he had made a vow and wouldn't cut his hair until it was fulfilled—a practice birthed long ago in Biblical times, the vow of a Nazirite. He'd never shared the details, and she hadn't asked. Now she was afraid to ask. She swallowed, fingers of fear scratching. Surely he didn't . . . "You told him?"

Clay pierced her with his dark eyes. "I told you I would. I needed to ask his forgiveness."

The fingers pressed against her throat. "What did he say?"

"He said, 'if Jesus can forgive the sins of the whole world, he can forgive me.'"

Karis fell silent. Her son put her to shame. Clay put her to shame. How long had she nurtured her hardened heart? How often had she crucified the Son of God afresh with her rebellion, her refusal to forgive? Her anger against Clay, her father, and her aunt had ultimately been aimed at the Lord Himself. Her sin was black. She was black. *Lord Jesus, forgive me. Again.*

"There's one more thing I want to show you." He grabbed her arm and pulled her through the back door, which opened onto a large deck with steps leading to the yard. Pumpkin's pen sat beside a large oak tree. Seth was throwing a tennis ball for the fast growing dog.

"Seth, we'll be in the garden."

"Watch this!" The boy tossed the ball in the air and the dog leaped and caught it in her mouth.

"Very cool."

Karis drank in the sight of the young boy, itching to touch him, to hold him. He was the true work of art. She followed Clay down a shaded pathway to a grassy clearing, which exploded with wild pinks, milkweed, and yellow sunflowers. A rustic wooden bench sat near a grove of forsythia in full bloom.

"Leila Stipes told me if a judge is going to take my request seriously for full custody, my chances would be better if I had a suitable mother for Seth." Clay captured her hand. "I was hoping for a tall, good-looking blonde."

"Clay—"

"I'm only going to ask you once."

"But I can't—"

He dropped to one knee and looked up. "Marry me, Karis. Like we should have done years ago. If not for me, for Seth."

She couldn't believe this was happening. The pain resurfaced as the fear assaulted. She could hardly speak. "He doesn't know who I am."

Clay's eyes held her. "God honors the truth, Karis."

She felt faint and could only whisper. "You didn't?" She pulled her hand away. "You told him?" Her lip quivered. "What did he say?"

"I'll let you ask him."

"You know I can't."

Clay rose and encircled her with strong arms. "There's nothing to fear, Karis. Trust me. Trust Seth. Trust God, for crying out loud."

But how could she? She would die if her son rejected her.

A ball landed near Karis' feet. The puppy entered the clearing with Seth following. Could this really be possible? Could they really belong to each other again?

Seth ran up, out of breath. "Pumpkin can really run."

Karis couldn't help but smile over the hammering of her heart. "Like the wind."

Seth looked up at her. The child always seemed to need a haircut. "Are you going to be my mom or not?" Just like that, he spit out the words.

She sucked in air. Maybe the little boy looked liked her, but he acted like his impetuous father. "Is that what you want?"

"Yeah, since you already are my mom. It makes sense."

She fell to her knees and grasped his right hand and the stub of his left arm. It was suddenly just the two of them again. She studied his face. "I wanted to keep you so badly when you were a baby, but I didn't have anything to give. Not a dad, not a family, not a home, not grandparents, not anything."

"But you could now."

The truth came rushing out. "I'm a coward, Seth."

He crinkled his nose. "What's that?"

"Someone who's afraid."

"I used to be afraid."

"What were you afraid of?"

"That no one would want me, but then I remembered God. He always wanted me. Do you want me now?"

Dear sweet Jesus. Karis fought to keep the tears at bay. What would he do if she tried to hug him? *Oh God, can I hug him?* She reached out her arms and gathered him close. He didn't draw away. "Oh Seth, more than anything in the world."

He pulled back and looked her straight in the eye. "Then you'll have to marry Clay cause he's gonna be my dad. That's the way it works."

Clay's deep voice tickled the air. "Sounds like a no-brainer to me, Dr. Henry."

Karis looked from the freckle-faced boy to the tall man. "On one condition. I want the wedding on May 7th."

"That's my birthday!" Seth's face was suddenly animated.

"How well I know that." And Karis' heart took flight.

*****

The day warmed as the sun peeked in and out of clouds during the afternoon, and a gentle breeze stirred the leaves of the trees. Karis had insisted on a simple outdoor ceremony, and though her mother had broached the subject of not being married in a church, she had stood her ground. Next to the lake, only close family, friends, and the Lord. White lawn chairs had been placed in the clearing in three neat rows with a small aisle down the middle. Feather Lake glistened in the distance.

She and Clay had thrown a big surprise birthday party for Seth — his first ever—at The Drop Zone and happily watched as Seth and his soccer team ran like maniacs around the play area, attacking the arcade games and cramming themselves full of pizza and soda.

After the party, they had rushed back to the bungalow to begin final preparations for the backyard wedding. Eden sparkled in her pale pink dress. The guests began arriving at half past three and were guided to the garden. Clay had enlisted a string quartet. With the bedroom window open, the music floated in. Her mother had just left to meet Micah who would escort her to her seat. Her dad would be coming soon. Karis looked in the mirror one more time and wondered if this was really happening. The simple tea dress, ivory satin overlaid with Chantilly lace and short sleeves, hung to her calves, its scoop neck a natural showcase for her mother's pearls. She'd elected to wear her hair down. It touched her shoulders in silky wisps. No veil, no garland, no pretense.

A knock on the door. She picked up the single white rose. Her father guided her out the back. She could see the guests, hear the sonata, and feel the warmth of the sun. Eden floated down the path, a gorgeous swan.

Then the moment arrived. Her eyes honed in on the tall man and the boy at his side. *You've never seen me in a tux.* She had to smile as she looked at her two men in matching black tuxedos with black bow ties and crisp white shirts. The quartet began "The Wedding March," and her eyes found Clay's. He stood straight and wore the most serious expression she'd ever seen, but then he winked, and Karis felt herself relax.

Her father placed her hand in Clay's strong one and then took his place before them. As birds called and the wind stirred the lake, a place where she had almost lost her life and then found it, they became husband and wife.

Afterwards, a catered dinner was served on the deck, followed by cake and music and dancing. By the time the sun had begun to dip into the horizon, the guests began making their way home. Seth was off to spend a few days getting to know both sets of grandparents, Mr. and Mrs. Montes first and then the Henrys. Clay's parents were slowly warming up. Relations weren't perfect, but held promise. While they were saying their goodbyes and taking pictures, Eden, Moira, Lou, and her parents cleaned up and then departed.

As she waved goodbye, Karis felt Clay's arms around her waist, his lips on her neck as he murmured softly. "Finally, I get you to myself."

Karis glanced up at the clear evening sky, sprinkled with twinkling diamonds. "The stars are coming out."

"Want to sit on the porch a while?"

"That would be nice."

They sat down on the swing, and Clay gathered her close to his side. He had shed his jacket, pulled off his tie, and unbuttoned his collar. She breathed in his musky scent and listened to the chirping of the night air. Was this a dream? His finger traced circles on her upper arm. Tingles danced along her spine.

"Are you sorry we didn't plan a honeymoon?"

She breathed in and shook her head. "There's no place I'd rather be than here. With you."

He stopped tracing. "Are you nervous?"

"Can't you tell?"

"I'm nervous too."

She turned toward him, expecting to see the tease in his eyes, but his face remained somber.

"I've never been a Christian husband. The way I read it, it's a pretty heavy responsibility. Love your wife as Christ loved the church."

She continued to marvel at the change in him. "I think you're doing a fine job so far."

"Oh, I'm just getting started." And then the rogue was back, his fingers fumbling with the top buttons of her dress.

She pulled away. "Shouldn't we go inside?"

A wolfish grin. "I thought you'd never ask."

He scooped her up and carried her across the threshold.

EPILOGUE

Outstretched hands, a gentle call
Lifted up for those who fall
Sweet drops of grace, poured out alone
He heals the lost to call His own

Present Day

THE WATERS OF FEATHER LAKE sparkled in the June sunlight as the morning mist dissipated. Karis slipped off her sandals and relished the softness of the sand. On her shoulder, baby Asher dozed beneath a cotton blanket, content from his last nursing. Clay had taken the kids for a boat ride, gracing her with time to walk along the shore and ponder the events of the last week.

She had been a wreck at Seth's high school graduation.

"Clay, I'm not helpless." But she had allowed Clay to put his arm around her waist and help her up the stadium steps. Almost thirty-nine years old and pregnant. When the test had come back positive, Clay had enjoyed her shock. "Don't look so surprised. You deserve it after the way you've been chasing me around." She had blushed and thrown a pillow at him.

Near the top of the steps, she had lost her balance and almost fell onto a silver-haired gentleman. Clay pulled her back. "Karis, why on earth did you wear those shoes?"

She had glanced at her swollen ankles in the strappy sandals. Though low heeled, she still wobbled. But her blue toenails looked nice—thanks to Clay and four-year-old Rachel who had given her a manicure the night before while she napped on the sofa during a Veggie Tale movie. Lydia, her toddler, had been too engrossed to notice. Samuel had been at baseball practice and Seth out with friends.

At the thought of her tall blond-haired son, she had felt tears threaten again. She had cried every day during her last trimester. Blasted hormones. Seth's high school years had zipped by at the speed of light.

Clay had noticed the tears sliding down her cheeks as he guided her up another step. "Babe, I didn't mean to criticize your shoe choice."

"It's not that, Clay!"

He had cocked an eyebrow, no doubt formulating an appropriate strategy for handling a hysterical pregnant wife in public. After eight years of marriage, he seemed to be a mind reader. "Karis, Seth will only be two hours away at Mizzou."

He might as well have said Mars. More tears. "It was only yesterday that he was a little boy."

Clay had gathered her close and squeezed at the exact moment her stomach contracted painfully. She gripped his arm. Clay narrowed his gaze. She smiled weakly and turned to wave at her little girls and seven-year-old Samuel as they neared the top of the bleachers. She would make it through her son's graduation. Period.

By the time Seth had walked across the stage an hour later, she was in agony, and Clay looked ready to sling her over his back. Her mother frowned every time she grabbed her seat. Sweat drenched the back of her dress. Fuzzy shapes floated before her eyes. She tried to focus, but merciless contractions were coming at three-minute intervals.

When the principal stood for the recessional, Clay clasped her elbows and lifted her up. "We're going. Now."

"But Clay, Seth—"

"Stop arguing, Karis or I'll throw you over my shoulder." It was her last conscious thought as Clay's strong arms caught her.

And then there was the hospital.

"Is Mommy alive?" Angel breath on her cheek. Rachel's sweet voice all but dulled by the heaviness.

"Mommy's just resting." Clay's deep voice.

"How come she has that tube in her arm?"

Her eyes opened to see Clay next to her in a rocking chair, holding a bundle with Rachel next to him.

Clay's daddy voice again. "If you sit down, you can hold the baby."

In her semi-conscious state, shards of memory flashed. The emergency room, speeding down the hospital corridor, Dr. Federoff's voice, the oxygen mask covering her nose, and then nothing. She heard Clay speak quietly to Rachel. What had happened? More voices. Her mom, Clay's parents, Samuel, Lydia, Seth. They spoke in hushed tones.

When Karis' eyes had finally obeyed, she found the room darkened. Clay sat nearby. His eyes were closed, his arms empty. Maybe she had dreamed it. She felt her jelly-like stomach and a row of staples. No baby.

"Clay?"

He turned instantly, leaned over, and ran a finger down her nose. "Finally decided to join us?"

"What happened?"

"A little delivery room drama. You were quite the story yesterday."

"Is everything—"

Clay grasped her hand. "Everything is fine now. The cord was wrapped around the baby's neck. Dr. Federoff had to do a C-section, but he's just fine."

"A boy?"

"A big, squalling boy."

"And the girls? Samuel? Seth?"

"All being spoiled like crazy by the grandparents. Stop worrying."

Clay was a sight—hair falling over his forehead, hollowed eyes, stained shirt, and as handsome as ever.

He gave her his killer smile. "I was thinking Mortimer. We could call him Mort. Mort Montes. Has a certain ring to it."

"Don't be ridiculous."

Just then the nurse came in. "I think this little guy is hungry."

Karis felt her heart melt as the tiny bundle was placed in her arms. She stroked his silky black hair and watched his heart-shaped lips pucker as he began to root.

Clay chuckled. "Better get that dairy barn open."

Karis would happily nurse 'til the cows came home. She snuggled him close and listened to him smack voraciously. "Seriously, what are we going to name him?"

"Well, Rachel is insisting on Bob, and Lydia wants Pongo. Samuel says Woody. Seth thought Butch sounded cool, and of course, I favor Mortimer."

"I love you, Clay Montes."

The lazy smile that always gave her goose bumps found its way to her husband's lips. "I am one blessed bum." He had leaned over and kissed her deeply. "What would you like to call him?"

"Asher."

Asher Mathias Montes. Their happy gift of God. It was perfect.

She heard the boat motor in the distance. Asher shifted but did not awaken. Clay powered the Freedom outboard toward their dock. His generous heart and creativity never ceased to amaze her. In 2013, he had partnered with *Sanctuary Homes* to build *The Tree House*, a log cabin by Feather Lake, especially for children awaiting adoption. Once staffed, it had filled up overnight. A year later, he envisioned *Mountain Top*, a special hospital camp for disabled and ill children. By 2015, it graced a wooded area just down the road from their house. Karis had resigned her clinic position to serve as one of the camp doctors. Never had she felt so fulfilled.

"Look at me, Mommy! I'm driving."

As Clay turned the boat eastward, she could see Samuel holding the steering wheel with his dad's strong arms about him. Towheaded, Samuel had come exactly nine months and four days after their wedding night. A "little Seth," he never went anywhere without his cowboy hat. Clay turned and called out to Rachel to sit down. Their black-haired pixie knew no fear. Once they had found her on top of the porch roof, putting acorns in her teapot. The lattice came down after that. Seth held Lydia and Poppy, Lydia's stuffed pig. She was feeding him "crackies." Karis still didn't know what to do with the toddler's wild honey curls.

Asher stirred and whimpered. Karis rubbed his back as Clay docked the boat, reminding the little ones to store their life jackets in the bench seat. While Clay assisted Samuel and Rachel, Seth helped Lydia, one-handed. He had never wanted a prosthesis, and the lack of one never stopped him. He was a perfect big brother—so patient with his younger siblings. A couple of tears slipped down her cheek as she thought of their recent conversation. He felt led to be a pastor, just like his Grandpa Henry who had passed away two summers ago.

Lydia held up her arms for a "piggy ride." Seth swung her up on his shoulders, smiling when she squealed with delight, and then turned. "Hey, Mom, what's for lunch?"

"Seth, we just ate breakfast."

"But that was an hour ago."

Before she could respond, they giddy-upped toward the house with Samuel and Rachel in hot pursuit.

Clay ambled up and pulled Asher from her shoulders, cradling him with one hand. "You sure have a cute family, Mrs. Montes."

She smiled at her husband. "I'll be sure and tell Mr. Montes you said so."

"Oh, you'd better do more than tell him." Clay's arm circled her waist, drawing her close. He kissed her neck. "Hmmm, you smell good."

"I smell like spit-up."

"That's the smell of love, hon." Clay shifted the baby to his shoulder, sniffed his diaper, and nearly choked. "Whoa, Asher! Toxic waste!"

"Clay, would you mind if I stayed here a little longer?"

He searched her face. "Are you alright?"

"I just need a little time alone."

He kissed her again. "Take all the time you need. I'll go see if the house is on fire yet."

He sang to Asher as he hiked up the path. It was pure delight watching him—with the kids, when he worked, and especially when he loved her.

A light westerly breeze rippled the waters. She waded out and breathed in the fresh scent of pine, enjoying the coolness of the lake. Along the far shore, a man stood in waders, fishing. For a moment, her mind replayed that morning long ago when she had felt so desolate. May 7, 2002. It was Seth's first birthday. But the Lord's love and mercy had lifted her to a place of healing and hope and complete restoration. She thought of Clay and the kids and her calling. How could life be so sweet? And why was she so blessed? She couldn't help but raise her hands in worship to the One who loved her and gave Himself for her. She was, and always would be, His very own.

A sparrow sang out suddenly. Karis turned and smiled at the tiny bird as it perched on a nearby branch. It was time to go home.

AUTHOR BIO

JOY CLEVELAND is a writer, histotechnologist, wife, mother of four, and shameless grandmother of two adorable granddaughters. She lives in Iowa where there are few distractions and tons of cornfields, and where she has spent twenty-one years in the medical field. She has written short stories, plays for children, and quirky newsletters. This is her first novel.

Please visit Joy at <u>joycleveland.com</u>.